Beastly Things

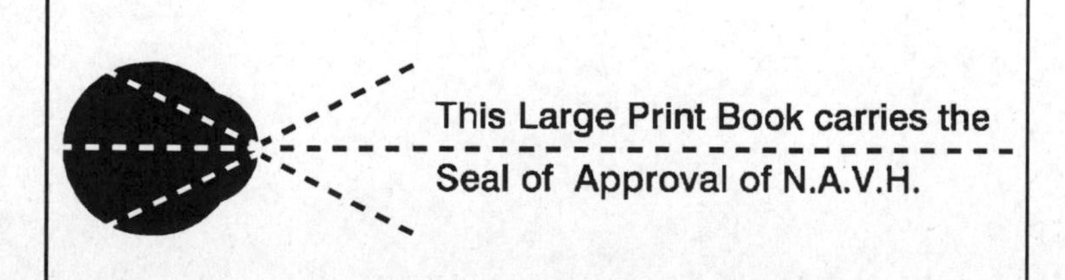
This Large Print Book carries the
Seal of Approval of N.A.V.H.

Beastly Things

Donna Leon

THORNDIKE PRESS
A part of Gale, Cengage Learning

GALE
CENGAGE Learning®

Detroit • New York • San Francisco • New Haven, Conn • Waterville, Maine • London

A Commissario Guido Brunetti Mystery.
Thorndike Press, a part of Gale, Cengage Learning.

Thorndike Press® Large Print Mystery.
The text of this Large Print edition is unabridged.
Other aspects of the book may vary from the original edition.
Set in 16 pt. Plantin.

LIBRARY OF CONGRESS CATALOGING-IN-PUBLICATION DATA

Leon, Donna.
Beastly things / by Donna Leon. — Large print ed.
p. cm. — (Thorndike Press large print mystery)
ISBN 978-1-4104-4879-8 (hardcover) — ISBN 1-4104-4879-7 (hardcover)
1. Brunetti, Guido (Fictitious character)—Fiction. 2. Police—Italy—Venice—Fiction. 3. Venice (Italy)—Fiction. 4. Large type books. I. Title.
PS3562.E534B43 2012
813'.54—dc23 2012011208

Published in 2012 by arrangement with Grove/Atlantic, Inc.

Printed in the United States of America
1 2 3 4 5 6 7 16 15 14 13 12

For Fabio Moretti and
Umberto Branchini

Va tacito e nascosto,
quand'avido è di preda,
l'astuto cacciator.
E chi è a mal far disposto,
non brama che si veda
l'inganno del suo cor.

When intent on his prey,
the clever hunter
moves silently and hidden.
And he who wants to do evil
is not eager
that the evil in his heart be seen.

Giulio Cesare
Handel

1

The man lay still, as still as a piece of meat on a slab, as still as death itself. Though the room was cold, his only covering was a thin cotton sheet that left his head and neck free. From a distance, his chest rose inordinately high, as though some sort of support had been wedged under his back, running the length of it. If this white form were a snow-covered mountain ridge and the viewer a tired hiker at the end of a long day, faced with the task of crossing it, the hiker would surely choose to walk along the entire length of the man to cross at the ankles and not the chest. The ascent was too high and too steep, and who knew what difficulties there would be descending the other side?

From the side, the unnatural height of the chest was obvious; from above — if the hiker were now placed on a peak and could gaze down at the man — it was the neck that was conspicuous. The neck — or perhaps more accurately the lack of one. In fact, his neck was a broad column running down straight from beneath his ears to his shoulders. There was no narrowing, no indentation; the neck was as wide as the head.

Also conspicuous was the nose, now barely evident in profile. It had been crushed and pushed to one side; scratches and tiny indentations patterned the skin. The right cheek, as well, was scratched and bruised. His entire face was swollen, the skin white and flaccid. From above, his flesh sank in a concave arc below his cheekbones. His face was pale with more than the pallor of death. This was a man who had lived indoors.

The man had dark hair and a short beard, grown perhaps in an attempt to disguise the neck, but there was no disguising such a thing for more than a second. The beard provided a visual distraction, but almost instantly it would be seen as camouflage, nothing more, for it ran along the jaw line and down that column of a neck, as if it did not know where to stop. From this height, it looked almost as though it had flowed down across the neck and off to the sides, an effect exaggerated by the way the beard grew increasingly white at the sides.

His ears were surprisingly delicate, almost feminine. Earrings would not have looked out of place there, were it not for the beard. Below the left ear, just beyond the end of the beard and set at a thirty-degree angle, was a pink scar. About three centimetres long, it was as wide as a pencil; the skin was rough, as though whoever had sewn the skin shut had been in a hurry or careless because he was a man, and a scar was nothing for a man to worry about.

It was cold in the room, the only sound the heavy wheeze of the air conditioning. The man's thick chest did not move up and down, nor did he stir uncomfortably in the cold. He lay there, naked under his sheet, eyes closed. He did not wait, for he was beyond waiting, just as he was beyond being late or being on time. One might be tempted to say that the man simply was. But that would be untrue, for he was no more.

Two other forms lay, similarly covered, in the room, though they were closer to the walls: the bearded man was in the centre. If a man who always lies tells someone he is a liar, is he telling the truth? If no one is alive in a room, is the room empty?

A door was opened on the far side and held open by a tall, thin man in a white lab jacket. He stood there long enough for another man to pass in front of him and enter the room. The first man released the door; it closed slowly, giving a quiet, almost liquid click that sounded loud in the cold room.

'He's over there, Guido,' Dottor Rizzardi said, coming up behind Guido Brunetti, Commissario di Polizia of the city of Venice. Brunetti stopped, in the manner of the hiker, and looked across at the white-covered ridge of the man. Rizzardi walked past him to the slab on which the dead man lay.

'He was stabbed in the lower back three times with a very thin blade. Less than two centimetres wide, I'd say, and whoever did it was very good or very lucky. There are two small bruises on the front of his left arm,' Rizzardi said, stopping beside the body. 'And water in his lungs,' he added. 'So he was alive when he went into the water. But the killer got a major vein: he didn't have a chance. He bled to death in minutes.' Then, grimly, Rizzardi added, 'Before he could drown.' Before Brunetti could ask, the pathologist said, 'It happened last night, some time after midnight, I'd say. Because he's been in the water, that's as close as I can come.'

Brunetti remained halfway to the table, his eyes going back and forth between the dead man and the pathologist. 'What happened to his face?' Brunetti asked, aware of how difficult it would be to recognize a photo of him, indeed, how difficult it would be even to look at a photo of that broken, swollen face.

'My guess is that he fell forward when he was stabbed. He was probably too stunned to put out his hands to break his fall.'

'Could you take a photo?' Brunetti asked, wondering if Rizzardi could disguise some of the damage.

'You want to ask people to look at it?' It was not an answer Brunetti liked, but it was an answer. Then, after a moment, the pathologist said, 'I'll do what I can.'

Brunetti asked, 'What else?'

'I'd say he's in his late forties, in reasonably good health, isn't someone who works with his hands, but I can't say more than that.'

'Why is he such an odd shape?' Brunetti asked as he approached the table.

'You mean his chest?' Rizzardi asked.

'And the neck,' Brunetti added, his eyes drawn to its thickness.

'It's something called Madelung's disease,' Rizzardi said. 'I've read about it, and I remember it from med school, but I've never seen it before. Only the photos.'

'What causes it?' Brunetti asked, coming to stand beside the dead man.

Rizzardi shrugged. 'Who knows?' As if he'd himself just heard a doctor saying such a thing, he quickly added, 'There's a common link to alcoholism, sometimes drug use, though not in his case. He wasn't a drinker, not at all, and I didn't see signs of drug use.' He paused, then went on, 'Most alcoholics don't get it, thank God, but most of the men who get it — and it's almost always men — are alcoholics. No one seems to understand why it happens.'

Stepping closer to the corpse, Rizzardi pointed to the neck, which was especially thick at the back, where Brunetti could see what appeared to be a small hump. Before he could ask about it, Rizzardi continued, 'It's fat. It accumulates here,' he said, pointing to the hump. 'And here.' He indicated what looked like breasts under the white cloth, in the place where they would be on the body of a woman.

'It starts when they're in their thirties or forties, concentrates on the top part of the body.'

'You mean it just grows?' Brunetti asked, trying to imagine such a thing.

'Yes. Sometimes on the top part of the legs, too. But in his case it's only the neck and chest.' He paused in thought for a moment and then added, 'It turns them into barrels, poor devils.'

'Is it common?' Brunetti asked.

'No, not at all. I think there's only a few hundred cases in the literature.' He shrugged. 'We really don't know very much.'

'Anything else?'

'He was dragged along a rough surface,' the pathologist said, leading Brunetti to the bottom of the table and lifting the sheet. He pointed to the back of the dead man's heel, where the skin was scratched and broken. 'There's evidence on his lower back, as well.'

'Of what?' Brunetti asked.

'Someone grabbed him under the shoulders and dragged him across a floor, I'd say. There's no gravel in the wound,' he said, 'so it was probably a stone floor.' To clarify things, Rizzardi added, 'He was wearing only one shoe, a loafer. That suggests the other one was pulled off.'

Brunetti took a few steps back to the man's head and looked down at the bearded face. 'Does he have light eyes?' he asked.

Rizzardi glanced at him, his surprise evident. 'Blue. How did you know?'

'I didn't,' Brunetti answered.

'Then why did you ask?'

'I think I've seen him somewhere,' Brunetti answered. He stared at the man, his face, the beard, the broad column of his neck. But memory failed him, beyond his certainty about the eyes.

'If you did see him, you'd be likely to remember him, wouldn't you?' The man's body was sufficient answer to Rizzardi's question.

Brunetti nodded. 'I know, but if I think about him, nothing's there.' His failure to remember something as exceptional as this man's appearance bothered Brunetti more than he wanted to admit. Had he seen a photo, a mug shot, or had it been a print in something he'd read? He'd leafed through Lombroso's vile book a few years ago: did this man do nothing more than remind him of one of those carriers of 'hereditary criminality'?

But the Lombroso prints had been in black and white; would eyes have shown up as light or dark? Brunetti searched for the image his memory must have held, stared at the opposite wall to try to aid it. But nothing came, no clear image of a blue-eyed man, neither this one nor any other.

Instead, his memory filled almost to suffocation with the unsummoned picture of his mother, slumped in her chair, staring at him with vacant eyes that failed to know him.

'Guido?' he heard someone say and turned to see the familiar face of Rizzardi.

'You all right?'

Brunotti forced a smile and said, 'Yes, I was just trying to remember where I might have seen him.'

'Leave it alone for a while and it might come back,' Rizzardi suggested. 'Happens to me all the time. I can't remember someone's name, and I start through the alphabet — A, B, C — and often when I get to the first letter of their name, it comes back to me.'

'Is it age?' Brunetti asked with studied lack of interest.

'I certainly hope so,' Rizzardi answered lightly. 'I had a wonderful memory in medical school: you can't get through without it: all those bones, those nerves, the muscles . . .'

'The diseases,' volunteered Brunetti.

'Yes, those too. But just remembering all the parts of this,' the pathologist said, flipping the backs of his hands down the front of his own body, 'that's a triumph.' Then, more reflectively, 'But what's inside, that's a miracle.'

'Miracle?' Brunetti asked.

'In a manner of speaking,' Rizzardi said. 'Something wonderful.' Rizzardi looked at his friend and must have seen something he liked, or trusted, for he went on, 'If you think about it, the most ordinary things we do — picking up a glass, tying our shoes, whistling . . . they're all tiny miracles.'

'Then why do you do what you do?' Brunetti asked, surprising himself with the question.

'What?' Rizzardi asked. 'I don't understand.'

'Work with people after the miracles are over,' Brunetti said for want of a better way to say it.

There was a long pause before Rizzardi answered. At last he said, 'I never thought of it that way.' He looked down at his own hands, turned them over and studied the palms for a moment. 'Maybe it's because what I do lets me see more clearly the way things work, the things that make the miracles possible.'

As if suddenly embarrassed, Rizzardi clasped his hands together and said, 'The men who brought him in said there were no papers. No identification. Nothing.'

'Clothing?'

Rizzardi shrugged. 'They bring them in

here naked. Your men must have taken everything back to the lab.'

Brunetti made a noise of agreement or understanding or perhaps of thanks. 'I'll go over there and have a look. The report I read said they found him at about six.'

Rizzardi shook his head. 'I don't know anything about that, only that he was the first one today.'

Surprised — this was Venice, after all — Brunetti asked, 'How many more were there?'

Rizzardi nodded towards the two fully draped figures on the other side of the room. 'Those old people over there.'

'How old?'

'The son says his father was ninety-three, his mother ninety.'

'What happened?' Brunetti asked. He had read the papers that morning, but no mention had been made of their deaths.

'One of them made coffee last night. The pot was in the sink. The flame went out, but the gas was still on.' Rizzardi added, 'It was an old stove, the kind you need a match for.'

Then, before Brunetti could speak, the doctor went on, 'The neighbour upstairs smelled gas and called the firemen, and when they went in they found the place full of gas, the two of them dead on top of the bed. The cups and saucers were beside them.'

In the face of Brunetti's silence, Rizzardi added, 'It's a good thing the place didn't blow up.'

'It's a strange place for people to drink coffee,' Brunetti said.

Rizzardi gave his friend a sharp look. 'She had Alzheimer's and he didn't have the money to put her anywhere,' then added, 'The son has three kids and lives in a two-bedroom apartment in Mogliano.'

Brunetti said nothing.

'The son told me,' Rizzardi continued, 'that his father said he couldn't take care of her any more, not the way he wanted to.'

'Said?'

'He left a note. Said he didn't want people to think he was losing his memory and had forgotten to turn the gas off.' Rizzardi turned away from the dead and moved towards the door. 'He had a pension of five hundred and twelve Euros, and she had five hundred and eight.' Then, like doom itself, he added, 'Their rent was seven hundred and fifty a month.'

'I see,' Brunetti said.

Rizzardi opened the door and let them into the corridor of the hospital.

2

They walked down the corridor in companionable silence, Brunetti's thoughts divided between his own lingering terror at his mother's fate and Rizzardi's talk of a 'miracle'. Well, who better to contemplate that than someone who had it under his hands every day?

He considered the note the old man had left for his son, words written from the heart of something Brunetti found so fearful that he could not bear to name it. It had been deliberately willed, this opting out of life, and the old man had chosen it for both of them. But first he had made their coffee. With a deliberate lurch of his mind, Brunetti freed himself from the room where the two old people had drunk their coffee and the inevitability of the choice that had moved them from that place to the chill room where he had seen them.

He turned to Rizzardi and asked, 'Is there

a way I could use this Marlung disease — if he's being treated for it — as a way to find out who he is?'

'Madelung,' Rizzardi corrected automatically, then went on, 'You might send an official request for information to the hospitals with centres for genetic diseases, with a description of him.' Then, after a moment's reflection, the doctor added, 'Assuming he's been diagnosed, that is.'

Thinking back to the man he had seen on the table, Brunetti asked, 'But how could he not be? Diagnosed, that is. You saw his neck, the size of him.'

Outside the door to his office, Rizzardi turned to Brunetti and said, 'Guido, there are people walking around everywhere with symptoms of serious disease so visible they'd cause any doctor's hair to catch fire if they saw them.'

'And?' Brunetti asked.

'And they tell themselves it's nothing, that it will go away if they just ignore it. They'll stop coughing, the bleeding will stop, the thing on their leg will disappear.'

'And?'

'And sometimes it does, and sometimes it doesn't.'

'And if it doesn't?' Brunetti asked.

'Then I get to see them,' Rizzardi said

grimly. He gave himself a shake, as if, like Brunetti, he wanted to free himself of certain thoughts, and added, 'I know someone at Padova who might know about Madelung: I'll call her. That's the likely place someone from the Veneto would go.'

And if he's not from the Veneto? Brunetti found himself wondering, but he said nothing to the pathologist. Instead, he thanked him and asked if he wanted to go down to the bar for a coffee.

'No, thanks. Like yours, my life is filled with papers and reports, and I planned to waste the rest of my morning reading them and writing them.'

Brunetti accepted his decision with a nod and started towards the main entrance of the hospital. A lifetime of good health had done nothing to counter the effects of imagination; thus Brunetti was often subject to the attacks of diseases to which he had not been exposed and of which he displayed no symptoms. Paola was the only person he had ever told about this, though his mother, while she was still capable of knowing things, had known, or at least suspected. Paola managed to see the absurdity of his uneasiness: it is too much to call them fears, since a large part of him was never persuaded that he actually had the disease in question.

His imagination scorned banal things like heart disease or flu, often upping the ante and giving himself West Nile Fever or meningitis. Malaria, once. Diabetes, though unknown in his family, was an old and frequently visiting friend. Part of him knew these diseases served as lightning rods to keep his mind from suspecting that any loss of memory, however momentary, was the first symptom of what he really feared. Better a night mulling over the bizarre symptoms of dengue fever than the flash of alarm that came when he failed to remember the number of Vianello's *telefonino.*

Brunetti turned his thoughts to the man with the neck: he had begun to think of him in those terms. His eyes were blue, which meant Brunetti must have seen him somewhere or seen a photo of him: nothing else would explain his certainty.

Mind on autopilot, Brunetti continued towards the Questura. Crossing over Rio di S. Giovanni, he checked the waters for signs of the seaweed that had, during the last few years, been snaking its way deeper into the heart of the city. He consulted his mental map and saw that it would drift up the Rio dei Greci, if it came. Certainly there was enough of it and to spare slopping out there against Riva degli Schiavoni: it hardly needed a strong tide to propel it into the viscera of the city.

He noticed it then, unruly patches floating towards him on the incoming tide. He remembered seeing, a decade ago, the flat-nosed boats with their front-end scoops, chugging about in the *laguna,* dining on the giant drifts of seaweed. Where had they gone and what were they doing now, those odd little boats, silly and stunted but oh, so voraciously useful? He had crossed the causeway on a train last week, flanked by vast islands of floating weed. Boats skirted them; birds avoided them; nothing could survive beneath them. Did no one else notice, or was everyone meant to pretend they weren't there? Or was the jurisdiction of the waters of the *laguna* divided up among warring authorities — the city, the region, the province, the Magistrate of the Waters — parcelled and wrapped up so tightly as to make motion impossible?

As Brunetti walked, his thoughts unrolled and wandered where they chose. In the past, when he encountered a person he had met somewhere, he occasionally recognized them without remembering who they were. Often, along with that physical recognition came the memory of an emotional aura —

he could think of no more apt term — they had left with him. He knew he liked them or disliked them, though the reasons for that feeling had disappeared along with their identity.

Seeing the man with the neck — he had to stop calling him that — had made Brunetti uneasy, for the emotional aura that had come with the memory of the colour of his eyes was uncertain, bringing with it a sense of Brunetti's desire to help him. It was impossible to sort his way through this. The place where he had just seen the man made it obvious that someone had failed to help him or that he had failed to help himself, but there was no reconstructing now whether it was the sight of him earlier that day or the sense of having seen him before that had prompted this urge in Brunetti.

Still mulling this over, he entered the Questura and headed towards his office. About to start up the final flight of steps, he turned back and went into the room shared by members of the uniformed branch. Pucetti sat at the computer, his attention riveted to the screen as his hands flew over the keys. Brunetti stopped just inside the door. Pucetti might as well have been on some other planet, so little was he conscious of the room in which he sat.

As Brunetti watched, Pucetti's body grew ever tenser, his breathing tighter. The young officer began to mutter to himself, or perhaps to the computer. Without warning, Pucetti's face, and then his body, relaxed. He pulled his hands from the keys, stared a moment at the screen, then raised his right hand, index finger extended, and jabbed at a single key in the manner of a jazz pianist hitting the final note he knew would bring the audience to its feet.

Pucetti's hand bounced away from the keys and stopped, forgotten, at the level of his ear, his eyes still on the screen. Whatever he saw there lifted him to his feet, both arms jammed above his head in the gesture made by every triumphant athlete Brunetti had ever seen on the sports page. 'Got you, you bastard!' the young officer shouted, waving his fists wildly over his head and shifting his weight back and forth on his feet. It wasn't a war dance, but it was close. Alvise and Riverre, standing together at the other side of the room, turned towards the noise and motion, their surprise evident.

Brunetti took a few steps into the room. 'What have you done, Pucetti?' he asked, then added, 'Who'd you get?'

Pucetti, radiant with a mixture of glee and triumph that took a decade off his face, turned to his superior. 'Those bastards at the airport,' he said, punctuating his statement with two quick uppercuts into the air above his head.

'The baggage handlers?' Brunetti asked, though it was hardly necessary. He had been investigating them and arresting them for almost a decade.

'Sì.' Pucetti failed to restrain a hoot of wild success, and his dancing feet took two more triumphant steps.

Alvise and Riverre, intrigued, moved towards them.

'What did you do?' Brunetti asked.

With an act of will, Pucetti brought his feet together and lowered his hands. 'I got into . . .' he began and then, glancing at his fellow officers, said, enthusiasm fading from his voice, 'some information about one of them, sir.'

All excitement disappeared from Pucetti's manner; Brunetti took the hint and responded with studied indifference. 'Well, good for you. You must tell me about it some time.' Then, to Alvise, 'Could you come up to my office for a moment?' He had no idea what to say to Alvise, so inadequate was the man's ability to grasp anything he was told, but Brunetti sensed he had to distract the two officers from paying any attention to what Pucetti had said or attributing to it any importance.

Alvise saluted and gave Riverre a look from which self-importance was not absent. 'Riverre,' Brunetti said, 'could you go down to the man on the door and ask him if the package has arrived for me?' To prepare for the inevitable, he added, 'If it hasn't come, don't bother to tell me. It'll come tomorrow.'

Riverre loved tasks, and to the degree that they were simple and explained clearly, he could usually perform them. He too saluted and turned towards the door, leaving Brunetti to regret he had not thought of some request that would have got them both out of the room. 'Come along, Alvise,' he said.

As Brunetti began to shepherd Alvise towards the door, Pucetti took his place at the computer and hit a few keys; Brunetti watched the screen grow dark.

3

Brunetti found it perversely fitting to be going upstairs with Alvise, since making conversation with him was so often an uphill climb. He tried to stay on the same step as the slower-moving officer so as not to make even more evident the difference in their height. 'I wanted to ask you,' Brunetti invented as they reached the top, 'how you think the mood of the men is.'

'Mood, sir?' Alvise asked with eager curiosity. To show his willingness to cooperate, he gave a nervous smile to suggest he would do so as soon as he understood.

'Whether they feel positive about the work and about being here,' Brunetti said, as uncertain as Alvise apparently was about what he might mean by 'mood'. Alvise fought to preserve his smile.

'Since you've known many of them for so long, I thought they might have spoken to you.'

'About what, sir?'

Brunetti asked himself if anyone in possession of all his faculties would confide in Alvise or ask his opinion about anything. 'Or you might have heard something.' No sooner had Brunetti said that than it occurred to him that Alvise might take this as an invitation to spy and be offended by the offer, though for Alvise to take offence was as unlikely as his ability to see a hidden meaning in anything.

Alvise stopped at Brunetti's door and asked, 'You mean, do they like it here, sir?'

Brunetti put on an easy smile and said, 'Yes, good way to put it, Alvise.'

'I think some of us do and some of us don't, sir,' he said sagely, then hastened to add, 'I'm one of the ones who do, sir. You can count on that.'

Prolonging the smile, Brunetti said, 'Oh, that was never in doubt: but I was curious about the others and hoped you'd know.'

Alvise blushed. Then he said, voice hesitant, 'I suppose you don't want me to tell any of the boys you asked, eh?'

'No, perhaps better not to,' Brunetti answered; Alvise must have expected this answer, for no disappointment showed in his face. Conscious of how easily the kindness came into his voice, Brunetti asked,

'Something else, Alvise?'

The officer put his hands in the pockets of his trousers, looked at his shoes, as if to find the question he wanted to ask written there, looked at Brunetti, and said, 'Could I tell my wife, sir? That you asked me?' He placed unconscious emphasis on the final word.

Only by force of will did Brunetti stop himself from putting his arm around Alvise's shoulder to give him a hug. 'Of course, Alvise. I'm sure I can trust her as much as I do you.'

'Oh, much more, sir,' Alvise said with accidental truth. Then, briskly, 'Is that package big, sir?'

Momentarily at a loss, Brunetti merely repeated, 'Package?'

'The one that's coming, sir. If it is, I could help Riverre bring it up.'

'Ah, of course,' Brunetti said, feeling like the captain of the school soccer team asked by a first-year student if he wanted him to hold his ankles while he did sit-ups. Then, quickly, 'No, thanks, Alvise. It's very generous of you to offer, but it's only an envelope with some files in it.'

'All right, sir. But I thought I'd ask. In case it was. Heavy, that is.'

'Thanks again,' Brunetti said and opened

the door to his office.

The sight of a computer on his desk drove all lingering concern with Alvise and his sensibilities from Brunetti's mind. He approached it with something between trepidation and curiosity. He had been told nothing. His request to have his own computer was so old that Brunetti had quite forgotten both about the request and the possibility that one of his own might someday materialize.

He saw that the screen carried the command: 'Please choose a password and confirm it. Then press "Enter". If you want me to have the password, press "Enter" twice.' Brunetti sat and studied the instructions, read them again, and considered their significance. Signorina Elettra — it could have been no one else — had organized this, had no doubt loaded the computer with those things he would need, and had set up a system that would make intrusion impossible. He began to consider the options: sooner or later, he would need advice, would work himself into a corner from which he would need to extricate himself. And she, being the mind behind the design, would be the one to help him. He did not know if she would need his password in order to untangle whatever mess he had made.

And he didn't care. He hit 'Enter' once, and then once again.

The screen flickered. If he expected some acknowledgement from her to flash across the screen, he was disappointed: all that appeared was the usual list of icons for the programs available to him. He opened his email accounts, both the official one at the Questura and his personal account. The first held nothing of interest; the second was empty. He typed in Signorina Elettra's work address, then the single word *'Grazie'*, and sent it off without signature. He waited for the answering ping of her reply, but nothing came.

Brunetti, proud of himself for having hit that second 'Enter' without having given it much thought, was struck by how technology had colonized human emotions: to tell someone your password was now the equivalent of giving them the key to your heart. Or at least to your correspondence. Or your bank account. He knew Paola's, always forgot it, and so had written it in his address book under James: 'madamemerle', no caps, all one word, an unsettling choice.

He connected to the internet and was astonished by the speed of the connection.

Soon no doubt he'd find it normal, and then he'd find it slow.

He typed in the correct name of the disease, Madelung, and was instantly confronted with a series of articles in Italian and in English. He chose the first and, for the next twenty minutes, doggedly read through the symptoms and proposed treatments, learning little more than Rizzardi had told him. Almost always men, almost always drinkers, almost always without a cure, with quite a high concentration of the disease in Italy.

He clicked the program closed and decided to take care of unfinished business: he called down to the officers' room to ask Pucetti to come up. When the young man arrived, Brunetti gestured to the chair in front of his desk.

Before sitting, Pucetti gave a look he could not disguise at Brunetti's computer. His eyes shot to his superior and then back to the computer, as if he had difficulty pairing the one with the other. Brunetti resisted the impulse to smile and tell the young officer that, if he did his homework and kept his room clean, he'd let him take it for a ride. Instead, he said, 'Tell me.'

Pucetti did not bother pretending not to understand. 'The one we've arrested three times — Buffaldi — has gone on two first-class cruises in the last two years. He has a new car parked in the garage at Piazzale Roma. And his wife bought a new apartment last year: declared price was 250,000 Euros, but the real price was 350,000.' Pucetti held up a finger with each fact, then folded his hands and put them in his lap to signify that he had nothing else to say.

'How did you get this information?' Brunetti asked.

The younger man looked down at his folded hands. 'I had a look at his financial records.'

'I think I could have figured that much out, Pucetti,' Brunetti said in a calm voice. 'How did you gain access to that information?'

'I did it on my own, sir,' Pucetti said in a firm voice. 'She didn't help me. Not at all.'

Brunetti sighed. If a safe-cracker files off a layer of skin to sensitize his pupil's fingertips or teaches him how to blow a lock, who's responsible for opening the safe? Each time Brunetti himself used his burglar tools to open a door, how much responsibility fell to the thief who had taught him how to use them? And, given that Brunetti had passed this skill on to Vianello, who bore the guilt for every door the Inspector managed to open?

'Your defence of Signorina Elettra is admirable, Pucetti, and your skill is a credit to her pedagogical capabilities.' He refused to smile. 'I had something more practical in mind with my question, however: what did you open and what information did you steal?'

Brunetti watched Pucetti fight down his pride and his confusion at his superior's apparent displeasure. 'His credit card records, sir.'

'And the apartment?' Brunetti asked, forbearing to remark that most people did not buy apartments with credit cards.

'I found out who the notary was who handled the sale.'

Brunetti waited, irony carefully placed aside.

'And I know someone who works in his office,' Pucetti added.

'Who?'

'I'd rather not say, sir,' Pucetti answered, his eyes in his lap.

'Admirable sentiment,' Brunetti said. 'This person confirmed the difference in price?'

Pucetti looked up at this. 'She wasn't sure, sir, but she said that when they discussed the sale with the notary, they made no secret that the difference in price would be at least a hundred thousand.'

'I see.' Brunetti allowed some time to pass, during which Pucetti twice glanced at the computer, as if memorizing the name and dimensions. 'And where does this lead us?'

Pucetti looked up eagerly. 'Isn't it enough to reopen the investigation? He makes about fifteen hundred Euros a month at that job. Where else does this money come from? He's been filmed opening suitcases and taking things from them: jewels, cameras, computers.' He paused, as though he were not the one who should be answering questions.

'The filming was dismissed as evidence during the last trial, as you know, Pucetti, and we are not yet at a place where the mere possession of large amounts of money is proof that it was stolen.' Brunetti kept calm, imitating the voice of the defence attorney the last time the baggage handlers had been accused of theft. 'He could have won the lottery, or his wife could have. He could have borrowed the money from members of his family. He could have found it in the street.'

'But you know he didn't, sir,' Pucetti pleaded. 'You know what he's doing, what the lot of them are doing.'

'What I know and what a prosecutor can prove in a court of law are entirely different matters, Pucetti,' Brunetti said, not without a note of reprimand in his voice. 'And I suggest very strongly that you consider this fact.' He saw the young man open his mouth to protest and raised his voice to stop him. 'Further, I want you to go back and very carefully cancel any traces you might have left during your investigation of Signor Buffaldi's finances.' Before Pucetti could object, he added, 'If you managed to find them, then someone else will be able to find that you have been there, and that information would render Signor Buffaldi untouchable for the rest of his career.'

'He's pretty much untouchable now, isn't he?' Pucetti said, voice just short of anger.

That was enough to spark Brunetti's own. Impetuous boy, thinking he could change things: so much the way Brunetti had been decades ago, just sworn into the force and keen to work for justice. The memory calmed Brunetti, who said, 'Pucetti, the system we have is the one we have to use. To criticize it is as useless as to praise it. You know and I know how limited our powers are.'

As if giving in to a force stronger than his

power to resist it, Pucetti said, 'But what about her? She finds out things, and you use them.' Brunetti was again conscious of Pucetti's zeal.

'Pucetti, I saw your face when I told you to cancel your traces: you know you left some. If you can't eliminate them, then ask Signorina Elettra to help you do so. I don't want this case made more difficult than it is.'

'But unless you use this . . .' Pucetti said in a high voice.

Staring him down, Brunetti continued in a tight voice. 'I have the information, Pucetti. I've had it since they booked the tickets for the cruises and bought the car, and bought the house. So go back and remove your traces, and don't ever think of doing something like this without my knowledge, without my authorization.'

'What's the difference?' Pucetti asked, in a voice that sought information, not sarcastic revenge. 'About how you got it?'

How much to trust him? How to stop Pucetti from dragging them into a legal swamp while still encouraging him to take chances? 'She doesn't leave traces and you do.'

Then Brunetti picked up his phone and dialled Signorina Elettra's number. When she answered, he said, 'Signorina. I'm just going out for a coffee. Do you think you could step up to my office while I'm gone? Pucetti has some changes he has to make to research he's been doing, and I wonder if you could help him.' He paused for a moment while she answered, then said, 'Of course I'll wait until you come up.' He replaced the phone and went to stand by the window until she arrived.

4

Brunetti, who had already had three coffees that morning and did not want another, went down to the lab in search of Bocchese and whatever information he might have about the man who had been found that morning. When he went in, he saw two technicians at a long table at the back, one pulling objects from a cardboard box with plastic-gloved hands while the other appeared to check something on a list each time he removed a new object. The gloved one took a step to his left as Brunetti entered, cutting off his ability to distinguish the objects.

Bocchese sat at his desk in the corner, his head bent over a sheet of paper on which he appeared to be making a drawing. The lab chief did not raise his head at the sound of approaching footsteps, and Brunetti saw that the bald spot on the top of his head had expanded in recent months. Draped in a shapeless white workman's tunic, Bocchese could easily have been a monk in some medieval monastery. Brunetti abandoned this idea as he grew near and saw that the man was drawing a thin blade and not illuminating the initial letter in some biblical text.

'Is that what killed him?' Brunetti asked.

Bocchese changed his grip on the pencil and used the side of the point to shade in the underside of the blade. 'It's what Rizzardi's report described,' he said, holding the paper up so that he and Brunetti could examine it. 'It's almost twenty centimetres long and widens to four near the handle.' Then, with gruff expertise, 'So it was a regular knife, not one he could fold closed and put in his pocket. Find it in any kitchen, I'd say.'

'The point?' Brunetti asked.

'Very narrow. But that's normal with knives, isn't it? Most of it is about two centimetres wide.' He tapped the eraser end of the pencil against the point of the blade in the drawing. Then he added a few lines, curving the cutting edge of the blade upward to the tip. 'The report says tissue at the top of the cuts showed evidence of being scraped, probably when the blade was pulled out,' he explained. 'The cuts were wider at the top, but knife wounds always are.' Again he tapped the drawing with the eraser. 'That's what we're looking for.'

'You didn't draw a handle,' Brunetti said.

'Of course not,' the technician said, putting the paper down on his desk. 'There's nothing in the report that would give me any idea of what it was like.'

'Does it make a difference, not knowing?' Brunetti asked.

'You mean in identifying what sort of knife it is?'

'Yes. I suppose so.'

Bocchese put his hand, palm down, on the paper, just at the wider end of the blade, as if to wrap it around whatever handle would be there. 'It would have to be at least ten centimetres long,' he said, his hand still flat on the paper. 'Most handles are.' Then, surprising Brunetti with the irrelevance of it, he added, 'Even potato peelers.'

He removed his hand and looked at Brunetti for the first time. 'You need at least ten to get a grip of any sort. Why'd you ask?'

'Because he'd have to carry it, and if the blade's twenty and the handle ten, then it would be an awkward thing to walk around with.'

'Folded in a newspaper, in a computer case, briefcase; it would even fit in a Manila folder if you put it in on the slant,' Bocchese said. 'Make a difference?'

'You don't walk around with a knife that long unless you have a reason to. You have to think about how to carry it so no one will see it.'

'And that suggests premeditation?'

'I think so. He wasn't killed in the kitchen or the workshop or wherever else a knife might be lying around, was he?'

Bocchese shrugged.

'What does that mean?' Brunetti asked, leaning one hip against the desk and folding his arms.

'We don't know where it happened. The ambulance report says he was found in Rio del Malpaga, just behind the Giustinian. Rizzardi says he had water in his lungs, so he could have been killed anywhere and put in the water, then drifted there.' Seeing some invisible imperfection in the drawing, Bocchese picked up his pencil and added another faint line halfway down the blade.

'It's not an easy thing to do,' Brunetti said.

'What?'

'Slip a body into a canal.'

'From a boat, it might be easier,' Bocchese suggested.

'Then you've got blood in a boat.'

'Fish bleed.'

'And fishing boats have motors, and no motors are allowed after eight at night.'

'Taxis are,' Bocchese volunteered.

'People don't hire taxis to dump bodies in the water,' Brunetti said easily, familiar with Bocchese's manner.

After only a second's hesitation, the technician said, 'Then a boat without a motor.'

'Or a water door from a house.'

'And no nosey neighbours.'

'A quiet canal, a place where there are no neighbours, nosey or otherwise,' Brunetti suggested, starting to examine the map in his head. Then he said, 'Rizzardi's guess was after midnight.'

'Cautious man, the Doctor.'

'Found at six,' Brunetti said.

" 'After midnight",' Bocchese said. 'Doesn't mean he went in at midnight.'

'Where behind the Giustinian was he found?' Brunetti asked, needing the first coordinate on his map.

'At the end of Calle Degolin.'

Brunetti made a noise of acknowledgement, glanced at the wall behind Bocchese, and sent himself walking in an impossible circular path, radiating out from that fixed point, jumping over canals from one dead-end *calle* to another, trying, but failing, to recall the buildings that had doors and steps down to the water.

After a moment, Bocchese said, 'Better ask Foa about the tides. He'd know.'

It had been Brunetti's thought, as well. 'Yes. I'll ask him.' Then he asked, 'Can I have a look at his things?'

'Of course. They should be dry by now,' Bocchese said. He walked over to the table where the two men were still listing the things taken from the box, passed them, and opened the door to a storeroom to their left. Inside, Brunetti was struck by the heat and by the smell: fetid, rank, a combination of earth and mould and abandoned things.

Neatly folded over an ordinary household drying rack were a shirt and a pair of trousers, a set of men's underwear and a pair of socks. Brunetti bent to look more closely and saw nothing peculiar about them. Underneath stood a single shoe, brown, about Brunetti's size. A small table held a gold wedding ring and a metal watch with an expandable metal band, a few coins, and a set of keys.

Brunetti picked up the keys without bothering to ask if he could touch them. Four of them looked like ordinary door keys, another one was much smaller and the last one had the distinctive VW that the manufacturer put on all of their keys. 'So he owns a car,' Brunetti said.

'Like about forty million other people,' Bocchese answered.

'Then I won't say anything about the house keys or the one for the mailbox,' Brunetti said with a smile.

'Four houses?'

'My house needs two,' Brunetti said. 'Most of the houses in the city do. And two more get me into my office.'

'I know,' Bocchese said. 'I'm trying to provoke you.'

'I noticed,' Brunetti said. 'What about the smaller one? Am I right to think it's for a mailbox?'

'Could be,' Bocchese admitted, in a tone that said it could just as easily not be.

'What else?'

'Small safe, not a serious one; tool chest; garden shed; door to a garden or courtyard; and I suppose I'm overlooking some other possibilities.'

'Anything engraved in the ring?'

'Nothing,' Bocchese said. 'Machine made — sold everywhere.'

'Clothes?'

'Most of them made in China — what isn't these days? — but the shoe is Italian: Fratelli Moretti.'

'Odd combination: clothing made in China and expensive shoes.'

'Someone could have given them to him,' Bocchese suggested.

'Anyone ever give you a pair of shoes?'

'Does that mean I should stop provoking you?' the technician asked.

'It would help.'

'All right.' Then, 'You want me to guess out loud?'

'That would help, too.'

'I've had a look at the things he was wearing, and it doesn't look like he was in a boat. His clothes are clean: no oil, no tar, none of the sort of thing you'd get on you if you were put in the bottom of a boat. Even if there's no motor, they're dirty things.'

'And so?'

'So I think he was killed on land, either on the street or in a house, and he was put in the water after he was stabbed. Whoever did it thought he was dead or was so sure of what they were doing that they knew he had no chance, and the canal was just a way to get rid of him. Maybe to give them more time to get out of the city, or maybe they wanted him to drift away from where they did it.'

Brunetti nodded. He too had been thinking about this. 'A man lying in the bottom of a boat would always be visible from above.'

'We'll check for fibres, to see if he was covered or wrapped in something. But I don't think that's the case,' Bocchese said, waving towards the shirt, simple white cotton, the sort of thing any man would wear.

'No jacket, eh?' Brunetti asked.

'No. All he was wearing was the shirt and trousers,' Bocchese said. 'He must have been wearing a jacket or a sweater. Too cold last night to go out without one.'

'Or he could have been killed in his own house?' Brunetti suggested. It was his turn to provoke: he wanted Bocchese to agree with him before remarking that most people did not walk around in their houses with their keys in their pockets.

'Yes,' Bocchese said, sounding very unconvinced.

'But?'

'Rizzardi's report says he has Madelung. He hasn't sent the photos yet, but I've seen it before. It's possible someone here has seen him. Or they'd know him at the hospital.'

'Perhaps,' Brunetti agreed, uncertain that anyone would recognize a photo of the battered face. Bocchese was being cooperative, so he decided not to mention the keys again.

'Anything else?' Brunetti asked.

'No. If I find anything or think of anything, I'll let you know, all right?'

'Thanks,' Brunetti said. Bocchese had mentioned the man's disease, certain that anyone who saw him would remember him. He wondered if a shoe salesman would. 'Can you send me an email with the information about the shoe?'

5

When he returned to his office, Brunetti found Signorina Elettra still sitting at his computer. She looked up when he came in and smiled. 'I'm almost finished, Commissario. As I was here, I thought I'd download a few more things, and then it's ready.'

'Dare I ask how you managed to procure this marvel, Signorina?' he asked, leaning forward with both hands on the back of a chair.

She held up one finger to ask him to wait and returned her attention to the keyboard. She was wearing green today, a light wool dress he did not remember her having worn before. She rarely wore green: perhaps her choice was in honour of springtime; even the Church used green as the ecclesiastical colour of hope. Trying not to appear to do so, he watched her work, struck by the totality of her concentration. He might as well have been somewhere else for all the attention she paid him. Was it the program or working on the new computer that enthralled her so? he wondered. And how was it possible that something so alien from the unruly mess of life could exert such an attraction on such a person? Computers failed to interest Brunetti: yes, he used them and was glad of being able to do so, but he was always much happier to send this green-clad hunter off in pursuit of the game that proved too elusive for his limited skills. He simply could not work up any enthusiasm for the concept, had no desire to spend endless hours sitting in front of the screen and seeing what he could make the computer do for him.

Brunetti was sufficiently attuned to the times in which he lived to realize how foolish his prejudice was and how it sometimes slowed down the pace at which he could work. Had it not been that way with the investigation into the protest against European milk quotas that had blocked the autostrada near Mestre for two days last autumn? Because Signorina Elettra had been on vacation when that happened, he had had to wait two days before learning that the men who had set fire to cars trapped by the farmers' roadblock were petty criminals from Vicenza, urban criminals who had probably never seen a cow in their lives. And it was not until her return that he found out they were also cousins of the head of the provincial association of farmers, the man who had organized the protest.

His memory drifted back to that protest, which his superior, Vice-Questore Patta, had ordered him to observe in case the violence spread to the bridge to Venice and thus into their territory. He remembered the helmeted Carabinieri with their Plexiglas shields and face masks and polished black boots that turned their legs into highly polished stems and thinking how much like giant bugs they looked. He recalled the sight of them marching forward, their shields locked together, pressing ahead to repel any protest from the assembled farmers.

And there he was, the man with the neck, leaping unsummoned into Brunetti's memory. He had stood in a group of people on the other side of the blocked road from Brunetti, milling around their stopped cars and looking across the road divider at the farmers and the police. Brunetti remembered the taurine neck and bearded face and the clear eyes that watched the two opposed lines of men with what seemed to be a mixture of confusion and exasperation, but then Brunetti's attention had been pulled away by the explosion of violence and vandalism into which the protest descended.

'. . . many graces with which we are favoured by a beneficent Europe,' he heard Signorina Elettra say and called his attention back to her.

'In what particular way, Signorina?' he asked.

'The funds to Interpol to combat the falsification of merchandise that is protected by patents from any country in the European Union,' she said with a smile, the one she used when at her most predatory. Brunetti gave an inner tremble at the thought of the patent authorizations that must be streaming out of the offices of certain countries.

'I thought the NAS took care of all of that,' he said.

'Yes, they do, at least in Italy.' She gave the computer keys an affectionate caress then whisked away a random mote of dust from the screen. Then, brightly, looking across at him, 'It seems there is a small clause near the end of the ministerial decree, making provision for local entities to apply for supplementary funding.'

Conscious of how formulaic their conversation sometimes became, he asked, 'Funding for what purpose, Signorina?'

'To help with research at the local level into . . .' she began. A quiet sigh escaped her lips and she held up a hand. The other, like the tongue of a mother cat too long prevented from licking its newest-born, began to smooth the keys, and her eyes fell to the screen. She tapped out a silent request.

Brunetti came around the desk and sat.

In less than a minute, she looked up at him, then back at the screen, and read, ' ". . . at the local level to ensure that all efforts on the part of the competent Ministry to investigate and impede the counterfeiting of patented products be initiated and supported by supplementary funding in accordance with Regulation blah blah blah, subsection blah blah, with supplementary reference to Ministerial Decree blah blah blah, of 23 February 2001." '

'And when that is not pretending to make sense, what might it mean?' Brunetti inquired.

'It creates another pig's trough where the clever can dine, sir,' she said simply, her eyes still on the screen as though they delighted in dining off some rich interpretation of those words. When Brunetti did not respond, she went on, 'And in essence it means that we are free to use the money as we please, so long as our intention is to investigate and impede the production of these products.'

'That would certainly give the agency doing the investigating and the impeding a great deal of latitude in how to spend the money.'

'They are not fools, these men in Brussels,' she observed.

'Meaning?'

'Meaning that it is another gift to bureaucrats who are as inventive as they.' Then, after a pause meant perhaps to give weight to what was to follow, she added, 'Or who have the perseverance to read through the four hundred and twelve pages of the decree to find that particular paragraph.'

'Or to those who might receive a quiet, private suggestion about where it would be most profitable to direct their attention?' Brunetti asked.

'Do I detect the voice of a Euro-sceptic, sir?'

'You do.'

'Ah,' she whispered; then, as if unable to prevent herself from asking, she added, 'But that won't stop you from keeping the computer?'

'In the presence of a trough, it is difficult

not to oink,' Brunetti replied.

She looked at him, eyes wide with delight. 'I doubt that I have ever heard a more apposite explanation of the failure of our political system, sir.'

Brunetti allowed a few moments to pass so that they might again enjoy the experience of having filled with rich meaning the spaces between their words. Signorina Elettra touched a few keys, then started to get to her feet.

Brunetti raised a hand to stop her. 'Do you remember that trouble on the autostrada last year?' Realizing how unclear his question was, he added, 'With the farmers?'

'About milk quotas?'

'Yes.'

'What about it, sir?'

'A man was killed this morning. I've just come from talking to Rizzardi.' She nodded to show that the news of the murder had already reached the Questura. 'When I saw him — the man, not Rizzardi — I realized he looked familiar, and then I remembered that it was out there on the autostrada that I saw him.'

'Was he one of the protestors?'

'No. He was on the other side of the autostrada; his car was one of the ones blocked by the protest. I saw him there, standing with the other people who got stuck.'

'And you remembered him?'

'When you read Rizzardi's report, you'll understand,' Brunetti said.

'What would you like me to do, sir?'

'Contact the Carabinieri. Lovello in Mestre was in charge of it. See if they've got photos or maybe a video.' So many charges of excessive violence had been brought against the police and the Carabinieri in recent years that some commanders insisted on filming actions with a potential for violence.

'And check with Televeneto,' he added. 'They had a crew out there, so they should have something: see if they'll give you a copy.'

'Was RAI there?'

'I don't remember. But the local people would know if the big boys showed up. If so, see if you can get them to send you copies of whatever they shot, as well.'

'What does this man look like?'

'He's big, very thick around the shoulders and neck. Beard: he had it then, too. Dark hair, light eyes.'

She nodded. 'Thank you, sir. I'll tell them that so they can sort through the shots before they send me any.'

'Good, good,' Brunetti said.

'He was stabbed, wasn't he?' she asked.

'Yes. But Rizzardi said he had water in his lungs. They found him in a canal.'

'Did he drown?'

'No, the knife killed him.'

'How old was he?' she asked.

'In his forties.'

'Poor man,' she said, and Brunetti could but agree.

6

That left Patta. The obligation to deal with his superior often filled Brunetti with an anticipatory weariness, as if he were a swimmer who had miscounted laps and suddenly realized he still had ten to do in water that grew increasingly chilly. Also, like any athlete in competition, Brunetti had made a study of the track record of his opponent. Patta was quick off the block, had no compunction about obstructing the path of other competitors so long as he could get away with doing so, but lacked staying power and often dropped back in any long competition. Unfortunately, no matter how far behind he might fall in a race, he could be depended upon to appear at the award ceremony, and the force did not exist that could prevent him from hauling himself up on to the podium the instant that medals started to be handed round.

To know this was to be forewarned, but to

be forewarned served little purpose when one's opponent was Vice-Questore Giuseppe Patta, Sicily's best gift to the forces of order, kept for more than a decade at his position in Venice in anomalous defiance of the rule that high police officials were transferred every few years. Patta's tenacity in his post had puzzled Brunetti until he realized that the only policemen who were systematically transferred away from the cities where they combated crime were those who met with success, especially those who were successful in their opposition to the Mafia. To manage the arrest of the highest members of a Mafia clan in a major city was to guarantee transfer to some backwater in Molise or Sardegna, where major crimes included the theft of livestock or public drunkenness.

Thus perhaps Patta's professional longevity in Venice, where the mounting evidence of Mafia infiltration did nothing to spur his efforts to combat it. Mayors came and went, all of them pledging to correct the ills their predecessors had ignored or encouraged. The city grew dirtier, hotels proliferated and rents increased, every available inch of sidewalk space was rented out to someone wanting to sell unusable junk from a portable stall, and still the waves of promises to sweep away all these ills rose up ever new and ever higher. And there, becalmed at a safe distance behind the breaking wave, was Vice-Questore Giuseppe Patta, friend to every politician he had ever met, the now-almost-permanent face of the forces of order in the city.

Brunetti, however, a tolerant and moderate man, had trained himself to count his superior's virtues rather than his faults, and so he acknowledged that there was no proof that Patta was in the pay of any criminal organization; he had never ordered the mistreatment of a prisoner; he would upon occasion believe incontrovertible evidence of the guilt of a wealthy suspect. Had he been a judge, Patta would surely have been a thoughtful one, always ready to weigh the social position of the accused. In the broad scale of things, Brunetti often reflected, these were not ruinous weaknesses.

Signorina Elettra sat at her desk outside her superior's office and smiled at Brunetti as he entered. 'I thought I'd report to the Vice-Questore,' he said.

'He'll be glad of the distraction,' she said soberly. 'His younger son just called to say he's failed his exam.'

'The less-bright one?' Brunetti inquired, forcing himself not to refer to the boy as stupid, though he was.

'Ah, Commissario, you force me to make a distinction that is beyond my powers,' she said with a straight face and serious voice.

Some years ago, Roberto Patta had more than once come close to being arrested, saved only by his father's position. His involvement with the sale of drugs, however, had come to an end in an early morning car crash in which his fiancée had died, and only his father's position had kept him from being tested for alcohol and drugs until almost a full day after the accident, when both tests proved negative. With her death, however, something seemed to have snapped inside the boy, and he had abandoned — according to the rumours that circulated in the Questura — both drink and drugs and devoted his limited energies to finishing his degree and becoming an accountant.

It was a hopeless attempt. Brunetti knew it; Patta probably did, as well, yet the boy persisted, taking the same exams year after year, always failing them and determining each time to study harder and take them again, probably never pausing to consider that the state exams — should divine intervention confer his degree — would be even more difficult. Various officers whose children were in the same class as he repeated the stories about his dogged efforts, and over the course of years the common mind of the Questura had gone from considering him the spoiled child of a negligent father to the hard working, if limited, son of a devoted parent. The mystery of it — fatherhood was always a mysterious thing to Brunetti — was Patta's devotion to his two sons and his desire that they succeed in life by their own merits, an idea that had formed in him in response to the accident.

'How long ago did he speak to him?' Brunetti asked.

'About an hour,' she answered and then added in a different voice, 'His father was busy talking on his *telefonino* so Roberto called me and asked me to put him through.' She pulled her lips together in resignation. 'He told me what had happened. He was crying.'

'How old is he now, do you know?'

'Twenty-six, I think.'

'God, he'll never make it, will he?'

She shook away the very possibility. 'Not unless someone can fix things for him with the examining committee.'

'He won't do it?' Brunetti asked, indicating with his chin the door to Patta's office. 'He's done it in the past.'

'He won't do it any more.'

'But why?'

'God knows. It would be easy enough. He's certainly cultivated the right people in the last decade.'

'Maybe they don't know whose son he is,' Brunetti suggested.

'Perhaps,' she answered, clearly not persuaded.

'So it's really true?' Brunetti asked, marvelling at a parent who would not bend a rule to help his child.

Brunetti crossed the room and knocked on Patta's door.

'Avanti!' came the response, and Brunetti went in.

Patta looked older than he had the day before. He was still a fine figure of a man: muscular, broad-shouldered, with a face that cried out to be immortalized in bronze or stone. But there were faint hollows under his cheekbones this morning, something Brunetti had never noticed before, and his skin looked taut and almost dusty.

'Good morning, Vice-Questore,' Brunetti said, approaching the desk.

'Yes, what is it?' Patta asked, as though a waiter had approached his table while he was deep in conversation.

'I wanted to tell you about the man who

was found over near the Giustinian this morning, sir.'

'The drowned man?' Patta asked.

'The report must have been confused, sir,' Brunetti said, remaining at some distance from Patta's desk. 'There was water in his lungs: that's in Rizzardi's report. But he was stabbed before he went into the water. Three times.'

'So it's murder?' Patta said in a voice that registered understanding but was devoid of interest or curiosity.

'Yes, sir.'

'You better take a seat, then, Brunetti,' Patta said, as though he had suddenly noticed that the man in front of him was still standing.

'Thank you, sir,' answered Brunetti. He sat, careful not to make any sudden moves, at least not until he figured out Patta's mood.

'Why would someone stab him and put him in the water?' Patta asked, and Brunetti refused to allow himself to answer that, if he knew why, he could go out and arrest the person who did it and thus save them all a great deal of time and effort.

'Do you have an identification?' Patta asked before Brunetti could respond to his first question.

'Signorina Elettra is working on it, sir.'

'I see,' Patta said and left it at that. Abruptly, the Vice-Questore got to his feet and walked over to the window. He stood gazing out of it for so long that Brunetti began to wonder if he should ask him something in order to recapture his attention, but he decided to wait it out. Patta opened the window and let a draught of soft air into the room, then closed it and came back to his chair. 'Do you want it?' he asked when he sat back down.

The options open to Brunetti made the question ludicrous. His choices were Pucetti's baggage handlers, the anticipated increase in pickpocketing that springtime and Easter were bound to bring to the city, the never-ending illegal harvesting of clams, or a murder. But softly, softly, he warned himself. Never let Patta know what you are thinking, and never ever let him know what you want. 'If there's no one else free to handle it, sir. I could pass the Chioggia case' — how much better than calling it the illegal clamming — 'to the uniformed branch. Two of them are Chiogiotti and could probably use their families to find out who's digging the clams.' Eight years at university to chase after illegal clammers.

'All right. Take Griffoni: she might like a

murder for a change.' Still, after all these years, Patta could astonish him with some of the things he said.

He could also astonish Brunetti with the things he did not know. 'She's in Rome, sir: that course in domestic violence.'

'Ah, of course, of course,' Patta said with the wave of a man so busy that he could not be expected to remember everything.

'Vianello isn't assigned to anything at the moment.'

'Take anyone you want,' Patta said expansively. 'We can't have something like this happening.'

'No, sir. Of course not.'

'A person can't come to this city and be murdered.' Patta managed to sound indignant, but there was no way to tell if his emotions were aroused by what had happened to the man or because of what would happen to tourism as a result. Brunetti did not want to ask.

'I'll get busy with it then, sir.'

'Yes, do,' Patta told him. 'Keep me informed of what happens.'

'Of course, sir,' Brunetti said. He glanced at Patta, but he had started to read one of the papers that lay on his desk. Saying nothing, Brunetti let himself out of the office.

7

He closed the door behind him. In response to Signorina Elettra's glance, Brunetti said as he approached her desk, 'He asked me to take the case.'

She smiled. 'Asked, or did you have to encourage him?'

'No, the suggestion was his. He even told me to ask Griffoni to work on it with me.' If her smile had been connected to a dimmer, his words had turned the knob down. He went on, as though he had noticed nothing peculiar about her response to the attractive blonde Commissario's name, 'Forgetting she's in Rome, of course. So I asked for Vianello, and he didn't object.'

Calm restored, Brunetti decided to hammer it into place and asked, the idea having come to him while he was with Patta, 'Isn't there a new rule, some sort of statute of limitations, for students at the university?' Even Patta did not deserve to be subjected, year after year, to the consequences of this farce.

'There's talk of changing the rules so that they have to leave after a certain time,' she answered, 'but I doubt that anything will come of it.'

Talk of normal things appeared to have restored her mood; to maintain it, Brunetti asked, 'Why?'

She turned towards him fully and rested her chin on her hand before she answered. 'Think about what would happen if everyone agreed to accept the obvious and hundreds of thousands of these students were sent away.' When he did not comment, she continued. 'They'd have to accept — and their parents would have to accept — that they are unemployed and likely to remain that way.' Before Brunetti could speak, she voiced the argument he was about to make: 'I know they've never worked, so they wouldn't appear in the statistics as having lost their jobs. But they'd have to face the fact, as would their parents, that they're virtually unemployable.' Brunetti agreed with her, with a brief nod. 'So for as long as they're enrolled in a university, government statistics can ignore them, and they in turn can ignore the fact that they're never going to have decent jobs.' He thought she was finished, but she added, 'It's an enormous holding pool of young people who live off their parents for years and never learn a skill that would make them employable.'

'Such as?' Brunetti inquired.

She raised her hand and ran it through her hair. 'Oh, I don't know. Plumbing. Carpentry. Something useful.'

'Instead of?'

'The son of a friend of mine has been studying Art Administration for seven years. The government cuts the budget for museums and art every year, but he's going to get his degree in Art Administration.'

'And then?'

'And then he'd be lucky to get a job as a museum guard, but he'd scorn that because he's an art administrator,' she said. In a kinder voice, she added, 'He's a bright boy and loves the subject, and for all I know would be perfect for a job in a museum. Only there are not going to be any jobs.'

Brunetti thought of his son, now in his first year, and his daughter, soon to enter the university. 'Does this mean my children face the same future?'

She opened her mouth to speak but stopped herself.

'Go ahead,' Brunetti said. 'Say it.'

He saw the moment when she decided to do so. 'Your wife's family will see that they're protected, or your father-in-law's friends will see that they're offered jobs.'

Brunetti realized she never would have said something like this a few years ago and probably would never have said it now had he not provoked her with his reference to Griffoni. 'The same as with the children of any well-connected family?' he asked.

She nodded.

Suddenly mindful of her politics, he asked, 'You don't object to this?'

She shrugged, then said, 'Whether I do or I don't won't change it.'

'Did it help you get your job at the bank?' he asked, referring to the job she had left, more than a decade ago, to come and work at the Questura, a choice no one who worked with her had ever understood.

She lifted her chin from her hand, saying, 'No, my father didn't help. In fact, he didn't want me to work in a bank at all. He tried to convince me not to do it.'

'Even though he was in charge of one?' Brunetti asked.

'Exactly. He said it had shown him how soul-rotting it was to work with money and to think about money all the time.'

'But you did it anyway?' Brunetti was still

surprised to be engaged in this sort of conversation with her: their exchanges of personal information were usually cushioned by irony or masked by indirection.

'For a number of years, yes.'

'Until?' he asked, wondering if he was about to unravel the secret that had rumbled through the Questura for years and aware that, should she tell him, he could never repeat it.

Her smile changed and began to remind him of a famous one, last seen disappearing amidst the branches of a tree. 'Until it began to rot my soul.'

'Ah,' Brunetti said, deciding that was all the answer he was going to get and probably all he wanted.

'Will there be anything else, Signore?' Before he could respond, she said, 'They've sent the photos and videos from the protest.'

Brunetti could not disguise his astonishment. 'So fast?'

Her smile was as compassionate as that of a Renaissance Madonna. 'By computer, sir. They're in your email.' She glanced over his shoulder and studied the wall behind him for a few seconds, then added, 'I have a friend who works in the central health office for the Veneto. I can ask him to have a look to see if there's some central record kept of cases of this disease . . .'

'Madelung,' Brunetti supplied. The look she gave him showed him that the repetition was not necessary.

'Thank you,' she said to show there were no hard feelings, and then, 'There might be numbers for the Veneto, if people are being treated.'

'Rizzardi said he'd call someone he knows in Padova,' Brunetti said, hoping to spare her the effort.

She made a dismissive noise. 'They might want an official request. Doctors often do,' she said, as though she were a biologist speaking of some lower order of insect. 'It could take days. Even longer.' Brunetti appreciated her discretion in not bothering to say how quickly her friend might do it.

'He was in the lane coming south when I saw him,' he suddenly said.

'Which means?'

'He might have been coming down from Friuli. Could you ask your friend if they have the same sort of records, too?'

'Of course,' she said amiably. 'The men who blocked the road were protesting about the new milk quotas, weren't they?' she asked. 'Lowering production?'

'Yes.'

'Greedy fools,' she said with emphasis that

surprised him.

'You seem sure of that, Signorina,' he remarked.

'Of course I am. There's too much milk, there's too much cheese, there's too much butter, and there are too many cows.'

'Compared to what?' he asked.

'Compared to common sense,' she said heatedly, and Brunetti wondered what he had stumbled into.

Paola cooked with oil, not butter; he'd be sick if he had to drink a glass of milk, they did not eat much cheese, and Chiara's principles had long since sent beef fleeing from their table, so Brunetti was — in terms of behaviour — on Signorina Elettra's side of whatever principle was under discussion here. What he did not understand, however, was the force underlying her fervour, nor did he want to stand there and discuss it.

'If you receive anything from your friend, let me know, would you?'

'Of course, Commissario,' she said with her usual warmth and turned to her computer. Brunetti decided to go and have a look for the dead man in the films they had been sent of the incident last autumn.

Brunetti climbed the stairs to his office, reminding himself he could now access any video file that had been put into the new system.

He opened his mail account and found the link. Within seconds, the screen showed him, first, the original report and the written notes of the individual officers who had been there. After he read those, he had no trouble opening the file containing the police videos and those from the television station. When he watched the first clip and saw the flames consuming the minivan bearing the Televeneto logo, he understood the station's eagerness to cooperate.

He watched the first two clips, each lasting only a few seconds, but there was no sign of the man, then another, without success. Then, in the fourth, the man appeared. He stood, as Brunetti now remembered him standing, at the edge of the traffic island that divided the north and south sections of the autostrada. He was on screen for only a few seconds, his head and his distinctive neck and torso visible in front of a red car stopped in the middle of the road. A few people, three men and a woman, stood next to him, all of them staring straight ahead. The camera panned back to show a single row of helmeted men moving forward, their transparent shields side by side, all of them united in lock step. The video ended.

Brunetti opened the next one. This time the camera shot from behind the rank of Carabinieri as they approached the ragged group of farmers, their advancing line opening to flow around a car that had been set on fire. The next clip had been taken, it seemed, from a *telefonino,* but there was no identification of source: it could as easily belong to a police officer as some bystander whose phone had been sequestered. It showed a man slinging a pail of brown liquid at a carabiniere and hitting him square in the chest with it. The carabiniere retorted with a sidearm slash with his stick that caught the protestor on the lower arm and sent the pail into the air, with splashes flying from it as it disappeared to the right. The man bent forward, grabbing at his arm with his other hand, and was shoved to the ground by two Carabinieri. The video ended.

He typed in Pucetti's address and forwarded the email and attached video clips, shut down his computer, and went downstairs in search of the man himself.

8

Brunetti paused at the door of the officers' squad room and had a look around. Vianello, talking to the new recruit, Dondini, had his back to the door. Pucetti, upon whose lowered face Brunetti could not help but read the results of their last interchange, seemed as oblivious to his surroundings as he was to the papers spread on the surface of his desk. The worst part of Brunetti was glad to see the younger man so preoccupied: it would spare the rest of them a lot of trouble in future if he learned greater discretion in breaking the rules and perhaps the law.

'Pucetti,' he called as he came in. 'I've got a favour to ask.' He walked towards the young man's desk, gesturing to Vianello to join them when he could.

Pucetti shot to his feet, but he no longer snapped out a salute at the sight of his superior. 'I've found the man who was in the canal this morning. Have you read the report?' Brunetti asked.

'Yes, sir,' Pucetti said.

'There's a series of videos from that incident with the farmers on the autostrada last year. He was there.'

'You mean we arrested him?' Pucetti asked with badly disguised astonishment. 'And no one remembered?' It was implicit in his tone that *he* would surely have remembered, but Brunetti let that pass.

'No. He was there, but only as a spectator. There's no mug shot,' Brunetti said. 'A video shows him standing at the side of the road, watching.'

Pucetti could not hide his interest.

'There's something I'd like you to help me with,' Brunetti said with a smile, and the younger man, much in the manner of a hunting dog who has heard a familiar whistle, all but went into point position.

Vianello came over to them then and asked, 'What did you find?'

'A video with the man Rizzardi worked on this morning,' Brunetti answered, disliking the verb as soon as he heard himself using it. 'He was caught on the autostrada in that farmers' protest last year.' He told Pucetti about the email he had just sent him and said, 'I'd like you to see if you can print out copies of specific frames.'

'Nothing easier, sir,' Pucetti said, in the eager voice Brunetti was accustomed to hearing him use. 'Which one is he in?'

'He's in the fourth clip. Man with a dark beard; very thick shoulders and neck. I'd like you to see if you can stop it and get a picture of him we can use for identification.' Before Pucetti could ask, Brunetti said, without explanation, 'We can't show a photo of him as he is.'

Pucetti looked over at the officers' computer, the same machine that had been there for years. 'It would be much easier if I could work on this on my own equipment at home, sir,' he said, not panting, but visibly keen to be let off the leash.

'Then go and do it. If anyone asks, tell them it's part of the murder investigation,' he said, knowing that the only person likely to ask was Lieutenant Scarpa, the looming nemesis of the uniformed branch, Patta's assistant, his eyes and ears. Then, in his automatic response to keep information from the Lieutenant, Brunetti amended this: 'No, if anyone asks, better to say I'm sending you over to San Marco to get some papers from the Commissariat there.'

'I'll be as vague as I can be, sir,' Pucetti said seriously. Brunetti caught Vianello's fleeting grin.

'Good.' Turning to Vianello, Brunetti said, 'There are some other things.' He glanced at his watch to suggest that it was time to go and get a coffee.

By the time Vianello had gone back to his desk and picked up his jacket, Pucetti had disappeared. On the way down to the bar at Ponte dei Greci, Brunetti told Vianello about the autopsy, the man's strange disease, and his own certainty that he had seen him before, confirmed by the video that Pucetti had taken home to watch and copy.

Still talking, Brunetti led the way into the bar. Bambola, the assistant to the owner, nodded as they passed him on their way to the booth at the back. Within minutes, he was there, carrying two coffees and two glasses of water, along with a plate with four pastries. He spread them on the table and went back to the bar.

Brunetti picked up a brioche. It would soon be time for lunch, but so far that day he had seen the body of a murdered man; strongly reprimanded Pucetti, his favourite among the uniformed branch; Signorina Elettra had had a personal conversation with him; and the man who brought him his coffee was a Black African in a long white dress. 'By the time we retire, Signorina

Elettra will be coming to work in a ball gown and tiara, and Bambola will be sacrificing chickens in the back room,' he observed to Vianello and took a bite of his brioche.

Vianello sipped at his coffee and picked up a raisin-filled snail-shaped pastry and observed, 'By the time we retire, we'll be a colony of China, and Bambola's children will be teaching at the university.'

'I like the second part,' Brunetti said, then asked, 'You been reading your catastrophe books again, Lorenzo?'

Vianello, as ever, had the grace to smile. He and Signorina Elettra were the declared ecologists at the Questura, though Brunetti had recently observed evidence that their ranks were growing; further, it had been some time since he had heard the epithet *talibano dell'ecologia* attributed to either of them. Foa had requested that fuel efficiency be made a consideration in all future purchases of police boats; fear of Signorina Elettra's wrath kept everyone from placing the wrong sort of garbage in the receptacles located on every floor; and even Vice-Questore Patta had upon occasion been persuaded to use public transportation.

'*A proposito,*' he went on, 'Signorina Elettra stopped herself just short of a denunciation of cows this morning; or rather, I stopped her. Do you have any idea what that's all about?'

Vianello picked up his second pastry, a dryish-looking thing covered with fragments of nuts. 'The days of Heidi are over, Guido,' he said and took a bite.

'Which means?' Brunetti asked, his own second pastry poised in the air.

'Which means that there are too many cows, and we can't afford to keep them or raise them or eat them any longer.'

' "We" being?' Brunetti inquired and took a bite.

' "We" being the people in the developed world — which is just a euphemism for rich world — who eat too much beef and too many dairy products.'

'Are you worried about health?' Brunetti interrupted to ask, mindful of cholesterol levels, something he had never given any thought to, and curious about when and where Vianello and Signorina Elettra had their cell meetings.

'No, not really,' said a suddenly serious Vianello. 'I'm thinking about those poor devils in what we aren't allowed to call backward countries any more who have their forests cut down so big companies can raise meat to sell to rich people who shouldn't be eating it anyway.' He saw that his coffee cup was empty and took a drink of water. Then he surprised Brunetti by saying, 'I think I don't want to talk about this any more. Tell me about the man.'

Brunetti pulled a pen from his jacket pocket and used a napkin to draw a rough duplicate of the sketch Bocchese had made of the murder weapon, careful to curve the blade up at the point. 'This is the sort of knife that killed him. It's about twenty centimetres long, very narrow. It went in three times. Lower back, right-hand side. The report — I haven't read it yet — will tell exactly what it cut, but Rizzardi said he bled to death.'

'In the water?' Vianello said, putting his pastry back on the plate.

'He was alive long enough to breathe in some water, but not long enough to drown. Bocchese and I talked about where it could have happened and how it could have been done. Either he was in a boat, which doesn't sound right to me — too much risk of being seen, and Bocchese said there's no sign of that sort of dirt on his clothing. Or they did it in a house and slid him in from the water door, or maybe it happened at the end of a *calle,* where it runs into the water, and they just tossed him in.'

'Big chance of being seen, either way,' Vianello observed. 'Or heard.'

'Less from a house, I think. Also less chance that anyone would have heard.'

Vianello stared through the window of the bar, his eyes on the passers-by, his attention on the possibilities of the murder. After some time, he returned his attention to Brunetti and said, 'Yes, a house sounds better. Any idea where?'

'I haven't seen Foa yet,' Brunetti said, reminding himself to do this as soon as possible. 'They found the man's body at about six at the back of the Giustinian, in Rio del Malpaga. Foa should be able to calculate . . .' Brunetti stopped himself from saying 'the drift', so appalling did he find the expression, and substituted 'where he might have started from.'

This time Vianello closed his eyes, and Brunetti watched him do exactly what he had: summon up the decades-old map the Inspector had in his memory and walk his way through the neighbourhood, checking the canals and, to the degree that he could, the direction of the water in the canals. He opened his eyes and looked at Brunetti. 'We don't know which way the tide was flowing.'

'That's why I have to talk to Foa.'

'Good. He'll know,' Vianello said and

pushed his way out of the booth. He went over to the bar and paid, waited for Brunetti to join him, then together they went back to the Questura, both of them keeping their eyes on the water in the canal that ran to their right, looking for motion and wondering which way the tide was flowing when the dead man went into the water.

9

As he entered the Questura, Brunetti glanced at his watch and saw that it was after one; if he left now, he might still reach home in time to eat something. Again, the events of the day flowed through his mind, this time coloured by too much caffeine and sugar: why had he eaten two pastries when he knew he was supposed to go home? Was he some untutored youth, unable to resist the lure of sweet things?

Turning to Vianello, he said, 'I'll be back after lunch. I'll talk to Foa then.'

'He's not on shift until four, anyway. Plenty of time.'

Brunetti, the two brioches rumbling at him from inside, decided to walk all the way home but then immediately changed his mind and walked up the Riva degli Schiavoni to get the vaporetto.

Within five minutes, he had begun to regret his decision. Instead of being able to walk untroubled and uncrowded through Campo Santa Maria Formosa and Campo Santa Marina before confronting the inevitable logjam of Rialto, he had chosen to launch himself directly into the flood of tourists, even here. As he turned right on the *riva*, he saw the onrushing wave of them, though they moved far more slowly than any wave he had ever encountered.

Like any man of sense, he fled to the vaporetto stop, got on the One, and found a seat inside, to the left. It was a far safer place from which to allow the assault of the beauty of the city. The sun jumped off the still surface of the *bacino,* forcing him to squint his eyes as they passed the newly restored Dogana and the church of the Salute. He'd been inside the first recently, thrilled to see how well it had been restored, appalled by what was on display inside.

When had they sneaked in and switched the rules? he wondered. When did the garish become artistic, and who had the authority to make that declaration? Why was banality of interest to the viewer, and where, oh where, had simple beauty gone? 'You're an old fart, Guido,' he whispered to himself, causing the man in front of him to turn around and stare. Brunetti ignored him and returned his attention to the buildings on the left.

They passed a *palazzo* where a friend of his had offered to sell him an apartment six years before, assuring him that he would make a fortune on the deal: 'Just keep it for three years and resell it to a foreigner. You'll make a million.'

Brunetti, whose ethical system was monosyllabic in its simplicity, had refused the offer because something about profiting from land speculation made him uncomfortable, as did the idea of being indebted to anyone for having earned an easy million Euros. Or, for that fact, ten Euros.

They passed the university, and Brunetti looked at it with double fondness: his wife worked there, and his son was now a student. Raffi had, to Brunetti's delight, chosen to study history, not the history of the ancients that so fascinated Brunetti, but the history of modern Italy which, though it also fascinated Brunetti, did so in a manner that led him close to despair.

Their arrival at the San Silvestro stop pulled his mind away from its continuing contemplation of the parallels to be found between the Italy of two thousand years ago and that of today. It was a matter of minutes until he was opening the front door of the building and turning into the first flight of steps. At each landing, Brunetti felt the weight of the brioche fall away from him, and by the time he got to his apartment he was sure he had burned it all off and was prepared to do justice to whatever remained of lunch.

When he entered the kitchen, he saw his children at their places, their untouched lunch in front of them. Paola was just placing a dish of what looked like tagliatelle with scallops in front of his place. Walking back to the stove, she said, 'I was late today: had to talk to a student. So we decided to wait for you.' Then, as if to prevent him from forming any idea of her occult powers, she added, 'I heard you come in.'

He bent to kiss both children on the head, and as he took his place, Raffi asked, 'Do you know anything about the war in Alto Adige?' Seeing Brunetti's surprise at the question, he added, 'The First World War.'

'You make it sound as long ago as the war against Carthage,' Brunetti said with a smile, opening his napkin and spreading it on his lap. 'Your great-grandfather fought in the war, remember.'

Raffi sat silently with his elbows on the table and chin propped on his folded fingers, a gesture in which his mother was reflected. Brunetti glanced in Chiara's direction and saw that she was sitting with her hands folded in her lap: how long had it taken to train them?

Paola came back to the table, set down her own dish, and took her place. '*Buon appetito,*' she said, picking up her fork.

Ordinarily, that injunction served as the starter's whistle for Raffi, who sprinted through his first course with a velocity that could still astonish both his parents. But today he ignored his food and said, 'You never told me.'

Brunetti had often repeated his grandfather's war stories, to the general uninterest of his own children. 'Well, he was,' he limited himself to saying and began to twirl up some noodles with his fork.

'Did he fight up there?' Raffi asked. 'In Alto Adige?'

'Yes. He was there for four years. He fought in most of the campaigns except, I think, once when he was wounded and sent to Vittorio Veneto to recover.'

'Not sent home?' Chiara asked, drawn into the conversation.

Brunetti shook the idea away. 'They didn't send wounded men home to recover.'

'Why?' she asked, fork poised over her plate.

'Because they knew they wouldn't go back,' Brunetti said.

'Why?' she repeated.

'Because they knew they'd die.' Before she could say that their great-grandfather, because they were there at the table talking about him, hadn't died, Brunetti explained, 'Most of them did; well, hundreds of thousands of them did, so they knew that the odds were pretty bad.'

'How many died?' Raffi asked.

Brunetti read little modern history, and when he read Italian history, he tended to read translations of books in other languages, so little confidence did he have that the Italian accounts would not be coloured by political or historical allegiance. 'I'm not sure of the exact number. But it was more than half a million.' He set his fork down and took a sip of wine, then another.

'Half a million?' Chiara repeated, stunned by the number. As if comment or question were useless, she could only repeat, 'Half a million.'

'Actually, I think it was more. Maybe six hundred thousand, but it depends on who you read.' Brunetti took another sip, replaced his glass, and said, 'That's not counting civilians, I think.'

'Jesus on the cross,' Raffi whispered.

Paola shot him a sharp glance, but it was clear to all of them that astonishment, not blasphemy, had provoked the remark.

'That's twelve Venices,' Raffi said in a small, astonished voice.

Brunetti, in his desire for clarity, even statistical clarity, said, 'Since it was only young men between the ages of sixteen and twenty-five or so, it's far more than that. It would go a long way to depopulating much of the Veneto in the next generation.' After a moment's reflection, he added, 'Which is pretty much what it did.' He remembered, then, listening as a child as his paternal grandmother chatted with her friends, a recurring topic their good luck in having found a man to marry — a good man or a bad man — when so many of their friends had never been able to find a husband. And he thought of the war memorials he had seen in the North, up near Asiago and above Merano, listing the names of the 'Heroes of the Nation', so often long lists of men with the same surname, all dead in the snow and the mud, their lives cast away to gain a metre of barren land or a medal for a general's chest.

'Cadorna,' he said, naming the supreme commander of that benighted campaign.

'We were told he was a hero,' Raffi said.

Brunetti closed his eyes for a moment.

'At least that's what we were told in *liceo,* that he held off the attack of the Austrian invader.'

It was with some effort that Brunetti quelled the impulse to ask if the same teachers praised the brave Italian troops who had quelled the invading Ethiopians or the invading Libyans. He contented himself with saying only, 'Italy declared war on Austria.'

'Why?' Raffi demanded, looking as though he could not believe this.

'Why do countries ever declare war?' Paola broke in to ask. 'To get land, to grab natural resources, to maintain their power.' It came to Brunetti to wonder why there was such fuss when parents explained the mechanism of sex to their children. Wasn't it far more dangerous for parents to explain to them the mechanism of power?

He intervened. 'You're talking about aggressive war, I assume. Not like Poland, the last time?'

'Of course not,' Paola agreed. 'Or Belgium, or Holland, or France. They were invaded and they fought back.' Looking at the children, she said, 'And your father's right: we did declare war on Austria.'

'But why?' Raffi repeated.

'I've always assumed from what I read that it was to get back land the Austrians had taken, or been given, in the past,' Paola answered.

'But how do you know who it belongs to?' Chiara asked.

Seeing that their plates were empty — Raffi having managed to clean his during some lightning pause in the conversation — Paola held up her hands in the manner of a soccer umpire calling 'Time'. 'I want to beg the indulgence of everyone here,' she said, meeting their eyes one by one. 'I spent my morning in the apparently futile attempt to defend the idea that some books are better than others, so I cannot bear a second serious discussion, certainly not at this table, not while I'm eating my lunch. And so I suggest we change the topic to something frivolous and stupid like liposuction or break dancing.'

Raffi started to protest, but Paola cut him off by saying, 'There are calamari *in umido* with peas to follow — and finocchio al forno for Chiara — and then there is a crostata di fragole, but it will be given only to those who are subject to my will.'

Brunetti watched Raffi consider his options. His mother always made more finocchio than one person could eat, and this was the best season for fragole. ‘My only joy in life,’ he said, picking up his plate and preparing to take it to the sink, ‘is to live in abject subservience to the will of my parents.’

Paola turned to Brunetti. ‘Guido, you read all those Romans: which goddess was it who gave birth to a snake?’

‘None of them, I fear.’

‘Left it to us humans, then.’

10

For all Brunetti managed to achieve at the Questura that afternoon, he might as well have stayed at home for the rest of the day. Foa, he learned at four, had been chosen to accompany the Questore and a delegation from Parliament on a tour of the MOSE project — that money-guzzler that would, or would not, save the city from *acqua alta* — and then to dinner in Pellestrina. 'This is why no one's ever in Rome to vote,' Brunetti muttered to himself when he hung up from receiving this news. He knew he could easily call the office of the Magistrate of the Waters and ask the question about the tides, but he preferred to keep within the confines of the Questura any precise information about the nature of the investigation.

He spoke briefly with Patta, who said that he, in the absence of the Questore, had spoken to the press and given the usual assurances that there was every expectation of a speedy arrest in the case and that they were following various leads. Things had been slow for the last month — few major crimes in the region — so the famished press was bound to fall upon this one. And how refreshing readers would find it to have a male victim for a change; it had been open season on women since the beginning of the year: one a day had been murdered in Italy, usually by the ex boyfriend or husband, the killer — according to the press — always driven by a *'raptus di gelosia',* which excuse was sure to appear as the main pillar of the subsequent defence. If Brunetti ever lost his temper with Scarpa and did him a deliberate injury, he would surely plead a *raptus di gelosia,* though he was hard pressed to think of a reason why he would feel jealous of the Lieutenant.

Pucetti called after six to say he had had a technical problem but had just managed to isolate some still photos from the first video and was sure to have the prints within an hour or so. Brunetti told him that the following morning would do.

He resisted the urge to call Signorina Elettra and ask what success she had had with her friend in the health office, sure that she would let him know as soon as she learned anything, but no less impatient for that.

Becalmed, Brunetti flicked on his computer and tapped in *mucche,* wondering what Vianello and Signorina Elettra found so objectionable in those poor beasts. His family was Venetian as far back as anyone could remember, and then well beyond, so there was no atavistic memory of a great-great somebody who had kept a cow in the barn behind the house and thus no explanation for the sympathy Brunetti felt for them. He had never milked one; to the best of his memory had never done more than touch the noses of friendly cattle safely behind fences when they went walking in the mountains. Paola, even more fully urban than he, admitted that they frightened her, but Brunetti had never been able to understand this. They were, he believed, perfect milk machines: grass went in one end and milk came out the other: it was ever so.

He chose an article at random from those listed and began to read. After an hour, a shaken Brunetti turned off the computer, made a steeple of his palms and pressed his lips against it. So that was it, and that was why intermittently vegetarian Chiara, though she would occasionally backslide when in the presence of a roast chicken, adamantly refused to eat beef. And Vianello and Signorina Elettra. He wondered how it was that he had not known all of this. Surely everything he had just read was public knowledge; to some people it was common knowledge.

He considered himself a broadly read man, and yet much of this he had not known. The destruction of the rain forest to clear it for cattle: of course, he knew about that. Mad Cow and Foot and Mouth: he was familiar with them, as well, with their coming and their going. Only it seemed they were not gone, not really.

Brunetti's ignorance had evaporated as he read the long account of a South American rancher who had attended an animal husbandry programme at a university in the United States. He painted a picture of animals that were born sick, kept alive only by massive doses of antibiotics, made productive by equal doses of hormones, and who died still sick. The writer ended the article by stating that he would never eat beef unless it was one of his own animals and he had overseen its raising and slaughter. Like Paola, who had heard too much that day about books, Brunetti suddenly decided he had read too much about beef. Soon before seven, he left his office, went downstairs and wrote a note for Foa, asking about the tides, and left the Questura; he started towards home, passing eventually through no-longer-crowded Campo Santa Maria Formosa. Campo San Bortolo was busy, but he had no trouble crossing it, nor were there many people on the bridge.

He arrived in an empty apartment before seven-thirty, took off his jacket and shoes, went down to the bedroom and retrieved his copy of the plays of Aeschylus — he didn't know what force had driven him back to read them again — and sprawled himself on the sofa in Paola's study, eager to read a book in which there was no risk of sentimentality — only bleak human truth — and eager to tell Paola about the cows.

Agamemnon was in the midst of greeting his wife after his decades-long absence by telling her that her speech of welcome, like his absence, had been much prolonged, and the hair on the back of Brunetti's neck had begun to rise at the man's folly, when he heard Paola's key in the lock. What would she do, he wondered, if he were to betray her, shame her, and bring a new lover into their home? Less than Clytemnestra did, he suspected, and without physical violence. But he had no doubt that she would do her best to destroy him with words and with the power of her family, and he was sure she would leave him with nothing.

He heard her set down some shopping bags by the door. While hanging up her jacket, she would see his. He called her name, and she called back that she'd be there in a minute. Then he heard the rustle of the plastic bags and her footsteps retreating towards the kitchen.

She wouldn't do it for jealousy, he knew, but from injured pride and a sense of honour betrayed. Her father, with a phone call, would see that he was quietly transferred to some stagnant, Mafia-infested village in Sicily; she'd have every sign of him out of the apartment in a day. Even his books. And she'd never speak his name again; perhaps with the children, though they'd know enough not to name him or ask about him. Why did knowing this make him so happy?

She was back, carrying two glasses of prosecco. He had been so preoccupied with their separation and her revenge that he had not heard the pop of the cork, though it was a sound that had the beauty of music for Brunetti.

Paola handed him a glass and tapped his knee until he pulled his feet up and made room for her. He sipped. 'This is the champagne,' he said.

'I know,' she said, sipping in her turn. 'I felt I deserved a reward.'

'What for?'

'Suffering fools.'

'Gladly?'

She gave a snort of contempt. 'Listening to their nonsense and pretending to pay attention to it or pretending to think their idiotic ideas are worthy of discussion.'

'The thing about good books?'

She pushed her hair back with one hand, scratched idly at the base of her skull. In profile, she was the same woman he had met and loved decades ago. The blonde hair was touched with white, but it was hard to see unless one were very close. Nose, chin, line of the mouth: they were all the same. Seen from the front, he knew, there were creases around her eyes and at the corners of her mouth, but she could still cause heads to turn on the street or at a dinner party.

She took a deep swallow and flopped against the back of the sofa, careful not to spill any wine. 'I don't know why I bother to keep teaching,' she said, and Brunetti did not remark that it was because she loved it. 'I could stop. We own the house, and you make enough to support us both.' And if things got rough, he did not say, they could always pawn the Canaletto in the kitchen.

Let her talk, let her get rid of it.

'What would you do, lie on the sofa all day in your pyjamas and read?' he asked.

She patted his knee with her free hand. 'You pretty much prevent my taking up residence on the sofa, don't you?'

'But what *would* you do?' he asked, suddenly serious.

She took another sip, then said, 'That's the problem, of course. If *you* quit, you could always be a security guard and walk around all night sticking little pieces of paper into the doorways of houses and stores to show you'd been there. But no one's going to ask me to come and talk to them about the English novel, are they?'

'Probably not,' he agreed.

'Might as well live,' she confused him by saying, but he was so eager to talk about the cows that he did not ask her to explain what she had said.

'How much do you know about cows?' he asked.

'Oh, my God. Not another one,' she said and sank down on the sofa, her hand pressed to her eyes.

11

'What do you mean, "Another one"?' he asked, though what he really wanted to know was whom she included among them.

'As I have told you at least twelve thousand times in the last decades: don't be smart with me, Guido Brunetti,' she said with exaggerated severity. 'You know exactly who they are: Chiara, Signorina Elettra, and Vianello. And from what you've said, I suspect those last two will soon have the Questura declared a no-meat zone.'

After what he had read that afternoon, Brunetti thought this might not be such a bad thing. 'They're just the lunatic fringe, though other people there are beginning to think about it, too,' he offered.

'If you ever set foot in a supermarket and saw what people are buying, you wouldn't say that, believe me.'

The few times he had had that experience, Brunetti had — he confessed to himself —

been fascinated by what he saw people buying, given the probability that they intended to eat those things. So rarely did he shop for groceries that Brunetti had been uncertain as to the nature of some of the products he saw and could not work out whether they were meant for consumption or for some other domestic purpose; scouring sinks, perhaps.

He remembered, as a boy, being sent to the store to get, for example, a half-kilo of limon beans. He had come home carrying them in the cylinder of newspaper in which the shopkeeper had wrapped them. But now they came in a clear plastic package bound with a bow of golden ribbon, and it was impossible to buy less than a kilo. His mother had lit the fire in the kitchen with the newspaper: the plastic and the bow went into the garbage after their fifteen minutes of freedom from the shelves.

'We don't eat as much meat as we used to,' he said.

'That's only because Chiara's too young to leave home.'

'Is that what she'd do?'

'Or stop eating,' Paola declared.

'She's really that convinced?'

'Yes.'

'How about you?' he asked. It was Paola,

after all, who decided what they would eat every day.

She finished her champagne and twirled the glass between her palms, as though hoping to start a fire with it.

'I like it less and less,' she finally said.

'Because of how it tastes or because of what you read about it?'

'Both.'

'You're not going to stop cooking it, are you?'

'Oh course not, silly.' Then, reaching to hand him her glass, 'Especially if you go and get us more champagne.'

Visions of lamb chops, veal cooked in marsala, and roast chicken dancing in his head, he went into the kitchen to obey her.

On the way to the Questura the following morning, Brunetti stopped in a bar for a coffee and read the *Gazzettino*'s account of the discovery of the body in the canal, followed by a brief description of the man and his probable age. In his office, he learned that there had been no report filed of a missing man, in the city or in the surrounding area. Within minutes of his arrival, Pucetti was at his door. Either the young man had managed to place a computer chip in Brunetti's ear or, more likely, the man at the door had phoned Pucetti when his superior arrived.

When Brunetti signalled him to enter, Pucetti came in and placed a photo of the dead man on his desk. Brunetti had no idea how he had managed to isolate just one frame, but the photo was entirely natural and showed the man gazing ahead of him with a completely relaxed expression on his face. He appeared a different man from the one now lying in a cold room at the Ospedale Civile.

Brunetti gave a broad smile and nodded in approval. 'Good work, Pucetti. It's him, the man I saw.'

'I've made copies, sir.'

'Good. See that one's scanned and sent to the *Gazzettino.* The other papers, too. And see if anyone downstairs recognizes him.'

'Yes, sir,' Pucetti said, left the photo on Brunetti's desk, and was gone.

In her office, Signorina Elettra had today decided to wear yellow, a colour very few women could get away with. It was Tuesday, flower day at the market, and so her office — and presumably Patta's — was filled with them, a civilizing touch she had brought to the Questura. 'They're lovely, the daffodils, aren't they?' she asked as Brunetti came in, waving in the direction of a quadruple bouquet on the windowsill.

The first stirrings of springtime would once have urged an unmarried Brunetti to say that they were not as lovely as the person who had brought them there, but this Brunetti limited himself to responding, 'Yes, they are,' and then asking, 'And what excess of colour has transformed the Vice-Questore's office?'

'Pink. I love it and he dislikes it. But he's afraid to complain.' She looked away for a moment, back at Brunetti, and said, 'I read once that pink is the navy blue of India.'

It took Brunetti a moment, and then he laughed out loud. 'That's wonderful,' he said, thinking how Paola would love it.

'Are you here about the dead man?' she asked, suddenly serious.

'Yes.'

'Nothing from my friend. Maybe Rizzardi will have better luck.'

'He could be from some other province,' Brunetti suggested.

'Possible,' she said. 'I've sent out the usual request to hotels, asking if they have a guest who's missing.'

'No luck?'

'Only a Hungarian who ended up in the hospital with a heart attack.'

Brunetti thought of the vast net of rental

apartments and bed and breakfasts in which the city was enmeshed. Many of them operated beyond all official recognition or control, paying no taxes and making no report to the police of the people who stayed there. In the event of the nonreturn of a guest, how likely were the owners to report his absence to the police and bring their illegal operations to the attention of the authorities? How much easier simply to wait a few days and then claim whatever the decamping client might have left behind in lieu of unpaid rent, and that's the end of it.

Earlier in his career, Brunetti would have assumed that any self-respecting, law-abiding citizen would contact the police, certainly as soon as they read of the discovery of a murdered man whose description sounded so very much like the man staying in room three, over the garden. But decades spent amidst the prevarications and half-truths to which law-abiding citizens were all too prone had cured him of such illusions.

'Pucetti has a photo from one of the videos. He's sending it to the papers, and he's asking if anyone recognizes him,' Brunetti said. 'But I agree with you, Signorina: people don't disappear.'

12

Brunetti found Vianello in the officers' room, speaking on the phone. When the Inspector saw him, a look of great relief crossed his face. He said a few words, shrugged, said a few more, and replaced the phone.

Approaching, Brunetti asked, 'Who?'

'Scarpa.'

'What's he want?'

'Trouble. It's all he ever wants, I think.'

Brunetti, who agreed, asked, 'What sort of trouble this time?'

'Something about the receipts for fuel and could Foa be using the police account to buy it for his own boat?' Under his breath, Vianello muttered something Brunetti pretended not to have heard. 'Isn't there something in the Bible about seeing things against other people when you don't see the same thing in your own eye?'

'Something like,' Brunetti admitted.

'Patta has Foa pick him up and take him to dinner in Pellestrina, and if it's not a nice day, take him home, and Scarpa's worrying that Foa's stealing fuel.' Then, as an afterthought, 'Everybody's nuts.'

Brunetti, who agreed with this proposition as well, said, 'Foa wouldn't do it. I know his father.' This assessment made sense to both of them and served as sufficient validation of Foa's integrity. 'But why's he going after Foa now?' Brunetti asked. Scarpa's behaviour was often confusing, his motives always inexplicable.

'Maybe he has some cousin from Palermo who knows how to pilot a boat and needs a job,' Vianello suggested. 'Fat chance he'd have navigating here.'

Brunetti was tempted to ask if Vianello's last remark had a double meaning, but instead he asked him to come out and sit on the *riva* with him and talk while they watched the boats pass.

When they were seated on the bench, the new sun warming their faces and thighs, Brunetti gave Vianello the folder that contained the photos. 'Pucetti show you this?'

Vianello nodded as he took the photo and looked at it. 'I see what you mean about the neck,' he said and handed it back, then returned to their previous subject and asked, 'What do you think Scarpa's really up to?'

Brunetti raised his palms in a gesture of helpless incomprehension. 'In this case, I think he's just trying to cause trouble for someone who's popular, but I don't think there's ever any understanding of what people like Scarpa do.' Then he added, 'Paola's teaching a class in the short story this year, and in one of them, the bad guy — all he's called is The Misfit — after he wipes out a whole family, even the old grandmother, he sits there calmly and says something like, "There's no pleasure except meanness." ' As if to emphasize the truth of this, two seagulls farther up the *riva* began to fight over something, both tearing at it while managing to squawk and flail violently at the same time.

'I tell you, when Paola read it to me,' Brunetti went on, 'I thought of Scarpa. He just likes meanness.'

'You mean that literally — that he *likes* it?' Vianello asked.

Before Brunetti could answer, they were disturbed by the appearance from the left of an enormous — did it have eight decks? Nine? Ten? — cruise ship. It trailed meekly behind a gallant tug, but the fact that the hawser connecting them dipped limply into the water gave the lie to the appearance of whose motors were being used to propel them and which boat decided the direction. What a perfect metaphor, Brunetti thought: it looked like the government was pulling the Mafia into port to decommission and destroy it, but the ship that appeared to be doing the pulling had by far the smaller motor, and any time the other one chose, it could give a yank on the hawser and remind the other boat of where the power lay.

When the boats were past, Vianello said, 'Well?'

'Yes, I think he does like it,' Brunetti finally said. 'Some people just do. No divine possession, no Satan, no unhappy childhood or chemical imbalance in the brain. For some people, there's no pleasure except meanness.'

'That's why they keep doing it?' Vianello asked.

'Has to be, doesn't it?' Brunetti asked by way of answer.

'Gesù,' Vianello whispered. Then, after being interrupted by the continuing fight between the seagulls, he said, 'I never wanted to believe that.'

'Who would?'

'And we've got him?' Vianello asked.

'Until he goes too far or gets sloppy.'

'And then?'

'And then we get rid of him,' Brunetti said.

'You make it sound simple.'

'It might be.'

'I hope so,' Vianello said with the sincerity that most people reserved for prayer.

'About this man — I still don't understand why no one's reported a missing person. People have families, for God's sake.'

'Maybe it's too soon,' Vianello said.

Brunetti, unconvinced, said, 'The photo should be in the papers tomorrow. With any luck, someone will see it and call us.' He didn't tell Vianello he had resisted the idea because the dead man looked so much like a dead person and so little like a man. 'Someone should react to Pucetti's.'

'And until then?' the Inspector asked.

Brunetti reached over and took the folder, closed it, and said, getting to his feet, 'Let's go shoe shopping.'

The Fratelli Moretti shop in Venice is conveniently close to Campo San Luca. Brunetti had been an admirer of their shoes for a generation but for some reason had never bought a pair. It was not their price — everything in Venice had grown expensive — so much as . . . Brunetti was suddenly forced to realize that there was no reason whatsoever: he had simply never gone inside the shop, kept out by no reason he could name. Using this as justification, he led Vianello to the shop, where they paused outside to study the men's shoes in the window. 'I like those,' Brunetti said, pointing to a pair of dark brown tasselled loafers.

'If you bought them,' Vianello said, having assessed the quality of the leather, 'and things got tough, you could always boil them and live off the stock for a few days.'

'Very funny,' Brunetti said and went inside.

The robust woman in charge glanced at their identification and studied the photo of the dead man but shook her head. 'Letizia might recognize him,' she said and indicated the stairs that led to the floor above. 'She's with some customers but will be down in a minute.' While waiting, Brunetti and Vianello busied themselves by trailing through the shop: Brunetti had another look at the loafers.

Letizia, younger and thinner than the other woman, came downstairs after a few minutes, preceded by a Japanese couple and holding four shoeboxes in her arms. She might have been in her late twenties, with boyishly short blonde hair combed up in whimsical spikes and a face that escaped from plainness by virtue of the intelligence evident in her gaze.

Brunetti waited while the sale was completed and the customers led to the door, where there followed an exchange of deep bows, seeming not at all forced on the part of the saleswoman.

When Letizia came across to them, the manager explained who they were and what they wanted her to do. Letizia's smile was interested, even curious. Brunetti handed her the photo.

At the sight of the face of the dead man, she said, 'The man from Mestre.'

'From Mestre?' Brunetti inquired.

'Yes. He was in here — oh, it must have been two months ago — and tried to buy a pair of shoes. I think he said he wanted loafers.'

'Is there any reason why you remember him, Signorina?'

'Well,' she began, then added, with a quick glance at the manager, who was listening to all of this, 'I don't want to talk badly about our customers, not at all, but it's because he was so strange.'

'His behaviour?' Brunetti asked.

'No, not at all. He was very pleasant, very polite. It was the way he looked.' Saying this, she glanced again at the other woman, as if asking permission to say such a thing. The manager pursed her lips and then nodded.

Visibly relieved, Letizia continued. 'He was so big. No, not big the way Americans are big. You know, all over, and tall. It was only his torso and his neck that were so big. I remember wondering what size shirt he'd wear and how he'd find one with a neck big enough for him. But the rest of him was normal.' She studied Brunetti's face, and then Vianello's. 'He must have a terrible time buying a suit, too, now that I think about it: his shoulders and chest are enormous. The jacket would have to be two or three sizes bigger than the trousers.'

Before either of them could remark on this observation, she said, 'He tried on a suede jacket, so I saw that his hips were like a regular man's. And his feet were normal, too: size forty-three. But the rest of him was all . . . oh, I don't know, all pumped up.'

'You're sure this is the man?' Brunetti asked.

'Absolutely,' she said.

'From Mestre?' Vianello interrupted to ask.

'Yes. He said he was in the city for the day and had tried to buy the shoes in our store in Mestre — but they didn't have his size so he thought he'd look for them here.'

'Did you have the shoes?' Brunetti asked.

'No,' she said, her disappointment evident. 'We had one size larger and one size smaller. We had his size only in brown, but he didn't want them — only black.'

'Did he buy another style, instead?' Brunetti asked, hoping that he had and hoping even more strongly that he had paid for them with a credit card.

'No. That's exactly what I suggested, but he said he wanted the black because he already had them in brown and he liked them.' These must be the shoes he had been wearing when he was killed, Brunetti thought, smiling at the young woman to encourage her to keep speaking.

'And the suede jacket?' he asked when he realized she was finished.

'It didn't fit over his shoulders,' she said. Then, in a softer voice, she added, 'I felt sorry for him when he tried it on and he couldn't even get his other arm into the sleeve.' She shook her head, her sympathy obvious. Then she added, 'We usually keep our eyes on people who try on the suede jackets so they don't steal them. But I couldn't. He seemed almost surprised by it, sort of, but sad, really sad that he couldn't make it fit.'

'Did he buy anything at all?' Vianello asked.

'No, he didn't. I wish he could have found a jacket that fitted him, though.' Then, so they wouldn't misunderstand: 'Not because I wanted the sale of anything, but just so that he could find one that would fit him. Poor man.'

Brunetti asked, 'Did he actually say he lived in Mestre?'

She looked at her colleague, as if to ask her please to remind her what the man had said to make her believe he was from Mestre. She tilted her head to one side in a very birdlike way. 'He said that he'd bought a few pairs there, and I just sort of assumed that he must live there. After all, you usually buy shoes where you live, don't you?'

Brunetti nodded his agreement, thinking that you usually don't have the good fortune to be served by such a kind person, no matter where you buy your shoes.

He thanked both her and her manager, gave Letizia his card and asked her to call him if she remembered anything else the man had said that might give further information about him.

As they turned towards the door, Letizia made a noise. It wasn't a word, little more than a voiced aspirant. Brunetti turned back and she asked, 'Was he the man in the water?'

'Yes. Why do you ask?'

She waved at him and Vianello, as though their presence, or their appearance, were sufficient answer, but then said, 'Because he seemed troubled, not only sad.' Before Brunetti could point out that she had said nothing about this, she went on. 'I know, I know, I said he was pleasant and friendly. But under it, he was troubled by something. I thought it was the jacket, or that we didn't have the shoes he wanted, but it was more than that.'

Someone as observant as she didn't need to be nudged, and so Brunetti and Vianello remained silent, waiting.

'Usually, when people are waiting for me to bring them something — a different size or a different colour — they look around at different shoes or get up and walk around, go and look at the belts. But he just sat there, staring at his feet.'

'Did he seem unhappy?' Brunetti asked.

This time, it took her a moment to answer. 'No, now that you ask me about it, I'd say he looked worried.'

13

Brunetti and Vianello decided to have lunch together, but both cringed at the idea of eating anywhere within a radius of ten minutes of San Marco.

'How'd this happen?' Vianello asked. 'We used to be able to eat well anywhere in the city, well, just about anywhere. And it was usually good and didn't cost an eye from your head.'

'How long ago was "used to", Lorenzo?' Brunetti asked.

Vianello slowed to consider this. 'About ten years.' But then he added, his surprise audible, 'No, it's a lot more than that, isn't it?'

They were passing in front of the place where the Mondadori bookstore used to be, only a few hundred metres from the arched entrance to Piazza San Marco, still undecided where to go for lunch. A sudden surge in the wave of milling tourists engulfed them, forcing them against the windows of the shop. Ahead of them, near the Piazza, the pastel wave defied tidal patterns and flowed both ways. Blind, slowly urgent towards no goal, it appeared to have no beginning and no end as it seeped from and into the Piazza.

Vianello turned to Brunetti and placed a hand on his forearm. 'I can't,' he said. 'I can't go across the Piazza. Let's take the boat.' They took the right turn and struggled down towards the *embarcadero.* Long lines snaked away from the ticket office, and the floating docks lay low in the water from the weight of the people standing on them, waiting for the arriving vaporetti.

A Number One approached from the right, and the line moved forward a step or two, though there was nowhere for it to go, save into the water. Brunetti took his warrant card from his wallet and slipped around the bar that blocked the entrance to the passageway reserved for disembarking passengers. Vianello followed. They hadn't gone four steps when a *marinaio* shouted at them from the landing ahead of them, waving them back and away.

Ignoring him, the two men approached, Brunetti holding out his card. *'Scusi, Signori,'* the workman said when he saw it, stepping back to allow them on to the floating dock. He was young, like most of them these days, short and dark but speaking Veneziano. 'They all try to sneak in this way, and I have to shout them back. Some day I'm probably going to hit one of them.' The smile with which he said this belied the possibility.

'The tourists?' Brunetti asked, surprised that they would show such initiative.

'No, it's us, Signore,' the man said, obviously meaning Venetians. 'The tourists are like sheep, really: very gentle, and all you have to do is tell them where to go. The bad ones, really the worst, are the old ladies: they complain about the tourists, but most of them are riding for free, if they're old enough, or not paying for a ticket anyway, if they're younger.' As if to prove him right, an old woman appeared behind Brunetti and Vianello and, ignoring all three of them, pushed past them and planted herself directly in front of the point where passengers would disembark.

The sailor who worked on the boat tied it to the bollard then waited with his hand on the sliding gate while he asked the old woman to step aside to let the passengers off; she ignored him. He asked her again, and still she stood there. Finally, giving in to the pressure and muttering of the people blocked behind him, he slid the gate open, and the mass surged forward. The old woman, like a piece of flotsam, was moved to one side by pressure and blows from shoulders, arms, and backpacks.

She responded in kind, though verbally, letting fly a long stream of abuse in Veneziano that had the accent of Castello, towards which the boat was headed. She condemned the ancestry of tourists, their sexual habits and state of personal hygiene, until finally the path was free, the deck clear, and she could walk into the cabin and take a seat, surrounding herself with a cloud of muttered complaints against the bad manners of these foreigners who came to ruin the lives of decent Venetian folk.

When the boat had left the dock, Brunetti slipped the doors to the cabin closed, cutting off the sound of her voice. Finally Vianello said, 'She's a nasty old cow, but she has a point.'

It wasn't a point Brunetti could bear talking about or listening to, so fundamental had it become as a subject of small talk in the city. 'You decide where we can go?' he asked, quite as if Vianello's response to the tourist mass had not interrupted their conversation.

'Let's go out to the Lido and eat fish,' the Inspector said with all the enthusiasm of a boy playing hooky.

Andri was only a ten-minute walk from the landing at Santa Maria Elisabetta, and the owner, a schoolmate of Vianello's, found them a table in the crowded restaurant. Without being asked, he brought them a half-litre of white wine and a litre of mineral water, and told Vianello he should have the salad with shrimp, raw artichoke and ginger and then the zuppe di pesche. Vianello nodded; Brunetti nodded.

'So, Mestre,' Brunetti said.

Before Vianello could speak, the owner was back with some bread. He set it on the table, asked if they'd like some artichoke bottoms, and was gone as soon as they said yes.

'I don't want to get into some territorial squabble about this,' Vianello finally said. 'You know the rules better than I do.'

Brunetti nodded. 'I think I'll use Patta's tactic of simply assuming that because I want to do something, I have the right to do it.' He poured them each some wine and some water and took a long drink of water. He opened a package of grissini and ate one of them, then another, suddenly aware of how hungry he was. 'But for the sake of correctness, I'll call them and say we're coming out to ask if anyone in the shoe shop recognizes the man in the photo.'

Vianello helped himself to a package of breadsticks.

The owner came back with the artichokes, set them down, and hurried away. It was one o'clock, and the place was full. Both men were happy to see that it seemed to be full of local people: three tables were crowded with dust-covered workmen with thick clothing and heavy boots.

'You think there are places where everyone cooperates?' Vianello asked.

Brunetti finished his first artichoke and set his fork down. 'Is that a rhetorical question, Lorenzo?' he asked, sipping at his wine.

The Inspector tore off some bread and wiped up the olive oil from his plate. 'These are good. I like them without garlic.' Apparently, it had been a rhetorical question.

'We go out in a car, be back in no time.'

The owner replaced their empty plates with the salad: slivers of artichoke, quite a large number of tiny shrimp, sprinkled with slivers of ginger.

'If no one at the shop recognizes him, then we ask the guys there to give us a hand,' Brunetti said.

Vianello nodded and speared a few shrimp.

'I'll call Vezzani and tell him we'll stop by after we go to the shop,' Brunetti said and pulled out his phone.

If Mestre had not had its city centre, small but attractive, any Venetian forced to move there would have seen his fate as tragic, or so Brunetti had always thought. 'To fall from high to low estate,' Aristotle had written, establishing the rules. Kings crashed down to become blind beggars; queens murdered their children; the powerful died for hopeless causes or went to live in abject misery. Had Mestre been a slum, had it contained only skyscrapers separated by bleak desolation; had it resembled Milano more and Venice less, then to be forced, or to choose, to move there from Venice would indeed have been the stuff of tragedy. The city centre, however, though it still allowed the move to be painful, even laceratingly sad, prevented it from being wholly tragic.

The shoe shop was as tasteful as its sister shop in Venice, and the shoes on display looked the same. So did the two women working there: an older one who was obviously in charge and a younger one who viewed their arrival with a smile. Brunetti, wise to the rules of precedence, approached the woman he took to be the manager and introduced himself. She seemed unsurprised by his arrival and had apparently received a call from Venice.

'I'd like to ask you, and your colleague, to look at the photo of a man and tell me if you recognize him.'

'You the men who went to the other shop?' the younger one asked as she came across the store, a remark that earned her a sharp look from her superior.

'Yes,' Brunetti answered. 'The woman we spoke to there said the man tried to buy the shoes here, but you didn't have his size.' He knew that they knew the man was the dead man in the canal, and they knew he knew, so none of them said anything.

The older woman, thin to the point of emaciation and with a bosom perhaps not placed there by the hand of nature, asked to see the photo. Brunetti gave it to her to acknowledge that she was in charge. 'Yes,' she said when she saw the photo of the dead man. She passed it to the younger woman and folded her arms under that bosom.

At the sight of the dead man, the young woman said, 'Yes, he's been here a few times. The last time was about two months ago.'

'Did you serve him, Signorina?' Brunetti asked.

'Yes, I did. But we didn't have his size, and he didn't want anything else.'

Turning to the other woman, Brunetti inquired, 'Do you remember him, Signora?'

'No, I don't. We get so many clients in here,' she said, and indeed just then two women, their arms laden with bags, entered the shop. Without bothering to excuse herself, the manager went over and asked if she could help them.

Brunetti asked the young woman — really little more than a girl — 'Do you remember anything about him, Signorina? You said he'd been in before?'

Brunetti's hopes were still set on a credit card purchase. The young woman thought for a moment and then said, 'A few times. In fact, once he came in wearing a pair of shoes and bought the same ones.'

Brunetti glanced at Vianello, whose manner was often better at encouraging responses. 'Do you remember anything special about him, Signorina? Or did he strike you in a particular way?' the Inspector asked.

'You mean that he had got so big and was so sad?'

'Was he?' Vianello asked with every appearance of deep concern.

Before answering, she seemed to think back to the man's time in the shop. 'Well, he'd gained weight: I noticed that, even under his winter jacket, and he didn't really say anything that would make me think he was lonely or sad or anything. But he seemed it; sort of quiet and not paying much attention to things.' Then, to make things clear to both of them, she said, 'He tried on about eight pairs of shoes, and the boxes were lying all around him on the floor and on the chair next to him. When he was finished, and he still couldn't find the ones he wanted, he said — I guess he felt guilty about making me go and get so many of them. Maybe that's why I remember him — he said that he'd help me put them back in the boxes. But he put a black one in with a brown one, and then when there was only one shoe left, a black one, and the only box left had a brown shoe in it, we had to open them all up again and put the right shoes in.

'He was very embarrassed and apologized for it.' She thought about this for some time and said, 'No one ever bothers with that, you know. They try on ten, fifteen pairs of shoes, and then they walk out without even saying thank you. So to have somebody who treated me like a real person, well, it was very nice.'

'Did he give you his name?'

'No.'

'Or say anything about himself that you remember?'

She smiled at this. 'He said he liked animals.'

'I beg your pardon,' Brunetti said.

'Yes, that's what he said. When I was helping him, a woman came in, one of our regulars. She's very rich: you can tell it by looking at her — the way she dresses and all, and the way she talks. But she has this really sweet old dog that she got from the shelter. I asked her about it once, and she said she always gets her dogs from the shelter, and she asks for old ones. You'd expect a woman like that to have an, oh, I don't know, one of those disgusting little things that sits on your lap, or a poodle or something. But she's got this silly little mutt; maybe it's part beagle, but you'd never know what the other part is. And she adores it, and the dog loves her. So I guess it's all right that she's so rich,' she said, causing Brunetti to wonder if the revolution was closer to hand than he thought.

'And why did he say he likes animals?' Vianello asked.

'Because when he saw the dog, he asked

the woman how old it was, and when she said it was eleven, he asked her if she'd had it checked for arthritis.

'She said she hadn't, and he said that, from the way the dog walked, he'd guess it had it. Arthritis.'

'What did the woman say?' the Inspector asked.

'Oh, she thanked him. I told you: she's very nice. And then, after she left, I asked him, and he said he liked animals, especially dogs, and knew a bit about them.'

'Anything else?' Brunetti asked, realizing that this was precious little to be going ahead with.

'No, only that he was a nice man. People who like animals usually are, don't you think?'

'Yes, I do,' Vianello said. Brunetti limited himself to a nod.

The manager was still busy with the two women, the three of them surrounded by expanding waves of boxes, shoes littering the floor in front of them. 'Did your colleague speak to him?' Brunetti asked.

'Oh, no. She took care of Signora Persilli.' At their blank looks, she said, 'The lady with the dog.'

Brunetti took out his wallet and gave her his card. 'If you think of anything else,

Signorina, please call me.'

They turned towards the door, but she called from behind them. 'Is he really the dead man? In Venice?'

Surprising himself with his frankness, Brunetti turned back and said, 'I think so.' Her mouth contracted in a small grimace and she shook her head at the news. 'So if you think of anything, please call us; it might help,' he said, not specifying how this might be possible.

'I'd like to help,' she said.

Brunetti thanked her again, and he and Vianello left the shop.

14

'A man with Madelung who likes animals and knows something about dogs,' Vianello said as they walked towards the car.

More practically, Brunetti said, 'We'll talk to Vezzani. He should be back from Treviso by now.' He had gone to the shoe shop in the full hope, even expectation, of discovering the man's name and identity. He felt not a little embarrassed, now, at how he had looked forward to being able to walk into Vezzani's office with the dead man's name in his possession. Now, that possibility gone, he accepted the fact that there was nothing to do save what both of them now knew they should have done before: go to the Mestre Questura and ask for their cooperation.

He got into the front seat of the car and asked the driver to take him to the Questura. The driver reminded him about the seat belt, and Brunetti, thinking it foolish to use it for what would prove such a short trip, put it on nevertheless. It was well past four, and the traffic seemed heavy, though Brunetti was hardly an expert on traffic.

Inside the building, he showed his warrant card and said he had an appointment with Commissario Vezzani. They had worked as part of the team investigating the baggage handlers at the airport some years ago — the investigation Pucetti was still involved with — had passed through those fires together and emerged, both of them wiser and more pessimistic, but with a far clearer understanding of the limits to which a clever lawyer could push the rights of the accused.

The officer on duty pointed to the elevator and told them the Commissario's office was on the third floor. Vezzani was from Livorno originally, but he had lived in the Veneto so long that his speech had taken on the singsong cadence, and he had once told Brunetti, during a break in the endless interrogation of two men accused of armed robbery, that his children spoke to their friends in the Mestre version of Veneziano.

He rose when they entered, a tall, thin man with prematurely grey hair, cut close to his skull in a vain attempt, perhaps, to disguise the colour. He shook hands with

Brunetti, clapped him on the arm in greeting, and extended his hand to Vianello, with whom he had also worked.

'You find out who he is?' he asked when they were seated.

'No. We spoke to the women in the shoe shop, but they couldn't tell us who he was. All one of them said was that he liked dogs and knew something about animals.'

If Vezzani found this an odd piece of information to divulge during the purchase of a pair of shoes, he did not remark on it and merely asked, 'And this disease you say he had?'

'Madelung. It happens to alcoholics or addicts, but Rizzardi said there were no signs this guy was a drinker or used drugs.'

'So it just happened to him?'

Brunetti nodded, recalling the thick neck and the arching torso of the dead man.

'Could I see the photo?' Vezzani asked.

Brunetti gave it to him.

'You said Pucetti did this?' Vezzani asked, picking up the photo to take a closer look.

'Yes.'

'I've heard about him,' Vezzani said; then, in a different tone, 'God, I'd like to have a few like him around here.'

'That bad?'

Vezzani shrugged.

'Or you don't want to say?' Brunetti asked.

Vezzani gave a humourless laugh. 'If I saw a job opening for a street patrolman in Caltanissetta, I'd be tempted, I tell you.'

'Why?'

Vezzani rubbed at his right cheek with the palm of his hand: his beard was so heavy that, by this time of day, Brunetti could hear a grating noise. 'Because so little happens, combined with the fact that, when it does, there's so little we can do.' Then, as if the subject were too annoying, Vezzani got quickly to his feet, taking the photo with him. 'Let me take this downstairs and show it to the boys. See if anyone recognizes him.' At Brunetti's nod, he left the room.

Brunetti got to his feet and walked over to a bulletin board on which were pinned notices bearing the seal of the Ministry of the Interior. He read a few of them and found they were the same memos and reports that flowed into and out of his own office. Perhaps he should put theirs in suitcases, take them to the railway station, and leave them unattended for a few minutes or until they were stolen. There seemed no other way they would ever be disposed of effectively. Should he propose it to Patta? he wondered. He stood and looked at them, inventing his conversation with Patta.

Vezzani came quickly into the room. 'He's a veterinarian,' he said.

As if he were channelling the voice of the young woman in the shoe shop, Brunetti said, 'Likes animals and knows something about dogs.' Then he asked, 'Who told you that?'

'One of our men. He'd seen him at his son's school.' Vezzani came farther into the room. 'There was some sort of special day when parents were invited to the school and told the kids about their jobs or their professions. He said they do it every year, and last year this guy talked about being a vet and taking care of animals.'

'Is he sure?' Brunetti asked.

Vezzani nodded.

'What's his name?'

'He didn't remember, said he heard only the last part of his talk. But only parents are invited, so if he talked at the school, they've got to know who he is.'

'Which school is it?'

'San Giovanni Bosco. I can call them,' Vezzani said, moving towards his desk. 'Or we can go and talk to them.'

Brunetti's answer was immediate. 'I don't want to show up there in a police car, especially if his kid's still enrolled there. People always talk, and it's no way for him to find out about his father.'

Vezzani agreed, and Vianello, who had children in school and, like the others, worked in a potentially dangerous profession, nodded.

The call was quickly made, and after being passed to two different offices, Vezzani learned the dead man's name. Dottor Andrea Nava, his son still at the school, though there had been some family trouble and the father hadn't come to the most recent parent meeting. Yes, he had been there last year and had talked about household pets and how best to take care of them. He'd suggested that the children bring their pets with them, and he'd used them as examples. The children had enjoyed his talk more than any of the others, and it was a real pity Dr Nava hadn't been able to come back this year.

Vezzani wrote down the address and phone number listed in the boy's contact information, thanked the person speaking without explaining why the police were looking for the doctor, and hung up.

'Well?' Vezzani said, looking from one to the other.

'God, I hate this,' Vianello muttered.

'Your man was sure?' Brunetti asked.

'Absolutely,' Vezzani answered. Then, after a pause, he asked, 'Do we call first?'

'How far is it?' Brunetti asked, indicating the paper in Vezzani's hand.

He looked at it again. 'Clear on the other side of the city.'

'Then we call,' Brunetti said, not wanting to spend time sitting in traffic, only to find that the man's wife or *fidanzata* or companion, or whoever it was men lived with these days, was not at home.

Vezzani picked up the phone, hesitated a moment, then handed it to Brunetti. 'You speak to them. It's your case.' He dialled for an outside line, and punched in the number.

A woman's voice answered on the third ring. *'Pronto,'* she said, but provided no name.

'Buon giorno, Signora,' Brunetti said. 'Could you tell me if this is the home of Dottor Andrea Nava?'

'Who's calling, please?' she asked in a voice with a lower temperature.

'Commissario Guido Brunetti, Signora. Of the Venice police.'

After a pause that did not seem inordinately long to Brunetti, she asked, 'Could you tell me why you're calling?'

'We're trying to locate Dottor Nava, Signora, and this is the only number we have for him.'

'How did you get it?' she asked.

'The Mestre police gave it to us,' he said, hoping she would not ask why the Mestre police should have it.

'He doesn't live here any more,' she said.

'May I ask with whom I'm speaking, Signora?'

This time the pause was inordinately long. 'I'm his wife,' she said.

'I see. Would it be possible for me to come and speak to you, Signora?'

'Why?'

'Because we need to speak to you about your husband, Signora,' Brunetti said, hoping the seriousness of his tone would warn her of what was coming.

'He hasn't done anything, has he?' she asked, sounding more surprised than worried.

'No,' Brunetti said.

'Then what is it?' she asked, and he heard the mounting irritation in her voice.

'I'd prefer to speak to you in person, if I might, Signora.' This had dragged on too long, and it was now impossible for Brunetti to tell her on the telephone.

'My son is here,' she said.

That stopped Brunetti cold. How to distract a child while you tell his mother that her husband is dead? 'One of my officers will be with me, Signora,' he said, not explaining why this would make a difference.

'How long will it take you to get here?'

'Twenty minutes,' Brunetti invented.

'All right, I'll be here,' she said, clearly bringing the conversation to a close.

'Could I confirm the address, Signora?' Brunetti asked.

'Via Enrico Toti 26,' she said. 'Is that the address you have?'

'Yes,' Brunetti confirmed. 'We'll be there in twenty minutes,' he said again, thanked her, and replaced the phone.

Turning to Vezzani, Brunetti asked, 'Twenty minutes?'

'Not even,' he said. 'Do you want me to come?'

'Two of us is enough, I think. I'll take Vianello because we've done these things together before.'

Vezzani got to his feet. 'I'll take you in my car. You can tell your driver to go back. This way, there won't be a police car parked outside.' Seeing Brunetti about to protest, he said, 'I don't want to come in with you. I'll go across the street and have a coffee and wait for you.'

15

Number 26 was one of the first in a row of duplex houses on a street leading away from a small cluster of shops on the outskirts of Mestre. They passed the house; Vezzani parked the unmarked car a hundred metres ahead. As the three men got out of the car, Vezzani pointed to a bar on the other side of the road. 'I'll be in there,' he said.

Brunetti and Vianello walked along the row of houses and climbed the steps of number 26. There were two doors and two bells, beneath both of which were slots holding the names of the residents. One, the script faded by the light, bore the names 'Cerulli' and 'Fabretti'; the other, handwriting fresh and dark, read 'Doni'. Brunetti pressed that bell.

A few moments later, the door was opened by a dark-haired boy of about eight. He was thin and blue-eyed, his expression surprisingly serious for so young a child. 'Are you the policemen?' he asked. In one hand he held some sort of futuristic plastic weapon: a ray gun, perhaps. From the other hand hung a faded teddy bear with a large bald spot on his stomach.

'Yes, we are,' Brunetti said. 'Could you tell us who you are?'

'Teodoro,' he said and stepped back from the door, saying, 'My *mamma* is in the big room.' They asked permission and entered; the boy closed the door behind them. At the end of a corridor that seemed to bisect the house, they entered a room that looked out on an explosively disordered garden. In this suburban setting, Brunetti expected to see gardens of military rigidity, with straight lines of growing things, whether flowers or vegetables, and, regardless of the season, everything kept well pruned and clean. This one, however, spoke of neglect, with vines overgrowing what might once have been neat rows of bushes or plants. Brunetti saw the wooden poles that had supported tomatoes and beans gobbled up and tipped aside by the slow invasion of vines and brambles, as if someone had abandoned the garden at the end of summer and had completely lost interest by springtime.

The room into which the boy led them, however, reflected none of this disorder. A machine-made Heriz covered most of the marble floor; a dark blue sofa stood against one wall. On a low table in front of it was a neat pile of magazines. Two easy chairs, covered in a flower print dominated by the same dark blue as the sofa, stood facing it. On the walls Brunetti saw dark-framed prints of the sort that are bought in furniture shops.

As the boy entered, he said, 'Here are the policemen, Mamma.' The woman got to her feet as they came in and took a step towards them, her hands at her sides. She was of moderate height, the rigidity of her posture making her appear taller than she was. She looked to be in her late thirties, with shoulder length dark hair. Rectangular glasses enforced the angularity of her face. Her skirt fell to just below her knee; her grey sweater might have been silk.

'Thank you, Teodoro,' she said. She nodded at them and said, 'I'm Anna Doni.' Her face softened, but she did not smile.

Brunetti gave both their names and thanked her for letting them come to speak with her.

The boy looked back and forth as the grown-ups talked. She turned to him and said, 'I think you can go and do your homework now.'

Brunetti saw the boy begin to protest, then decide not to bother with it. He nodded and left the room without saying anything, taking both his weapon and his friend with him.

'Please, gentlemen,' the woman said, waving towards the sofa. She sat in one of the chairs, then rose halfway to straighten her skirt. When they were seated, she said, 'I'd like you to tell me why you've come.'

'It's in relation to your husband, Signora,' Brunetti said. He paused but she asked nothing. 'Could you tell me the last time you saw him or heard from him?'

Instead of answering, she asked, 'You know that we're separated?'

Brunetti nodded as if he did know but did not ask about it. Eventually she said, 'I saw him a bit more than a week ago when he brought Teodoro home.' In explanation, she added, 'He has visiting rights, and every second weekend he can take Teo to sleep at his house.' Brunetti relaxed to hear her finally use the boy's nickname.

'Is yours an amicable separation, Signora?' Vianello broke in to ask, signalling to Brunetti that he had decided to play the role of good cop, should that become necessary.

'It's a legal separation,' she said tersely. 'I don't know how amicable they can ever be.'

'How long were you married, Signora?' Vianello asked with every sign of sympathy for what she had just said. Then, as if to suggest she had the right to refuse to answer, he added, 'Excuse me for asking.'

That stopped her. She unfolded her hands and gripped the arms of her chair. 'I think that's enough, gentlemen,' she said with sudden authority. 'It's time for you to tell me what this is all about, and then I'll decide which of your questions I want to answer.'

Brunetti had hoped to delay telling her, but there was no chance of that now. 'If you've read the papers, Signora,' he began, 'you know that the body of a man was found in the water in Venice.' He paused for long enough for her to grasp what was bound to come next. Her hands tightened on the arms of her chair, and she nodded. Her mouth opened, as if the air around her had suddenly changed to water and she could no longer breathe.

'It appears that the man was murdered. We have reason to believe that the man is your husband.'

She fainted. During all his years in the police, Brunetti had never seen a person faint. He had seen two suspects, a man and a woman and at separate times, pretend to faint, and both times he had known instantly that they were only trying to buy time. But she fainted. Her eyes rolled upwards; her head fell against the back of the chair. Then, like a sweater placed carelessly on a piece of furniture, she slithered to the floor at their feet.

Brunetti reacted before Vianello did, pushed her chair aside and knelt beside her. He grabbed a cushion from the sofa and placed it under her head and then — and only because he had seen it done in the movies — took her hand and felt for her pulse. It beat, slow and steady; her breathing seemed normal, as though she had simply fallen asleep.

Brunetti looked up at Vianello, who had come to stand above him. 'Should we call an ambulance?' the Inspector asked.

Signora Doni opened her eyes, then raised a hand to straighten her glasses, which had been knocked askew by her fall. Brunetti saw that she looked around her, as if to ascertain where she was. A full minute passed before she said, 'If you'll help me, I think I can sit.'

Vianello knelt on her other side, and together, holding her as though she were sure to collapse, they helped raise her to her feet. She thanked them and waited until they released her, then she lowered herself into her chair, supporting herself with one hand.

'Would you like something to drink?' Brunetti asked, repeating what sounded like the script of a romantic comedy.

'No,' she said. 'I'm all right. I just need to sit quietly for a moment.'

Both men turned from her when she said that and went to the window to stare out at the desolate garden. Time passed while they waited for some word or sound from the woman behind them.

Finally she said, 'I'm all right now.'

They returned to the sofa. 'Please don't tell Teo,' she said.

Brunetti nodded and Vianello shook his head, both meaning the same thing.

'I don't know how . . . about his father,' she said, her voice growing unsteady. She took a few deep breaths, and Brunetti stifled the impulse to ask her again if she would like something to drink. 'Tell me what happened,' she said.

Brunetti saw no way to dress it up to make it more palatable. 'Your husband was stabbed and put in a canal. His body was found early on Monday morning, and he was taken to the Ospedale Civile. There was no identification: that's why it's taken us so long to find you.'

She nodded a number of times, then considered everything she had heard. 'There was no description of him in the papers,' she said. 'Or his disease.'

'We gave them the only information we had, Signora.'

'I read that,' she said angrily. 'But it didn't mention Madelung. Surely your pathologist would have recognized something like that.' She had chosen not to hear him or not to believe him, Brunetti realized as her voice lost the fight against sarcasm. Then, speaking more to herself than to them, she said, 'If I'd seen that, I would have called.' Brunetti believed her.

'I'm sorry, Signora. Sorry you had to learn it this way.'

'There's no way to learn it,' she said coolly, but seeing his response, added, 'is there?'

'How long did he have the disease?' Brunetti asked from simple curiosity.

'That's hard to say,' she told him. 'At first he thought he was just gaining weight. Nothing helped: no matter how little he ate, he kept getting heavier. It went on for almost a year. So he asked a friend. They'd been at university together, but Luigi went on to study medicine: human medicine, that is. He said what he thought it was, but we didn't believe him at first. We couldn't, really: Andrea never drank more than a glass or two of wine with dinner, often nothing, so it didn't seem possible.' She shifted her legs and moved around on her chair.

'Then about six months ago, he had a biopsy and a scan. And that's what it was.' All emotion scoured from her voice, she said, 'There's no treatment and no cure.' Then, with a false smile, she added, 'But it's not life-threatening. It turns you into a barrel, but it doesn't kill you.'

The false smile now forgotten, she said, 'But you didn't come here to talk about that, did you?'

Brunetti tried to assess how much he could ask of her and decided to risk speaking frankly. 'No, we didn't, Signora.' He paused, then asked, 'Is there anyone who might have wanted to do your husband an injury?'

'Besides me, you mean?' she asked with absolute lack of humour. Brunetti was taken aback by her remark and, glancing at Vianello, saw that the Inspector was, as well.

'Because of the separation?' Brunetti asked.

She looked out of the window, studying the mess in the garden. 'Because of what caused the separation,' she finally answered.

'Which was?' Brunetti asked.

'The oldest cliché in the world, Commissario. A woman where he worked, who is more than ten years younger than he is.' Then, with real rancour, she added, 'Or I am, which is perhaps closer to the point.' She looked at Brunetti directly, as if to suggest that he lived with a woman, too, and was merely biding his time before doing the same thing.

'He left you for her?' Brunetti asked.

'No. He had an affair with her, and when he told me about it — I suppose the right word here is "confessed" — he said he hadn't wanted to do it, that she'd seduced him.' Like a thermometer on to which the morning sun begins to shine, the bitterness in her voice rose as she spoke.

Brunetti waited. This was not a moment when a man could interrupt a woman who was speaking.

'He said he thought she planned it.' Abruptly, she raised one hand and made a waving gesture, as though she wanted to shoo away her husband, or the woman, or the memory of what he had said. Then, voice just over the edge of bitterness, she added, 'It wouldn't be the first time a man's claimed that, would it?'

Vianello, in his good-cop voice, slipped in to ask, 'You said he told you about it, Signora. Why was that?'

She glanced at the Inspector, reminded that he was there. 'He said the woman was going to tell me, so he wanted to be the one to do it before she did.' She raised her hand and rubbed at her forehead a few times. 'To tell me, that is.'

She gave the Inspector a level glance, then turned to Brunetti. 'So he didn't leave me for her, Commissario. I told him to get out.'

'And he left?' Brunetti asked.

'Yes. He left the same day. Well, the next day.' She sat quietly for some time, apparently reflecting on those events. 'We had to talk about what to tell Teo.' Then, in a softer voice, she said, 'I don't think there's anything you can tell them — children — not really.'

Brunetti was tempted to ask her what they had told their son, but he could not justify that and so he asked, instead, 'When did this happen?'

'Three months ago. We've both spoken to lawyers and signed papers.'

'And where was this leading, Signora?'

'Do you mean was I going to divorce him?'

'Yes.'

'Of course.' More slowly and far more

thoughtfully, she added, 'Not for the affair; please understand that. But because he didn't have the courage of it, because he had to play the victim.' Then, in a savage voice, she said, one arm raised across her breast and hand grabbing her shoulder as if to contain her rage, 'I hate victims. I hate people who don't have the courage of their own foul behaviour and blame it on someone else or something else.' She fought herself into silence, but lost the fight and went on: 'I hate the cowardice of it. People have affairs. They have affairs all the time. But for God's sake, at least admit that you did it. Don't go blaming the woman or the man. Just say you did it and, if you're sorry, say you're sorry, but don't go blaming some other person for your own weakness or stupidity.'

She stopped, exhausted, perhaps not so much by what she had said as by the circumstances in which she had said it. Two complete strangers, after all, and policemen, to boot, who had come to tell her that her husband was dead.

'Assuming that you are not the person responsible, Signora,' Brunetti said with the smallest of smiles, hoping that his irony would turn her away from the path this conversation seemed to have taken, 'can you think of anyone else who might have wanted to harm your husband?'

She weighed his question, and her face softened. 'Before I answer that, let me tell you one thing,' she said.

Brunetti nodded.

'The papers said the man in Venice — Andrea — was found on Monday morning,' she said, but it was a question.

Brunetti answered it. 'Yes.'

'I was here with my sister that night. She brought her two kids over, and we had dinner together, and then they all spent the night here.'

Brunetti permitted himself a glance in Vianello's direction and saw that the good cop was nodding. Signora Doni's voice called his attention back as she said, 'As to your other question, I don't know of anyone. Andrea was a . . .' She paused here, perhaps conscious that she had now to speak his epitaph. 'He was a good man.' Taking three deep breaths, she went on. 'I do know he was troubled at work or because of work. It was only during the last months we were together that I realized this; that's when he was . . .' Her voice trailed off, and Brunetti left her to remember what she chose. But then she spoke again. 'It might have been guilt about what he was doing. They were doing. But it might have been more than that.' Another long pause. 'We didn't talk much in the months before he told me.'

'Where does he work, Signora?' Brunetti asked, then cringed at the realization that he had used the present tense. To attempt to correct it would make things worse.

'His office isn't far from here. But two days a week he works at another job.' Unconsciously — perhaps because she had heard Brunetti do it — she had also fallen back into the present tense.

Brunetti assumed the work of a veterinarian must be pretty standard; he wondered what extra work Dr Nava could have done, aside from his private practice. 'Was he working as a veterinarian at this other job, too?'

She nodded. 'He was offered it about six months ago. With the financial crisis, there was less work at his clinic. That's strange, really, because people will usually do anything or pay anything to take care of their pets.' She twisted her hands together in a cliché gesture of helplessness, and Brunetti found himself wondering if she worked or whether she stayed home to take care of their son. And if so, then what would become of her now?

'So when they offered him the job, he took

it,' she said. 'We had the mortgage for the house and the costs of the clinic, and then there were the medical bills.' Seeing their surprise, she said, 'Andrea had to do it all privately. The waiting time for a scan at the hospital was more than six months. And he paid for all the visits to specialists. That's the reason he took the job.'

'Doing what, Signora?'

'Working at the slaughterhouse. They have to have a vet there when the animals are brought in. To see that they're healthy enough to be used.'

'As meat, do you mean?' Vianello asked.

She nodded again.

'Two days a week?' Brunetti asked.

'Yes. Monday and Wednesday. That's when the farmers bring them in. He arranged things at the clinic so that he didn't have to be there in the morning, though his staff would accept patients if necessary.' She stopped there, hearing herself describing this. 'Doesn't that sound strange: "patients", when you're talking about animals?' She smiled and shook her head. 'Crazy, really.'

'Which slaughterhouse, Signora?' Brunetti asked.

'Preganziol,' she said and then added, as though it still made a difference, 'It's only fifteen minutes by car.'

Thinking back to what she had said about what people would do for their pets, Brunetti asked, 'Did any of the people who took their pets to your husband ever display anger at him?'

'You mean, did they threaten him?' she asked.

'Yes.'

'He never told me about anything as serious as that, though a few did accuse him of not having done enough to save their pets.' She said this in a level voice; the coolness of her face suggested her opinion of such behaviour.

'Is it possible that your husband might not have told you about something like that?' Vianello asked.

'You mean to keep me from worrying about him?' she asked. It was a simple question, not a trace of sarcasm in it.

'Yes.'

'No, not before things got bad. He told me everything. We were . . .' she began, then paused to search for the proper word. '. . . close,' she said, having found it. 'But he never said anything. He was always happy with his work there.'

'Was the trouble you mentioned at the other job, then, Signora?' Brunetti asked.

Her eyes seemed to drift out of focus, and

she turned her attention to the neglected garden, where there were no signs of returning life. 'That's when his behaviour started to change. But that was because of . . . other things, I'd say.'

'Is that where he met the woman?' Brunetti asked, having for some reason thought she was someone who worked in his practice.

'Yes. I don't know what she does there: I wasn't interested in what her job was.'

'Do you know her name, Signora?'

'He had the grace never to use it,' she said with badly withheld anger. 'All he said was that she was younger.' Her voice turned to iron on the last word.

'I see,' he said, then asked, 'How did he seem, the last time you saw him?'

He watched her send her memory back to that meeting, watched as the emotions from it played across her face. She took a deep breath, tilted her head to one side to look away from both of them, and said, 'It was about ten days ago.' She took a few more deep breaths, and her arm again moved across her chest to anchor her hand on her shoulder. Finally she said, 'He'd had Teo for the weekend, and when he brought him back, he said he wanted to talk to me. He said something was bothering him.'

'About what?' Brunetti asked.

She released her hand and joined it to the one in her lap. 'I assumed it was about this woman, so I told him there was nothing he could say to me that I wanted to hear.'

She stopped, and both of them could see her recall saying those words. Neither of them spoke, however, and she eventually went on, 'He said there were things that were going on that he didn't like, and he wanted to tell me about them.' She looked at Vianello, then at Brunetti. 'It was the worst thing he did, the most cowardly.'

There was a noise from somewhere else in the house, and she half rose from her chair. But the noise was not repeated, and she sat down again. 'I knew what he wanted to tell me. About her. That maybe it wasn't going well and he was sorry. And I didn't care. Then. I didn't want to listen to it, so I told him that anything he had to tell me, he could say to my lawyer.'

She took a few breaths and went on. 'He said it wasn't really about her. He didn't use her name. Just called her "her". As if it was the most natural thing in the world for him to talk to me about her. In my home.' She had been looking between the two men as she spoke, but now she addressed her attention to the hands she kept folded in her lap. 'I told him he could leave.'

'Did he, Signora?' Brunetti asked after a long silence.

'Yes. I got up and left the room, and then I heard him leave the house, heard his car drive away. And that was the last time I saw him.'

Brunetti, who was looking at her hands, was startled by the first drop. It splashed on the back of her hand and disappeared into the fabric of her skirt, and then another drop, and another, and then she got to her feet and walked quickly from the room.

After some time, Vianello said, 'Pity she didn't listen to him.'

'For her reasons or for ours?' Brunetti asked.

Surprised by the question, Vianello answered, 'For hers.'

16

There was nothing for them to do but wait for her to return. Keeping their voices low, they discussed what she had said and the possibilities it created for them.

'We need to find this woman and see what was going on,' Brunetti said.

Vianello's look was easily read.

'No, not that,' Brunetti continued with a shake of his head. 'She's right: it's a cliché, one of the oldest ones. I want to know if he was bothered by anything other than the affair he was having with her.'

'You don't think that's enough to worry a married man?' Vianello asked.

'Of course it is,' Brunetti conceded. 'But most married men who are having affairs don't end up floating in a canal with three stab wounds in their back.'

'That's true enough,' Vianello agreed. Then, with a backward nod towards the door Signora Doni had used, he said, 'If I had her to contend with, I think an affair would make me very nervous.'

'What would Nadia do?' Brunetti asked, not sure how much criticism of Signora Doni lay in Vianello's question.

'Take my pistol and shoot me, probably,' Vianello answered with a small grin from which pride was not entirely absent. 'And Paola?'

'We live on the fourth floor,' Brunetti answered. 'And we have a terrace.'

'Crafty, your wife,' Vianello said. 'Would she leave an unsigned note in the computer?'

'I doubt it,' Brunetti said. 'Too obvious.' Entering into the puzzle, he gave it some thought. 'She'd probably tell people I'd been depressed for months and had recently talked about ending it all.'

'Who would she persuade to agree with her and say they'd heard you say the same thing?'

'Her parents.' Brunetti spoke before he thought about it, then quickly amended this: 'No, only her father. Her mother wouldn't lie.' Something occurred to him and he said it, his pleasure evident in his face and voice. 'I don't think she'd lie about me. I think she likes me.'

'Doesn't her father?'

'Yes, but in a different way.' Brunetti knew it was impossible to explain this, but he was much cheered at this sudden recognition of the Contessa's regard.

They heard Signora Doni's steps in the corridor and stood as she came back into the room. 'I had to check on Teo,' she said. 'He knows something big is wrong, and he's worried.'

'You told him we were policemen?' Brunetti asked, though the boy had told them so.

She met his gaze directly. 'Yes. I thought you'd come in uniform, and I wanted him to be prepared for that,' she said too quickly, as if she had been waiting for his question. Perhaps encouraged by their silence, she finally got to it: 'And I was afraid when you asked about Andrea. He usually called once or twice during the week. But I hadn't heard from him since he left.' She placed her palms on her thighs and studied them. 'I suppose I knew what you were going to tell me.'

Ignoring this, Brunetti said, 'You told us that his behaviour changed after he started the other job.' Brunetti knew he had to go carefully here, find a way to work himself through the tangle of her emotions. 'You said that you and he were close, Signora.'

He paused to let that sink in. 'Do you remember how soon after he began to work there he showed signs of being worried?'

He read in the stiffness of her mouth that she was close to the end of what she would accept and answer. She started to speak, coughed lightly, then went on: 'He hadn't been there long; maybe a month. But by then the disease had grown worse.

'He'd started eating less to try to lose weight, and that made him cranky, I'm afraid.' She frowned at the memory of this. 'I couldn't get him to eat anything except vegetables and pasta, and bread and some fruit. He said that would work. But it didn't do any good: he kept getting bigger.'

'Did he ever talk about a problem?' Brunetti asked. 'Other than the disease.'

She had grown visibly restless, so Brunetti forced himself into a more relaxed posture, hoping it would prove contagious.

'He didn't like the new job. He said it was hard to do both, especially now that the disease had got worse, but he couldn't leave because we needed the extra money.'

'That's quite a burden for a man who isn't in good health,' Vianello offered sympathetically.

She looked at him and smiled. 'That's the way Andrea was,' she said. 'He worried about the people who worked for him at the clinic. He felt responsible and wanted to keep it open.'

Brunetti left this alone. Years ago, less versed in the ways of emotions, he might have pointed to the dissonance between her behaviour towards her husband and these remarks, but the years had worn away his desire to find consistency, and so he never assumed it nor questioned its absence. She was aboil with emotions: Brunetti suspected the most powerful of them might be remorse, not anger.

'Could you tell us where his clinic is, Signora?' Brunetti asked. Vianello pulled a notebook from his pocket.

'Via Motta 145,' she said. 'It's only five minutes from here.' Brunetti thought she looked embarrassed. 'They called me yesterday and told me Andrea hadn't come in. I told them I didn't . . . didn't know where he was.' In the manner of a person not accustomed to lying, she looked down at her hands, and Brunetti suspected she had also told them she didn't care.

She forced herself to look at him and went on. 'He was living in a small apartment on the second floor of the building. Should I call them and tell them you're coming?' she asked.

'No, thank you, Signora. I think I'd like to go there unannounced.'

'To see if anyone tries to run away when they hear you're policemen?' she asked, only half joking.

Brunetti smiled. 'Something like that. Though if your husband hasn't been there for two days, and we show up without an animal, they'll probably guess who we are.'

It took a few moments for her to decide that he was exaggerating. She did not smile.

'Is there anything else?' she asked.

'No, Signora,' Brunetti said, then added, speaking with great formality, 'I'd like to thank you for being generous with your time.' Speaking as a father, he said, 'I hope you can find a way to tell your son,' unconsciously using the plural when he spoke.

'He is, isn't he?' she asked.

'What?'

'Ours.'

Vezzani was waiting for them in the bar, watching an afternoon cooking programme, the *Gazzettino* open on the table in front of him, a coffee cup placed to its side.

'Coffee?' he asked.

They nodded, and Vezzani waved to the barman and asked for two coffees and a glass of water.

They came and sat at his table. He folded the newspaper and tossed it on the empty fourth chair. 'What did she tell you?'

'That he was having an affair with a woman at work,' Brunetti answered.

Vezzani opened his mouth in a gasping O and held up both hands. 'Well, who ever heard of such a thing? What's the world coming to?' The waiter approached with the coffees and a glass of water for Vezzani.

They drank and then Vezzani, in a more serious voice, asked, 'What else?'

'He was also working at the slaughterhouse,' Vianello began.

'The one at Preganziol?' Vezzani asked.

'Yes,' Brunetti answered. 'Are there others?'

'I think there's one in Treviso, but that's a different province. Preganziol's the closest one to us.'

Vezzani asked, 'Why do they need a vet at a slaughterhouse? It's not as if he's there to save the lives of the animals, is it?'

'To check that they're healthy, and I imagine he also has to see that they slaughter them in a humane way,' Brunetti said. 'There's got to be some EU regulation about that.'

'Name the activity about which there is no EU regulation and win a prize,' Vezzani said, gave a mock toast with his glass, and took a sip of water. Then, his glass still held in the air in front of him, 'Did he have any trouble with clients at his practice?'

'His wife didn't know of any,' Brunetti said, but then added, 'She did say that some people were unhappy with the way their animals were treated. But that's not trouble.'

'I've heard people say awful things,' Vianello jumped in to say. 'Some of them would be capable of violence to anyone who hurt their animals. I think they're nuts, but we don't have a pet, so maybe I don't understand.'

'It does seem exaggerated,' Vezzani agreed, 'but I've lost the ability to understand what people do. If they'll kill you because you damage their car,' he said, referring to a recent case, 'think what they'd do if you hurt their dachshund.'

'You know where his clinic is?' Brunetti asked. He put some coins on the table and got to his feet. 'Via Motta 145. It seems he was living there, too.'

Vezzani stood, saying, 'Yes, I know the place. Let's go and talk to them.'

At one time, the clinic must have been a two-floor suburban residence large enough for two families. Similar houses stood on either side of it, each surrounded by a broad expanse of grassed land. As they slowed in front of it, they could hear the sound of a dog barking from behind the building, then another one answering: a human voice intervened; a door slammed, and then silence.

Vezzani had trouble parking the car. He drove ahead a hundred metres or so, but there were cars everywhere and no chance of finding a space. Is this, Brunetti wondered, what it is to live out here on *terraferma?* He turned to Vianello in the back seat; the two men exchanged a glance, but neither said a word.

With an irritated noise, Vezzani pulled the car into a sudden U-turn and drove back to the clinic. He parked on the wrong side of the road directly in front. He pulled down a plastic ticket from the windscreen, set it on the dashboard and got out of the car, slamming the door behind him. Brunetti and Vianello got out but did not slam the doors.

The three men walked up the short pavement to the front door. To one side a metal plaque bore the name 'Clinica Amico Mio', with below it the hours of operation. Dott. Andrea Nava was listed as the director.

Vezzani opened the door without ringing and entered; Brunetti and Vianello followed him inside. There was nothing, Brunetti realized, that could be done to eliminate the smell of the animals. He had smelled it before in the homes of friends of theirs who had pets, in the apartments of people he arrested, in abandoned buildings, and once in an antique shop where he had gone to question a witness. Sharp, rich with the tang of ammonia, it gave him the feeling that it would sink into his clothing and linger for hours after he left. And Nava had been living for some time above this.

The entrance was brightly lit, the floor covered with grey linoleum, and at one side stood a desk, behind which sat a young man in a white lab jacket. *'Buon dì,'* he said, smiling. 'May I help you?'

Vezzani stepped aside and allowed Brunetti to approach the desk. The boy could not have been eighteen and filled the air around him with a sense of health and well-being. Brunetti saw matched rows of perfect teeth, brown eyes so large his mind flashed to the description of 'ox-eyed Hera', even though he was looking at a boy. If roses had skin, his was the same.

'We're looking for the person in charge,' Brunetti said, smiling back, as who could not?

'Is it about your pet?' the young man

asked, not managing to sound as if he expected a positive response. He leaned to the side to see around them.

'No,' Brunetti said, letting his smile disappear. 'It's about Dottor Nava.'

At those words, the boy's smile went the way of Brunetti's, and he studied each of them more closely, as if in search of some new odour they might have carried into the room. 'Have you seen him?' he finally brought himself to ask.

'Perhaps I could speak to the person in charge,' Brunetti said.

The boy got to his feet, suddenly in a hurry. 'That would be Signora Baroni,' he said. 'I'll get her.' Abruptly he turned away from them to open a door just behind him. Leaving it open, he walked down a short corridor and entered a room on the right. Animal sounds came from the open door: barking and a thumping sound that could have been anything.

After less than a minute, a woman emerged and came towards them. Leaving the door open behind her, she approached Brunetti, who was closest to her. Though her face suggested she was a generation older than the receptionist, there was no sign of this in the ease and fluidity of her motions.

'Clara Baroni,' she said, shaking Brunetti's hand and nodding to the others. 'I'm Dottor Nava's assistant. Luca said you came to talk about him. Do you know where he is?'

Brunetti was struck by the awkwardness of the situation, the four of them standing in the room. It did not seem the best setting for what he had to say, but he saw no alternative. 'We've just come from speaking to Dottor Nava's wife,' he began. Then, in case it was still necessary, 'We're policemen.'

She nodded, encouraging him.

'The doctor's been killed.' He could find no better way to say it.

'How?' she asked, face blank with shock. 'In an accident?'

'No, Signora. Not an accident,' Brunetti said evasively. 'He had no identification, so it's taken us this long to trace him.' As he spoke to her, the focus of her eyes drifted away from him while she studied some interior place. She braced herself with one hand against the receptionist's desk. None of the men said anything.

After what seemed an interminable time, she stood upright and turned back to Brunetti. 'Not an accident?' she asked.

'It doesn't appear that way, Signora,' Brunetti said.

Like a dog coming out of the water, she

gave a shake of her entire body and asked in a tight voice, 'What was it, then?'

'He was the victim of a crime.'

She bit at her upper lip. 'Was he the man in Venice?'

'Yes,' Brunetti said, wondering why, if she had had any suspicion, she had not contacted them. 'Why do you ask that, Signora?'

'Because no one's heard from him for two days, and even his wife doesn't know where he is.'

'Did you call us, Signora?'

'The police?' she asked in honest astonishment.

Brunetti was tempted to ask her who else, but he resisted temptation and answered with a simple 'Yes.'

As if she were only now aware of the three men standing in the room, she said, 'Perhaps we could go back to my office.'

They followed her down a corridor, where the smell of animal grew even stronger, and into the room on the right. Against one wall, the receptionist sat in a straight-backed chair, a black and white rabbit on his lap. The rabbit had only one ear but, aside from that, seemed well-fed and sleek. A large grey cat was asleep in the sun on the windowsill behind them. It opened one eye when they came in but then closed it.

At their arrival, the boy leaned down and set the rabbit on the ground, then left the room without speaking. The rabbit hopped over to Vianello and sniffed at the bottom of his trousers, then did the same with Vezzani's, and then Brunetti's. Unsatisfied, it hopped over to Signora Baroni and raised itself on its hind legs against her leg. Brunetti was surprised to see that its front paws reached well above her knees.

She bent down and picked it up, saying, 'Come on, Livio.' The animal settled comfortably into her arms. She went and sat behind her desk. Vianello leaned against the windowsill, leaving the two chairs in front of the desk to the commissari. As soon as Signora Baroni sat and created a lap, the rabbit fell asleep in it.

As if there had been no interruption, the woman said, the fingers of one hand idly scratching the belly of the rabbit, 'I didn't call because Andrea's been gone from here only one full day, and then again today. I was going to call his wife again, but then you came.' Her attention left the rabbit and she looked at all three of them in turn, as if to assure herself that they were all listening and had understood. 'Then, when you said he'd been the victim of a crime, my first thought, obviously, was that man in Venice.'

'Why "obviously", Signora?' Brunetti asked in a pleasant voice.

Her fingers returned their attentions to the rabbit, which appeared to have been transformed into a piece of splay-legged drapery. 'Because the article said the man had not been identified, and Andrea's missing, and you're the police, and you're here. So that's the conclusion I came to.' She shifted the rabbit, who refused to emerge from his coma, to her other knee and asked, 'Am I mistaken?'

Brunetti said, 'We don't have a definite identification yet,' but quickly added, 'There's little doubt, but we need a positive identification.' He told himself he had forgotten to ask Nava's wife, but that was not the truth.

'Who has to do it?' she asked.

'Someone who knew him well.'

'Does it have to be a relative?'

'Not necessarily, no.'

'His wife's the obvious person, isn't she?'

'Yes.'

Signora Baroni picked up the rabbit, shook him into something resembling consciousness, and lowered him gently on to his feet. He hopped as far as the wall beside her, stretched out on the floor, and was immediately asleep. She sat upright, met

Brunetti's eyes, and said, 'Could I do it? I worked with him for six years.'

'Yes, of course,' he said. 'Why?'

'It would be too much for Anna.'

Though he was surprised, Brunetti was relieved that Nava's wife would be spared at least this.

Signora Baroni seemed to know a great deal about Nava's life, both personal and professional. Yes, she knew about his separation from his wife, and yes, she thought he was not happy with his job at the slaughterhouse. Here she sighed and added that Nava had made it clear that, no matter how disagreeable he might find the job, he felt obliged to keep it in order, among other reasons, she explained, 'to pay my salary here'. Saying that, she closed her eyes for a moment and rubbed at her forehead with her fingers.

'He said it as a joke, of course,' she said, looking up at Vianello. 'But it wasn't.'

Brunetti asked, 'Did he say anything else about his work there, Signora?'

She reached down and picked up the sleeping rabbit, whose eyes did not open. She began to stroke the rabbit's single ear. Finally she said, 'He never told me, but I think it was more than the job that was bothering him.'

'Do you have any idea what it might have been?' Brunetti asked.

She shrugged, disturbing the rabbit with the motion. It jumped to the floor again but this time walked over to a radiator and lay down beside it.

'I suppose it was a woman,' she said at last. 'It usually is, isn't it?'

None of the men answered her.

'He never spoke about it, if that's what you want to know. And I didn't ask him because I didn't want to know. It was none of my business.'

After that, she explained to them what her business was: make appointments; send samples to the labs and register the results for each animal; send bills and keep the accounts; occasionally help with exams and treatments. Luca and another assistant, who was not there that day, greeted patients, fed the animals, and helped Doctor Nava with procedures; no, he had never been threatened by the owner of a pet, though some had been distressed by the death of their animals. On the contrary, most people saw his concern for their pets and liked him as a result.

Yes, he lived upstairs, had been there for the last three months or so. When Brunetti told her that they had keys and wanted to have a look at his apartment, she said she saw no reason why they couldn't do so.

She led them to a door at the far end of the corridor, explaining, 'Because it was originally all one house, the entrance to his apartment is from here.'

Brunetti thanked her and opened the door with a key from the set that had been in Nava's pocket and that he had taken from the evidence room. At the top of the stairs another door, unlocked, opened into a large, open space running from the back of the building clear to the front, as though the original builders had stopped before dividing it into separate rooms. To say it was sparsely furnished was to understate the case: a two-seat sofa faced a small television placed on the floor, a neat pile of DVDs on the floor in front of it. A wooden table stood in front of the window that gave on to the back of the house and provided a view of the houses opposite. To the left of the window was a two-ring electric cooker on a narrow wooden table; frequent scrubbing had worn away the enamel. Clean pots hung from hooks above a small sink. On top of a small refrigerator was a ceramic bowl filled with apples.

A single bed stood under the eaves at the back of the room, blanket and sheet tucked in with military precision. Opposite it, along the other wall, was another bed covered with a tightly tucked Mickey Mouse blanket and a hillock of toy animals.

A cardboard wardrobe stood against the back wall. Brunetti looked inside and saw a few suits and an overcoat whose weight was turning the closet's crossbar into a U. Below these were a few pairs of small sneakers and to their right three pairs of larger shoes, one pair of which, Brunetti observed, were well-worn brown tasselled loafers. Plastic-wrapped white shirts lay stacked on a shelf above the clothes bar. The shelf below held the neatly folded underwear and clothing of a small boy.

The bathroom was just as spartan as the rest of the apartment but surprised Brunetti by being very clean. In fact, the apartment held no empty cups, old clothing, food wrappers, dirty plates, or any of the detritus Brunetti associated with the homes of the abandoned or solitary.

A few magazines and books lay on the table next to the man's bed. Brunetti drifted over and picked them up. There was a book about vegetarianism and, stuck into it, a photocopied chart of the combinations of grains and vegetables that would best create protein and amino acids. There was a printout of an article about lead poisoning and what appeared to be a veterinarian textbook on bovine diseases. Brunetti flicked through this, looked at two photos, and set the book down again.

The other men walked around the apartment, but neither stooped to pick up anything interesting or stopped to point out an object or an incongruity. The bathroom held nothing but soap, razors, and towels. A chest of drawers at the end of the bed held clean and folded men's underwear and, in the bottom drawer, clean towels and sheets.

There was none of the mess left behind by the permanent residence of a child. Only the clothing said anything about the persons using the apartment, and all it said was that it was a man of a certain size and a small boy.

'You think it's just the way he lived, or has someone been in here?' Brunetti finally asked.

Vezzani shrugged, reluctant to answer. Vianello gave another long look around and then said, 'I hate to say it, but I think he lived like this.'

'Poor devil,' Vezzani said. Soon after, none of them having found anything further to say, they left.

17

The men agreed it would be wiser to go to the slaughterhouse the following morning, when the place would be at work. As Vezzani drove them across the bridge to Piazzale Roma, Brunetti stared from the right side of the car at the vast industrial complex of Marghera. His thoughts were not on the daily ration of death pumped out by the chimneys he viewed but on the slaughterhouse and the idea of early morning as the best time for sudden death. Had not the KGB taken people off in the dark of night, their victims' senses dulled with sleep?

The ringing of Vianello's phone broke into these reflections, and from his seat in the back of the car the Inspector said, 'That was Foa. He says he can't pick us up. He's docked below Patta's place, waiting for him and his wife to come down. He's got to take them to Burano.'

'Police business, no doubt,' Vezzani commented, giving evidence that Patta's reputation extended even to the Questura in Mestre.

'If the police have to investigate a restaurant, it is,' Vianello answered. Brunetti told him to tell the pilot he was still waiting for a report on the tides for the night of Nava's murder. Vianello passed on the message and snapped his phone closed.

'You guys have any idea how lucky you are?' Vezzani asked.

Brunetti turned to him and asked, 'To work for Patta?'

Vezzani laughed. 'No, to work in Venice. There's hardly enough crime worth talking about.' Before either of them could protest, he said, 'I don't mean this Nava guy, but in general. The worst criminals are the politicians, but since there's nothing we can do about them, they don't count. So what do you get? A few break-ins, some tourist who gets his wallet stolen? The guy who kills his wife and calls you up to confess? So you spend your days reading notices from the idiots in Rome, or waiting for the next Minister of the Interior to be arrested so you get a new boss and new notices, or you walk down the street to have a coffee and sit in the sun and read the newspaper.' He tried to make it sound like a joke, but

Brunetti suspected he meant every word of it.

Brunetti took a quick glance into the rear-view mirror but saw only Vianello's left shoulder. In a level voice, he said, 'People pray for rain. Perhaps we should pray for murder.'

Vezzani took his eyes off the road and glanced quickly at Brunetti, but there was nothing to read in Brunetti's face, just as there had been nothing to read in his voice.

At Piazzale Roma, Brunetti and Vianello got out of the car and reached in to shake Vezzani's hand, then Brunetti said they'd get one of their own drivers to take them to the slaughterhouse the next morning. Vezzani did not bother to protest, said goodbye, and drove off.

Brunetti looked at Vianello, who shrugged.

'If that's the way he thinks, there's nothing we can do about it,' Brunetti said.

Vianello followed him towards the *embarcadero* of the Number One. The Inspector could get home more quickly by taking the Number Two, so Brunetti took this as a sign that Vianello wanted to continue the conversation.

People hurried towards them, most of them keeping to the left but some swerving closer to the water to get past faster and arrive a few seconds earlier at the buses that would take them to their homes on the mainland.

They passed the taxis bobbing in the water. Finally Vianello said, 'I suppose I can understand him. After all, the *calli* aren't lined with whores, and we don't get called to go out to the Chinese factories and arrest everyone. Or their whorehouses, for that matter.'

'And we don't have drunk drivers,' Brunetti offered.

'That's for the *Polizia Stradale,* Guido,' Vianello said with false reproach.

Undeterred, Brunetti added, 'Or arson. People don't set fire to factories.'

'That's because we don't have any factories any more. Only tourism,' said a dispirited Vianello, quickening his steps at the sound of the approaching vaporetto. The Inspector flashed his warrant card at the uniformed young woman on the boat landing.

The gate slid shut just behind them and they went inside to sit. Neither of them spoke until they passed under the Scalzi bridge, when Vianello said, 'You think he's jealous?'

On the left, the church of San Geremia slid towards them, and after a moment they could see, ahead of them on the right, the columned façade of the Natural History Museum.

'He'd be crazy if he weren't, don't you think?' Brunetti asked.

Only when he reached the door to his apartment did Brunetti realize how profoundly tired he was. He felt like a billiard ball that had been sliding around all day, first to this side and then to that. He'd learned too much and travelled too much, and now all he wanted to do was sit quietly and eat his dinner while listening to his family discuss subjects that had nothing to do with crime or death. He wanted a peaceful, uncontentious evening.

However much this might have been Brunetti's wish, it was not that of his lady wife, something he realized at the first sight of her and by the greeting she gave him when he went into her study.

'Ah, there you are,' she said with a broad smile that was perhaps too graced with teeth. 'I want to ask you a legal question.'

Brunetti sat on the sofa, and only then did he say, 'After eight at night, I function only as a private legal consultant and expect to be paid for my time and for any information I might provide.'

'In prosecco?'

He kicked off his shoes and extended himself to his full length on the sofa. He pummelled a pillow until its shape suited him, and lay back. 'Unless it is a serious or a nonrhetorical question, in which case I am to be paid in champagne.'

She removed her glasses, placed them on the open pages of the book she had been reading, and left the room. Brunetti closed his eyes and let his mind wander through the day in search of something restful he could contemplate until Paola's return. He found himself remembering the teddy bear in Teo's hand, its stomach fur rubbed or chewed away by childish adoration. Brunetti emptied his mind of everything else and considered the bear, which led him to the bears his children had loved and then to the one he could still remember having, though where he came from and where he went were mysteries long removed from his memory.

The clink of glass on glass brought him back from childhood to adult life. The fact that his eyes opened to a bottle of Moët in the hand of his wife did a great deal to ease the transition.

She filled the second glass and came towards the sofa. He pulled back his feet to give her room and took the glass she offered him. He held it toward her and joyed in the sound the glasses made as they touched, then took the first sip. 'All right,' he said as she sat down beside him, 'tell me.'

She shot him a look, tried to inject it with surprise, but when his expression remained unmoved, she abandoned the attempt and drank some of her wine. She pushed herself back in the sofa and let her left hand fall on to his calf. 'I want to know whether it's a crime to know that something illegal is going to take place and not report it.'

He took another sip of champagne, decided not to try to distract her with compliments for it, and considered her question. In similar manner to that with which he had conjured up Teo's teddy bear, though casting his net much farther into the past, he ran through those elements of criminal law he had studied at university.

'Yes and no,' he finally said.

'When is it a yes?' she asked.

'For example, if you are some sort of public official, you have to inform the authorities.'

'And ethically?' she asked.

'I don't do ethical,' Brunetti said and returned to his champagne.

'Is it right to stop a crime from being

committed?' she asked.

'You want me to say yes?'

'I want you to say yes.'

'Yes.' Then Brunetti added, 'Ethically. Yes.'

Paola considered this in silence, then got up and went over to fill both of their glasses. Still silent, she came back and handed him his and sat down again. Out of the habit of decades, her left hand returned to his leg.

Sitting back in the sofa she crossed her legs, then took another sip of champagne. Looking at the painting on the far wall, the portrait of an English naturalist holding a tufted grouse they had found years ago in, of all places, Seville, she said, 'Aren't you going to ask me what this is all about?'

He looked at his wife, not at the naturalist and not at the tufted grouse, and said, 'No, I'm not.'

'Why?'

'In the immediate sense, because I've had a long day and I'm very tired, and I don't have room in my brain or in my sensibility for anything that might lead to trouble. And from the way you ask, I suspect that possibility exists.'

'And in the larger sense or longer sense, why don't you want to hear about it?' she asked.

'Because if it does lead to trouble, I'll

learn about it sooner or later, so there's no need for you to tell me about it now.' He leaned forward and placed his hand on hers. 'I really can't do this now, Paola.'

She turned up her palm, gave his a strong squeeze, and said, 'Then I'll go and start dinner, shall I?'

18

Brunetti woke a few times in the night, thinking about what Paola had asked him and trying to imagine what it might mean, what she was up to, for he knew she was up to something. He knew the signs from long exposure and long experience: once she started on one of what he thought of as her missions, she grew intense, sought specific information rather than concepts or ideas, and seemed to lose her sense of irony and humour. Over the years, she had had attacks of zeal, and they had often led to trouble. Brunetti sensed that another one was on the way.

Each time he woke, he had but to sense the presence of the inert lump beside him to marvel anew at her gift of plunging into sleep, no matter what was happening around her. He thought of the nights he had spent lying awake and worrying about his family or his job or his future or the future of the planet, or simply kept awake by the inability to digest his dinner. While beside him rested a monument to peace and tranquillity, motionless, barely breathing.

He woke again a bit before six and decided it was useless to try to go back to sleep. He went down to the kitchen and made himself coffee, heated milk to pour into it, and went back to bed.

Having finished the *Agamemnon* and in need of a break before continuing that familiar family saga, Brunetti did what he often did in such circumstances: he picked up the *Meditations of Marcus Aurelius* and, much in the way devout Christians were said to consult the Bible, opened it at random. It was rather like playing a slot machine, he had to admit: sometimes what came up was sententious pap that led to nothing and certainly provided no riches. But sometimes the words came at him like a stream of coins, flooding out of the trough in the slot machine and splashing across his feet.

He opened to Book Two and found this: 'Failure to read what is happening in another's soul is not easily seen as a cause of unhappiness: but those who fail to attend to the motions of their own soul are necessarily unhappy.' He looked up from the book and out the window, where the curtain was only half drawn; he was conscious of the light, not from the approaching dawn, but from the ambient illumination with which the city was filled.

He considered the words of the wise emperor, but then he thought of Patta, of whom many things could be said, among which was the undeniable fact that he was happy. Yet if ever man had been made who was unconscious of the motions of his own soul, that man was Vice-Questore Giuseppe Patta.

In no way deterred by the failure of the book to spin up a winning combination, Brunetti opened to Book Eleven. 'No thief can steal your will.' This time he closed the book and set it aside. Again, he gave his attention to the light in the window and the statement he had just read: neither provided illumination. Government ministers were arrested with frightening frequency; the head of government himself boasted, in the middle of a deepening financial crisis, that he didn't have financial worries and had nineteen houses; Parliament was reduced to an open shame. And where were the angry mobs in the piazzas? Who stood up in Parliament to discuss the bold-faced looting of the country? But let a young and virginal girl be killed, and the country went mad; slash a throat and the press was off and running for days. What will was left among the public that had not been destroyed by television and the penetrant vulgarity of the current administration? 'Oh, yes, a thief can steal your will. And has,' he heard himself say aloud.

Brunetti, trapped in the mixture of rage and despair that was the only honest emotion left to the citizenry, pushed back the covers and got out of bed. He stayed under the shower for a long time, indulging in the luxury of shaving there without giving a thought to the consumption of water, the energy expended to heat it, nor yet to the fact that he was using a disposable razor. He was tired of taking care of the planet: let it take care of itself for a change.

He went back to the bedroom and dressed in a suit and tie, but then he remembered where it was he and Vianello were going that morning and replaced the suit in the closet and put on a pair of brown corduroy trousers and a heavy woollen jacket. He searched around on the floor of the closet until he found a pair of Topsiders with thick rubber waffle soles. He had little idea of the proper attire for a slaughterhouse, but he knew a suit was not it.

It was seven-thirty before he left the house, stepping out into an early morning crispness that gave promise of clean air and growing warmth. These really were the best days of the year, with the mountains sometimes visible from the window in the kitchen, the nights cool enough to summon a second blanket from the closet.

He walked, stopped to get a newspaper — *La Repubblica* and not either of the local papers — and then in Ballarin for a coffee and a brioche. The *pasticceria* was busy, but not yet crowded, so most people could still find a place to stand at the bar. Brunetti took his coffee to the small round table, placed the paper to the left of his cup, and studied the headlines. A woman about his age, with hair the colour of marigolds, set her cup not far from his, studied the same headlines while sipping at her coffee, looked at him, and said, speaking Veneziano, 'It makes a person sick, doesn't it?'

Brunetti held up his brioche and tilted it in the equivalent of a shrug. 'What can we do?' had come from his lips before he remembered the words of Marcus Aurelius. The thief, it seemed, had stolen his will during the short time since he had left his home. Thus, as if he had intended his first remark as a rhetorical flourish, he looked at her directly and said, 'Other than to vote, Signora.'

She looked at him as if she had been stopped on the street by one of the patients from Palazzo Boldù, some raving lunatic who would now reveal the Secret of the Ages. Disgust at his own moral cowardice swept Brunetti, forcing him to add, 'And throw small coins at them if we see them on the street.'

She considered this and, seeming gratified that this man had so quickly come to his senses, set her cup in her saucer and carried it over to place it on the bar. She smiled at him, wished him good day, paid, and left.

At the Questura, he went directly to the officers' room, but none of the day shift had arrived. In his own office, he checked for new files, but his desk was as he had left it the day before. He used his new computer to check the other newspapers, but they had no further information about the murdered man nor about the progress of the case, nor had they bothered to print the photo that had been sent to them. Interest in the dead man had been supplanted by the news that the decomposing body discovered in a shallow grave near Verona two days before had turned out to be that of a woman who had been missing for three weeks. She was young, and her photo showed her to have been attractive, so her death had blotted out the other.

Vianello's entrance cut short his reflections. 'Foa's assistant's waiting,' he said, then by way of explanation, 'He's not on till the afternoon. There's a car at Piazzale Roma.' Brunetti saw that the Inspector, too, had given some thought to their destination and was wearing a pair of much-laundered jeans, a brown leather jacket, and a pair of shoes that looked as if they were made for walking in rough country.

Brunetti glanced over the surface of his desk, wondering if there was anything he should be taking with him, but he could think of nothing. Cowardly delay: his search was no more than cowardly delay. 'Right. Let's go,' he said and started down towards the boat.

It took them an hour to get to Preganziol, what with the seemingly stationary agglomeration of cars and buses at Piazzale Roma and the dense traffic on the Ponte della Libertà and in the outskirts of Mestre. Traffic didn't begin to move at a steady pace until they passed under the autostrada and started north on Highway 13.

They passed the entrances to Villa

Fürstenberg and Villa Marchesi and then found themselves running parallel to the train tracks. They slowed to go through Mogliano Veneto, and then passed another villa; the name sped by too fast for Brunetti to read it. Their driver looked neither right nor left: the villa could have been a circus tent or an atomic reactor, and still he would not have taken his eyes from the road. They crossed a small stream, passed another villa, and then the driver turned to the right and into a narrow two-lane road, eventually drawing to a stop in front of what looked like an industrial park.

The world in front of them was a world of cement, chain-link fences, anonymous buildings, and moving trucks. The buildings for the most part were naked: unpainted, flat-roofed rectangles with very few windows; each was surrounded by an apron of stained cement, and most of those were surrounded by fences. The only brightness came from the lettering on some of the trucks and an open-sided kiosk where workers stood, drinking coffee and beer.

The driver turned to speak to Brunetti. 'This is it, sir,' he said, pointing to a gate in the metal fence around one of the buildings. 'Here on the left.' Only then, seeing him full face, did Brunetti notice the smear of a broad, glossy scar that could have been caused only by a burn; it began above his left eye and widened as it ascended until it disappeared, broad as three fingers, under the brim of his hat.

Brunetti opened the door. As soon as he was outside, he heard the noise: a distant growling sound that might have come from New Year's noisemakers or from the exultation of passionate lovers, or even from a badly played oboe. Brunetti, however, knew what it was, and if he had not, the iron-strong smell would have told him what went on behind those gates.

Vezzani had called Brunetti while he was in the car: the Director was not there, so he had explained to his assistant that two officers from Venice were on their way. She would meet them. When Brunetti conveyed this message to Vianello, the Inspector repeated, 'she' and shrugged.

The driver sounded the horn a few times: Brunetti doubted that it would be heard. But after a few seconds, and as in a film, a new sound began, rougher and more mechanical than the other, and the two sides of the gate began to open inwards.

Brunetti waited until the gates had stopped moving to decide whether to get back into the car or to walk through the gate. The metallic odour grew stronger. The gates and the noise of the mechanism propelling them stopped at the same moment, leaving audible only the original sound, now louder. One high-pitched squeal that must have come from a pig rose above all the other noises, then ended as quickly as it had begun, as though the sound had run into a wall. Yet this in no way diminished the level of noise: perhaps it resembled the noise from a playground of excited children let out to play, but there was nothing playful in the sound. And no one was going to be let out.

Brunetti turned towards the car just as Vianello got out of the back seat and walked over to join him. Brunetti was vaguely conscious that something was odd, and it was only when he glanced down and saw that the ground was covered with gravel that he realized Vianello's footsteps were obliterated by the sounds coming from beyond the open gates.

'I told the driver to go and get a coffee and that we'd call him when we're finished,' the Inspector said. Then, in answer to Brunetti's expression, he added, neutrally, 'The smell.'

As they walked towards the gate, Brunetti was amazed that he could feel the gravel slide beneath his feet while he could not hear the sound his feet made. When they passed through the gate, a door opened in the building just to their right, a large rectangle built from cement blocks, roofed with aluminium panels. A small woman paused a moment in the doorway, then came down the two steps and walked towards them, her footsteps also eliminated by the sounds that came from behind her.

Her dark hair was cut close to her head, suggesting a boyishness that was quickly dispelled by her full bosom and the tight-waisted skirt she wore. Her legs, Brunetti noticed, were good, her smile relaxed and welcoming. When she reached them, she raised her hand and offered it, first to Vianello, who was closer to her, and then to Brunetti, then tilted her head back to get a better view of the two men, each so much taller than she.

She indicated the building and turned towards it, not bothering to waste words against the noise.

They followed her up the steps and into the building, where the noise grew less, and even less again when the woman reached behind them to close the door. They now stood in a small vestibule about two metres by three, cement-floored, utterly utilitarian.

The walls were white plasterboard, without decoration. The only object in the room was a video camera suspended from the ceiling and aimed at the door, where they were standing. 'Yes,' she said, watching the relief on both their faces, 'it's quieter in here. If not, we'd all be driven mad.' She was close to thirty, but not yet there, and had the easy grace of a woman at home in her body and with no anxieties about it.

'I'm Giulia Borelli,' she said, 'I'm Dottor Papetti's assistant. As I explained to your colleague, Dottor Papetti is in Treviso this morning. He's asked me to help you in any way we can.' She gave a small smile, the sort one gives to visitors or prospective clients. How many women would work at a slaughterhouse? Brunetti asked himself.

Then, with a look of open curiosity, she asked, 'You're really the police from Venice?' Her voice was curiously deep for so small a woman, musical with the cadence of the Veneto.

Brunetti said that they were. Closer to her, he saw the freckles sprayed across her nose and cheeks; they added to the general impression of health. She ran the fingers of her right hand through her hair. 'If you come to my office, we can talk,' she said.

The iron-rich odour had diminished here,

as well. Would air conditioning do that? Brunetti wondered, and, if so, what would happen in the winter, when this part of the building was heated? He and Vianello followed her through a door and into a corridor that led to the back of the building. He was aware that his senses had been both battered and starved since he left the car. His hearing and sense of smell had been overloaded with sensation, shocked into a state where they might not be capable of registering any new smell or sound, while his sense of sight had been heightened by the blank room and corridor.

Signorina Borelli opened a door, then stepped back to let them go in ahead. This room, too, was close to naked. There was a desk with a computer and some papers on it, a chair behind it and three in front, and nothing else. More unsettling, there were no windows: all light came from multiple neon strips in the ceiling that created a textureless, dull illumination that deprived the room of any sense of depth.

She went behind the desk and sat, leaving them to take their places in front. 'Your colleague said you wanted to talk about Dottor Nava,' she said in a level voice. She leaned forward, body bent towards them.

'Yes, that's correct,' Brunetti answered.

'Could you tell me when he came to work here?' he asked.

'About six months ago.'

'And his duties?' Brunetti asked, continuing to evade the use of either the present or the past tense and hoping he did so naturally. Vianello took out his notebook and began to write.

'He inspects the animals that are brought in.'

'For what purpose?' Brunetti asked.

'To see if they're healthy,' she answered.

'And if they're not?'

Signorina Borelli seemed surprised at the question, as though the answer should be self-evident. 'Then they aren't slaughtered. The farmer takes them back.'

'Any other duties?'

'He inspects some of the meat.' She sat back and raised one arm to point behind her to the left. 'It's refrigerated. Obviously, he can't inspect it all, but he does look at samples and decides if it's safe for human consumption.'

'And if it's not?'

'Then it's destroyed.'

'How?'

'It's burned.'

'I see,' Brunetti said.

'Any other duties?'

'No, only those two things.'

'How many days a week is he here?' Brunetti asked, as if he had not already had this information from the dead man's wife.

'Two. Monday and Wednesday mornings.'

'And the other days? What does he do?'

If she was puzzled by the question, she did not hesitate to answer it. 'He has a private practice. Most of the examining veterinarians do.' She smiled and shrugged, then said, 'It would be hard to live on what they earn here.'

'But you don't know where?'

'No,' she said regretfully, then said, 'But it's probably in our files, on his application. I could easily find out for you.'

Brunetti held up a hand both to acknowledge and decline her offer. In a friendly voice, he asked, 'Could you give me a clearer idea of how things work here? That is, how is it that he inspects animals on only two days?' He spread his hands in a gesture of confusion.

'It's quite simple, really,' she said, using an expression most commonly chosen to begin an explanation of something that was not simple. 'Most farmers get their animals here the day before the slaughtering, or the same day. That saves them the cost of keeping and feeding and watering the animals while they wait. Dottor Nava inspects them on Monday and Wednesday, and they're processed after that.' She paused to see if Brunetti was following, and Brunetti nodded. He was, as well, mulling over the verb 'processed'.

'And if he doesn't see them?' Vianello broke in to ask, also using the deliberately deceptive present tense.

She raised her eyebrows, either at the discovery that the Inspector could speak or at the question itself. 'That's never happened before. Luckily, his predecessor has agreed to come in and do the inspections and continue with them until Dottor Nava comes back.'

Imperturbable, Brunetti asked, 'And the name of his predecessor?'

She could not disguise her surprise. 'Why do you want to know that?'

'In case it becomes necessary to speak to him,' Brunetti answered.

'Meucci. Gabriele Meucci.'

'Thank you.'

Signorina Borelli straightened up, as though she thought that would be the end of it, but Brunetti asked, 'Could you give me the names of the other people Dottor Nava is in contact with here?'

'Aside from me and the Director, Dottor

Papetti, there's the chief knacker, Leonardo Bianchi. He might know other people, but we're the ones he deals with most frequently.'

She smiled, but the wattage was now dimmer. 'I think it's time you explained why you're asking all these questions, Commissario. Perhaps I watch too much television, but usually this kind of conversation takes place when someone has died and the police are trying to get information about him.'

Her glance went back and forth between the two men. Vianello kept his head bent over his notebook, leaving it to his superior to answer.

'We have reason to believe that Dottor Nava has been the victim of violence,' Brunetti said, unable to resist the bureaucrat's need to release information in small portions.

Just then, as if to draw attention to the phrase, a shrill noise penetrated whatever acoustical insulation was meant to protect this room from the reality beyond it. Unlike the previous long cry, this one was not drawn out, only three short blasts like the ones that on the vaporetti were a command to abandon ship. There were three more cries, muffled this time, and then the animal making them was forced to abandon ship, and the noises stopped.

'Is he dead?' Signorina Borelli asked, visibly shaken.

Confused for an instant by the object of her curiosity, it took Brunetti a moment to answer. 'We think so, yes.'

'What does that mean: you think so?' she demanded, looking back and forth between them. 'You're the police, for heaven's sake. If you don't know, then who does?'

'We still don't have a positive identification,' Brunetti said.

'Does that mean you're going to ask me to make one?' she asked, voice hot with the outrage ignited by Brunetti's last remark.

'No,' Brunetti said calmly. 'We've already found a person to do that.'

She leaned forward suddenly, her head extended like a snake about to strike, and said, 'You're cold-hearted, aren't you? You tell me he's been the victim of violence, but the fact that you're here means he's dead, and the fact that you're asking all these questions means someone killed him.' She wiped at her eyes as she spoke and seemed to have trouble finishing some of her words.

Vianello looked up from his notebook and studied Signorina Borelli's face.

She propped her elbows on the desk and lowered her face into her upraised palms.

'We find a good man, and this happens to him,' she said. Brunetti had no idea how to interpret 'good', and there was no hint in her voice. Did she judge Nava to be a competent man or a decent one?

After a short time, and still not completely in control, she said, 'If you have more questions, you'll have to ask Dottor Papetti.' She slapped both palms on the desk, and the noise seemed to calm her. 'What else do you want?'

'Would it be possible to look at your facility?'

'You don't want to,' she said without thinking.

'I beg your pardon?' Brunetti said.

'You don't want to see what we do here.' She sounded entirely calm and reasonable. 'No one does. Believe me.'

Few remarks could have as effectively steeled Brunetti's intention to see what went on here.

'We do,' he said and got to his feet.

19

For all the care they had taken in dressing, Vianello and Brunetti might as well have worn tuxedos to the slaughterhouse. The first thing Signorina Borelli did, in the face of Brunetti's adamant insistence that they be taken to see where Dottor Nava had worked, was to phone the chief knacker, Leonardo Bianchi, and ask him to meet them in the changing room. Then she led them from her office, down a cement-floored corridor, up a double flight of stairs and into a spartan room that reminded Brunetti of the ones he had seen in American films of high schools: metal lockers lined the walls, a table in the centre was chipped and scarred with cigarette burns and spills of thick, dried liquid. Benches held crumpled copies of *La Gazzetta dello Sport* as well as discarded socks and empty paper cups.

She led them silently across the room to a

locker, took a key ring from her pocket and used a small key to open the padlock on the door. She reached in and pulled out a folded white paper jumpsuit of the sort worn by the men on the crime squad, shook it open and handed it to Brunetti, another to Vianello. 'Take your shoes off to put it on,' she said.

Brunetti and Vianello obeyed the instructions. By the time they had their shoes on again, she had found two sets of transparent plastic shoe covers. Silently she handed them to Brunetti. He and Vianello slipped them on. Next came transparent plastic caps that looked like the ones Paola wore in the shower. They pulled them over their hair.

Signorina Borelli looked them up and down, saying nothing. The door opposite the one they had used opened, and a tall bearded man came into the room. He wore a long smock that had once been white but was now grey: there were broad red smears across the front and sides. Brunetti looked at his feet and was glad she had given them the plastic covers.

The man, whom Brunetti understood must be the chief knacker, nodded to Signorina Borelli and looked at the two men indifferently. She made no attempt to introduce them. The man said, 'Come with me, gentlemen.' Brunetti and Vianello followed Bianchi towards the door. When he opened it, cries and howls were newly audible, and heavy thumps and clangs came from beyond it.

He led them down a narrow corridor towards a door about five metres ahead of them. Brunetti was intensely aware of the ruffling noise made by his protective suit and the slippery feel under his feet as his shoes slid around inside their plastic covers. He looked down to see what the surface of the floor was, the better to calculate the sort of purchase his feet would have. His step faltered for the briefest instant when he saw a bloody sole-print on the floor, heading their way. He moved his right foot quickly to the side and came down heavily in order to avoid stepping on the other print, too late realizing that it wouldn't make any difference, not really; at least not beyond the level of superstition.

Brunetti shot a quick glance behind him and caught sight of Vianello's strained face; he quickly returned his attention to Bianchi's back. Brunetti shivered: the increasing noise had obliterated other sensitivities, and he had not noticed the cold until now. Vianello made a humming noise that was barely audible. Noise and cold intensified as they got closer to the door. Bianchi stopped in front of it and put his hand on the metal bar that stretched across it. Push down, and the door would open.

He stared at Brunetti, looked beyond him to Vianello, saying nothing, his question in his eyes. Brunetti had a moment's uncertainty about the wisdom of all of this, but Nava's wife had said that the veterinarian was troubled by something taking place here.

Brunetti lifted his chin in a signal that could have been command or encouragement. Bianchi turned away from him and pushed down on the bar, swinging open the door. Sound, cold, and light spilled over them. The cries and howls, whimpers and thuds mingled in a modern cacophony that assaulted more than their sense of hearing. Most sounds are neutral. Footsteps all sound the same, really: the menace comes from the setting in which they are heard. Running water, too, is no more than that. Bathtub overfilling, mountain stream: context is all. Unweave a symphony and the air is filled with odd, unrelated noises that no longer follow one another. A howl of pain, however, is always that, whether it comes from a beast with two or four legs, and a human voice raised in anger causes the same reaction regardless of the language in which the anger is expressed or whom it is directed at.

The stimuli given to the other senses did not permit of pretty word or thought games: Brunetti's stomach contracted away from a smell that was as strong as a blow, and his eyes attempted to flee from red in all its varieties and all its striations. His mind intervened, forcing him to think and in thought to find some escape from what surrounded him. He thought it was William James: yes, William James, the brother of the man his wife loved, a half-memory of something he'd written more than a hundred years ago, that the human eye was always pulled to 'things that move, things that something else, blood'.

Brunetti attempted to hold those words up in front of him, like a shield from behind which he could look at what was happening. He saw that they were on a grated catwalk protected on both sides by handrails and raised at least three metres from the work area beneath them. Seeing and not seeing, perceiving and failing to perceive, he guessed, from the sight of so much empty space beneath them, that the work was nearing its end. Six or seven yellow-booted men in white rubber coats and yellow hardhats moved below them in the cement-floored cubicles and did things with knives and pointed instruments to pigs and sheep; hence the noise. Animals fell at the feet of the men, but some managed to flee, crashing into the walls before slipping and falling. Others, wounded and bleeding and unable to get to their feet, continued to flail about with their legs, feet scrambling against floors and walls, while the men dodged their hooves to deliver another blow.

Some of the sheep, Brunetti noticed, were protected from the knives by their thick coats and had to be struck repeatedly on the head by what looked like metal rods that ended in hooks. Occasionally the hooks were used for other purposes, but Brunetti looked away before he could be sure of that, though the wail that always followed the desertion of his eyes left no doubt about what went on.

The sheep made low, animal noises — grunts and bleats — while the pigs struck him as sounding not unlike what he, or Vianello, would sound like, were they down there and not up here. The calves bleated.

The smell bored into his nose: it was not only the iron-sharp tang of blood but the invasive stench of offal and excrement. Just as Brunetti realized that, he heard the water and gave unconscious, unknowing thanks for the sound. He looked to the source and saw one of the white-coated men below them spray an empty cubicle with what seemed to be a fire hose. The worker stood, legs widespread, the better to brace his body against the force of the jet of water that he sprayed across the floor of the cubicle, waving the stream back and forth so as to wash everything down an open grille in the cement.

The walls of the cubicles were made of wire fencing, so water coursed into the adjacent one, swirling away the blood that ran from the nose and mouth of a pig that lay against a wall, feet scraping across the floor in a vain attempt to push himself farther from the man who stood above him. The man there used his metal pole, and when Brunetti looked back, the pig appeared to have taken flight and was ascending towards them, perhaps to leave this place behind and continue — who knew where? Brunetti turned away as the pig's twitching body appeared beside him, joined to a metal chain by a hook through its neck. Brunetti looked for and found Vianello, but before either could speak, a rash of sudden red spots splashed across the Inspector's chest. Vianello, stunned, glanced down and raised a hand to try to wipe the red away, but he never completed the gesture: the hand fell to his side, and he looked at Brunetti, face blank.

A cranking noise made them return their attention to the twitching pig, which was now moving away from them towards the double plastic flaps of a broad door at the other end of the room. When he saw the pig's body push the door open and disappear, Brunetti abandoned his quaint idea of intervention or salvation for the doomed beast.

Brunetti cleared his throat and tapped Bianchi on the shoulder. 'Where do they go from here?' he asked above the clanks and cries.

The knacker pointed farther back in the building and started in that direction. Brunetti, careful to keep his eyes on the man's back, followed, and a dazed Vianello trailed along behind them. At the end of the catwalk they came to a thick metal door with a horizontal metal handle. Bianchi appeared hardly to break his stride, so quickly did he push it open and pass through. The others followed, and Vianello pushed the door closed behind them.

At first, Brunetti wondered if they had managed to escape outside and had somehow walked directly into a forest, though he could recall having seen no growth of trees behind the building. It was dark, with light filtering down from above, as in a forest in the early morning. He saw a field of thick shapes just ahead of them, seeming to rise up from the earth. Bushes, perhaps, or young poplar trees in full leaf? Surely they were not tall enough to be full-grown trees, yet they were thick, and that brought his sense-assaulted mind back to the idea of bushes. The three men separated and began to walk about on their own.

If they were outside, however, the day had changed and it had grown terribly cold. Gradually Brunetti's eyes adjusted to the diminished light, and the bushes or trees began to take on finer definition. His first thought was of autumnal leaves until he saw that the red was muscle and the yellow was streaks of fat. He and Vianello had become so dependent upon Bianchi's guidance that they had followed him unthinkingly into the midst of the hanging sides of beef and pig and sheep, the headless beasts distinguishable only by their size, and who could differentiate between a large sheep and a small calf? Red and yellow and the frequent streak of white fat.

Vianello broke first. He pushed past

Brunetti, no longer concerned with Bianchi and his opinion, or any opinion at all, and staggered drunkenly to the door. He pushed at it uselessly, then pounded it twice and gave it a kick. The knacker materialized from the thicket of bodies, pulled at some handle Vianello could not make out in the dimness, and the door opened. Looking into the greater light of the other room, Brunetti could see Vianello walking away from them, one hand raised to shoulder height beside him, as if to keep it there, ready to grab on to the wire wall of the walkway should he not be able to continue.

Forcing himself to move slowly and keeping his eyes on Vianello's retreating back, Brunetti went through the door but did not wait for Bianchi to join him. He walked towards the other end of the catwalk, making the same humming noise he heard Vianello making and now understanding that it succeeded in blocking out some of the noise that rose up from what was still going on below them. Something appeared beside him, at shoulder height, appearing to keep pace. Brunetti broke step for a moment but quickly regained control and kept walking, his eyes straight in front and not for an instant giving in to the temptation to look at what was floating alongside him.

He found Vianello slumped on one of the benches in the changing room, one arm removed from his protective suit, the other forgotten, or trapped, inside it. He looked to Brunetti like one of the heroes of the *Iliad,* broken in defeat, armour hanging half slashed from his body, the enemy about to slay him and strip him clean. Brunetti sat beside him, then slumped forward and rested his forearms on his thighs and remained like that, staring at his shoes. Anyone seeing them from the doorway would see two middle-aged but oddly dressed athletes, exhausted by the game they had just played, waiting for the coach to come in and tell them how they'd done.

But there was no sign of Coach Bianchi. Brunetti leaned down and slipped off the plastic shoe covers and kicked them aside, then shoved himself to his feet and fumbled to unzip his suit. He slipped his arms out, then pushed it down below his knees and sat down again to rip it over his shoes. For want of anything else to do, he picked it up and made a sloppy attempt to fold it, then simply dropped it in a heap on the bench beside him.

Turning to Vianello, Brunetti noticed that he had not moved. 'Come on, Lorenzo. The driver's outside.'

Moving like a man asleep or under water, Vianello pulled his other arm free and used both hands to push himself upright. He yanked the suit down, failing to notice that he had not unzipped it down to the bottom. It stuck at his waist and hips and hard as he pushed at it, he could not force himself free.

'The zipper, Lorenzo,' Brunetti said, pointing to it, reluctant to try to help him. Vianello saw what he had to do, and did it. He too sat down, first to remove his shoes, then to slip the suit over his feet, and then to replace his shoes. He had a moment of confusion before he figured out he had to remove the plastic covers before he put his shoes back on, but once he saw that, he was quickly finished. Like Brunetti, he bunched his suit together and left it on the bench beside where he had been sitting.

'Bene,' Vianello said. *'Andemmo.'*

In the continued absence of Bianchi and Signorina Borelli, the two men retraced their steps towards the entrance. When they walked outside, the sun fell across their bodies, their heads, their hands, even their feet, with a generosity and grace that made Brunetti think of the carvings he had seen of Akhenaten receiving the radiant blessing of Aten, the sun god. They stood there, as silent as Egyptian statues themselves, letting the sun warm them and cleanse them of the miasmic air of the building.

Soon enough the car appeared just in front of them, neither having heard it approach, their ears still attuned to the things they had heard inside.

The driver lowered the window and called to them, 'You ready to leave?'

20

This time, both of them got into the back seat of the car. Though the day was by no means warm, Brunetti and Vianello rolled down the windows of the car and sat, heads leaning back against the seat, to let the air wash over them. The driver, aware of something he did not understand, remained silent but had the sense to use the car phone to call the Questura and ask that a boat be sent to pick the two men up when they got to Piazzale Roma.

On the way to the city, they passed through quiet countryside that was preparing to expand into the richness of summer. The trees had put out their first green shoots that would unfurl into the magic of leaves. Brunetti gave thanks for the green and for its promise. Birds Brunetti recognized but could not name sat amidst the green shoots, chatting with one another about their recent flight north.

They did not notice the villas this time, only the cars that came towards them or those that passed them and fell into line in front of them. Nor did they speak; neither to one another nor to the driver. They let time pass, knowing that time would take away the brightness of some of their memories. Brunetti returned his attention to the landscape. How lovely it was, he thought: how lovely growing things were: trees, grapevines just waking from the winter, even the water in the ditch at the side of the road would soon help the plants in their scramble back to life.

He turned back to face the oncoming traffic and closed his eyes. After what seemed only a moment, the car came to a halt and the driver said, 'Here we are, Commissario.' Brunetti opened his eyes and saw the ACTV ticket office and, beyond it, water and the *embarcadero* of the Number Two.

Vianello was already getting out of the other side of the car as Brunetti thanked the driver and closed the door gently. He was pleased to see Vianello say something to the driver. The Inspector smiled, smacked his hand lightly on the roof of the car, and turned towards the water.

They went down the low steps and off to the left, where they saw Foa's assistant, talking to a taxi driver while keeping his eye on the place from which they were likely to appear. Brunetti was astonished to see that the young man looked exactly as he had some hours before. The pilot raised a hand to the brim of his cap, but it might as easily have been a wave of friendly recognition as a salute: Brunetti found himself hoping it was the first.

The pilot reached to hand him that morning's *Gazzettino,* folded and stuck behind the wheel. But Brunetti needed to see distance and colour and beauty and life, not the close-together lines of the printed word, so he made no gesture to take it, and the pilot bent to turn on the engine.

'Don't go around the back of the station. Let's go up the canal.' That way, though the trip would take longer, they would avoid having to make the turn next to the causeway, where they would see the smokestacks of Marghera; they would also avoid having to pass between the hospital and the cemetery. Neither Brunetti nor Vianello spoke, though both chose to remain on deck in the sun. It beat down on them, warming their heads and causing them to sweat under their jackets. Brunetti felt his damp shirt clinging to his back, even felt a faint trickle just over his temple. He had forgotten his sunglasses and so, like some eighteenth-century sea captain, he shielded his eyes with his hand and looked off into the distance. And he saw, not a tropical atoll surrounded by pristine beaches and not the tempestuous waters of the Cape of Good Hope, but the Calatrava Bridge, appearing diaper-clad in its current state, with short-sleeved tourists hanging over the side to take a photo of the police launch. He smiled up at them and waved.

None of the three men spoke as they passed under the bridge, nor when they passed under the next one and the others, nor when they passed the Basilica, and San Giorgio on the right. What would it be, Brunetti tried to imagine, to see all of this for the first time? Virgin eyes? It came to him that this assault of beauty was the opposite of what had happened in Preganziol, though each experience was overwhelming, each ravishing the viewer in its own way.

The pilot glided the launch up to the dock in front of the Questura, hopped out with the mooring rope in his hand, and hitched it over the bollard. As Brunetti stepped from the boat, the pilot started to say something to him, but the engine gave a sudden burp and he jumped back on deck. By the time he cut the motor, Brunetti and Vianello were already inside the building.

Brunetti didn't know what to say to Vianello: he could not remember ever being in this position, as though what they had just experienced together was so intense as to render all comment, almost to render all future conversation, futile. This awkwardness was broken by the man at the door, who said, 'Commissario, the Vice-Questore wants to see you.'

The thought of having to talk to Patta came almost as a relief: the predictable unpleasantness of that experience was sure to nudge Brunetti back towards ordinary life. He glanced at Vianello and said, 'I'll talk to him, then come and get you, and we'll go down to the bar.' First the reintroduction to ordinary life and then the enjoyment of ordinary humanity.

Because Signorina Elettra was not at her desk, Brunetti knocked on Patta's door with no advance warning of the level, or cause, of his superior's irritation. He had no doubt that this was the Vice-Questore's mood: it was only in moments of severe displeasure with his subordinate that the Vice-Questore could be moved to leave an order downstairs telling Brunetti to see him as soon as he came in. Before their meeting, Brunetti, like a gymnast about to leap up to grab the rings, took a few deep breaths and did his best to prepare himself for his performance.

He knocked firmly, made it as manly a sound as he could muster: three quick shots of noise announcing his arrival. Brunetti interpreted the responding shout as a request that he enter. Patta, he saw, was costumed for the role of country squire. The instant he saw him, Brunetti realized his superior had finally gone too far in pursuit of sartorial perfection, for he was today arrayed in a proper shooting jacket. A light brownish tweed, cut long and close to the body, it had the requisite brown suede patch at the right shoulder, a single pocket opposite on the left. Below were envelope pockets that could be easily unbuttoned to allow the wearer to reach for more shotgun cartridges. The white shirt Patta wore with it had a discreet check, and the green silk tie was covered with tiny yellow sheep that put Brunetti in mind of the ones in the mosaic behind the main altar in the Basilica of Saint' Apollinaire in Classe in Ravenna.

Much in the manner of Saint Thomas, incapable of believing in Christ's Resurrection until he put his hand into the wound in his Master's side, Brunetti was overcome with the urge to go and place his cheek on the brown suede patch on Patta's shoulder, for the patch was evidence, however outrageous, of all existence. In this instant, still battered by the experiences of the afternoon, Brunetti's spirit needed proof that the ordinary, indeed, all of life, was still there, and what better proof was there than this absurd display? Here was Patta talking on the phone, here was consistency, here was Proof. The Vice-Questore glanced up and, seeing who it was, said something and replaced the phone.

Brunetti resisted the temptation to bend down and look under the desk to see if the Vice-Questore had chosen to wear what Brunetti's reading of English novels had trained him to think of as 'sturdy brogues'. At the desk, with an effort he fought down the urge to thank his superior for calling him back to life. Instead, Brunetti said, 'Di Oliva said you'd like to speak to me, sir.'

Patta picked up a copy of *Il Gazzettino,* the newspaper that Brunetti had chosen not to read on the boat. 'Have you seen this?' Patta asked.

'No, sir,' Brunetti said. 'My wife is making me read *L'Osservatore Romano* this week.' He was going to add that it was the only newspaper that gave him a daily account of the appointments of the Holy Father, much in the manner of the *Times* with its calendar of the doings of the royals, but he was not sure — not having read the paper for decades — whether this was the case, nor would his gratitude allow him to goad Patta any farther. He contented himself, therefore, with the shrug of a true weakling and reached for the paper.

Patta surprised him by handing it to him gently and saying, 'Sit down and read it. It's on page five. Then tell me where the motive came from.'

Hastening to obey, Brunetti sat and opened the paper and quickly found the headline, 'Mystery Man in Canal Identified as Local Veterinarian'. The article gave Nava's name and age, said that he lived in Mestre, where he ran a private veterinarian clinic. It reported that he was separated from his wife and had one son. The police investigating his death were considering the possibility of a private vendetta.

' "Vendetta privata"?' Brunetti looked up to ask.

'That's exactly what I wanted to ask you about, Commissario,' Patta said with sarcasm that halted just short of a leer. 'Where did that idea come from?'

'From his wife, from her relatives, or anyone that the reporter spoke to, or maybe he just liked the sound of it. God knows.'

Brunetti weighed for a moment the wisdom of suggesting that it could just as easily have been someone at the Questura, but wisdom and the knowledge that life was long silenced him.

'You deny suggesting it?' Patta asked, level-voiced.

'Vice-Questore,' Brunetti said in his calmest, most reasonable voice, 'it doesn't matter where they got the idea.' Knowing the crannies and dark corners of Patta's brain as he did, Brunetti went on to say, 'If you think about it, "personal vendetta" is far better than the idea that it was random assault.' He was careful to keep his eyes on the paper and pay no attention to Patta as he said this, speaking as though he were engaged in idle reflection. It probably didn't matter to Patta that a man had been stabbed and tossed into a canal, so long as the man was a local. Had he been a tourist, then the crime would have disturbed Patta, and had the victim been a tourist from a wealthy European country, there was no saying how strong the Vice-Questore's response would have been.

'Possibly,' Patta said grudgingly; Brunetti translated this immediately into an unspoken 'You're probably right.' He folded the paper closed, and set it in front of Patta. He pasted a look of dutiful eagerness across his face.

'What have you done?' Patta finally asked.

'I spoke to his wife. His widow.'

'And?' Patta asked, but he said it in such a way that Brunetti decided that this was not the day to continue sparring with Patta.

'She told me they were separated; there's no question she wanted a divorce. He was involved with a woman colleague. Not at his clinic but at the *macello* where he worked: it's just outside of Preganziol.' He paused to give Patta the opportunity to ask questions, but his superior merely nodded. 'His wife said he was troubled.'

'Other than with this woman?' Patta asked.

'So it would seem from what she said, or from the way she said it. I wanted to get a sense of the place.' More than that, Brunetti could not bring himself to say.

'And?'

'It's not a nice place: they kill animals and cut them up,' Brunetti said bluntly. 'I spoke to the woman who must have been his lover.'

Before he could continue, Patta cut him off, demanding, 'You didn't tell her you know about their affair, did you?'

'No, sir.'

'What did you tell her?'

'That he was dead.'

'How did she react?'

Brunetti had been thinking about this for some time. 'She was angry that it took us so long to tell her, but she didn't say anything particular about him.'

'No reason to, really, I suppose,' Patta said. Then, seeing Brunetti's reaction and displaying a remarkable sensitivity to it, Patta hastened to add, 'From her point of view, that is.' Returning to his usual self, he demanded, 'What's a woman doing working there, anyway?'

'I don't know, sir,' Brunetti said, ignoring this echo of his own thoughts.

'It doesn't sound like you got much information,' Patta said, sounding gratified to be able to say it.

Brunetti had, on the contrary, got too much information, but this was not something he wanted to discuss with Patta or, indeed, with anyone. He contented himself with giving Patta a serious look, then said, 'I suppose you're right, Vice-Questore. I didn't learn much about what he did out there, nor how this woman might enter into things. If at all.' He was suddenly too tired and — much as it disgusted him to admit it — too hungry to dispute things with Patta. He allowed his gaze to drift towards the window of Patta's office, the one that looked out on the same *campo* as his.

He was suddenly tempted to ask Patta if he had ever considered the view from his window as a metaphor for the difference between himself and Brunetti. They both looked at the same thing, but because Brunetti's view came from a higher place, it was better. No, perhaps wiser not to ask Patta this.

'Well, get busy with it, then,' Patta said in the voice he used when urged to be a mover of men and a creator of dynamic action.

Brunetti knew from long experience that this was the voice that was most in need of deference, and so he answered, *'Sì, Dottore,'* and got to his feet.

Downstairs, Vianello was at his desk. He was not reading, nor talking with his colleagues nor on the phone. He sat at his desk, motionless and silent, apparently deep in consideration of its surface. When Brunetti came in, the other men in the room looked at him uneasily, almost as if they feared he was coming to take Vianello away because of something he had done.

Brunetti stopped at the desk of Masiero and asked in a normal voice if he had had any luck with the break-ins to the cars parked in the Municipal Garage at Piazzale Roma. The officer told him that, the night before, three of the video cameras in the garage had been vandalized, and six cars had been broken into.

Though he was not involved in the case and had no interest in it, Brunetti continued to question the officer about it, speaking more loudly than he ordinarily would. As Masiero explained his theory that the thefts must be the work of someone who worked there or of someone who parked his car there, Brunetti kept the edge of his attention on Vianello, who remained still and silent.

Brunetti was about to suggest disguising or camouflaging the cameras when he sensed motion from Vianello, and a moment later the Inspector was at his side. 'Yes, a coffee would be good.'

Without another word to Masiero, Brunetti left the squad room and led the way down to the front door and then along the *riva* towards the bar up near the bridge. Neither had much to say, though Vianello did observe dully that it would probably be easier simply to check the schedule of the people working at the garage for the nights of the thefts. That failing, he went on, it would be easy enough to check the computer list of those who had used their entrance cards to park or remove their cars on the nights in question.

They entered the bar and, united in their hunger, stood and studied the *tramezzini* on offer. Bambola asked what they would like. Brunetti asked for a tomato and egg and a tomato and mozzarella. Vianello said he'd have the same. Both asked for white wine and took their glasses to the booth at the far end of the bar.

It was only a moment before Bambola was there with the sandwiches. Ignoring them, Vianello drank half his wine; Brunetti did the same, then nodded to Bambola, holding up his glass and pointing to Vianello's.

He set his glass down and picked up one of the *tramezzini,* not bothering to see which it was. Hunger demanded haste, not consideration. Less mayonnaise than Sergio used, Brunetti determined with the first bite, and all the better for that. He finished his glass and handed it to the returning Bambola.

'Well?' Brunetti finally said as the barman went off with the empty glasses.

'What did Patta say?' Vianello asked, then smiled at Brunetti's look. 'Alvise saw you going in.'

'He told me to get on with it, without specifying what he meant. I take it to mean the Borelli woman.'

'It didn't look like a place a woman would

want to be,' Vianello said, echoing his and Patta's thought while somehow managing to make it sound less objectionable. Then the Inspector surprised him by saying, 'My grandfather was a farmer.'

'I thought he was Venetian,' Brunetti said, one thing making the other impossible.

'Not until he was almost twenty. He came here just before the First World War. My mother's father. His family was starving to death on a farm in Friuli, so they took the middle boy and sent him to the city to work. But he grew up on a farm. I remember, when I was a kid, he used to tell me stories about what it was like to work under a *padrone.* The man who owned the farm would ride over on his horse every day and count the eggs, or at least count the chickens and then demand more eggs if he didn't get the number he thought was right.' Vianello looked out the window of the bar at the people walking up and down the bridge. 'Think of it: the guy owned most of the farms in the region, and he spent his time counting eggs.' He shook his head at the thought and added, 'He told me the only thing they could do, sometimes, was drink some of the milk while it was set out to settle overnight.'

Caught by memory, Vianello placed his

glass on the table, his sandwiches forgotten. 'He told me he had an uncle who starved to death. They found him in his barn one morning, in the winter.'

Brunetti, who had heard similar stories when he was a boy, asked nothing.

Vianello looked across at Brunetti and smiled. 'But it doesn't help anything, does it, talking about these things?' He picked up one of his sandwiches, took a tentative bite, as if to remind himself what eating was, apparently liked it, and finished the *tramezzino* in two more quick bites. And then the other.

'I'm curious about this Borelli woman,' Brunetti said.

'Signorina Elettra will find whatever there is,' Vianello observed, repeating one of the Seven Pillars of Wisdom of the Questura.

Brunetti finished his wine and set down his glass. 'Patta wouldn't like it to have been a robbery,' he said, repeating another one. 'Let's go back.'

21

The relief of sitting and talking while eating and drinking restored their spirits, and when they left the bar, it seemed the lingering odour was gone from their jackets. Walking along the *riva,* Brunetti said he would ask Signorina Elettra to have a look into the life of Signorina Borelli. Vianello offered to see what there was to be found out about Papetti, the director of the slaughterhouse, both from official sources and from 'friends on the mainland', whatever that might mean. When they entered the Questura, the Inspector went into the officers' room and Brunetti continued up to Patta's office.

Signorina Elettra was behind her computer, her arms raised over her head, hands clasped. 'I hope I'm not disturbing you,' Brunetti said as he came in.

'Not at all, Dottore,' she said, lowering her arms but continuing to wiggle her fingers as she did so. 'I've been sitting behind this screen all day, and I suppose I'm tired of it.'

Had his son said he was tired of eating, or Paola said she was tired of reading, Brunetti could have been no more astonished. He wanted to ask if she was tired of . . . but he failed to find the word that adequately named what she did all day. Snooping? Unearthing? Breaking the law?

'Is there something else you'd rather do?' he asked.

'Is that a polite question or a real question, Signore?'

'I believe it's a real one,' Brunetti admitted.

She ran her hand through her hair and considered his question. 'I suppose if I had to choose a profession, I'd like to have been an archaeologist.'

'Archaeologist?' he could only repeat. Oh, the secret dream of so many people he knew.

She put on her most public smile and voice. 'Of course, only if I could make sensational discoveries and become very, very famous.'

Aside from Carter and Schliemann, Brunetti thought, few archaeologists became famous.

Refusing to believe her about this part of her desire, he asked, with audible scepticism, 'Only for fame?'

She was silent a long time, considering, then smiled and admitted, 'No, not really. I'd like to find the pretty trinkets, of course — that's the only reason archaeologists become famous — but what I'd really like to know is how people lived their daily lives and how much they were like us. Or different, in fact. Though I'm not sure it's archaeology that tells us that.'

Brunetti, who believed that it wasn't and that literature had far more to tell about how people were and lived, nodded. 'What do you look at in the museums?' he asked. 'The beautiful pieces or the belt loops?'

'That's what's so perplexing,' she answered. 'So much of their everyday stuff was beautiful that I never know what to look at. Belt loops, hairpins, even the clay dishes they ate from.' She thought about this and then added, 'Or maybe we consider them beautiful only because they're handmade, and we're so accustomed to seeing mass-produced things that we say they're beautiful only because each one is different and because we've come to place a higher value on handmade objects.'

She gave a quick laugh and then added, 'I suspect most of them would be willing to trade their beautiful clay drinking cup for a glass jam jar with a lid, or their hand-carved ivory comb for a dozen machine-made needles.'

To show that he agreed, he upped the ante and said, 'They'd probably give you anything you asked for in exchange for a washing machine.'

She laughed again. '*I'd* give you anything you asked for in exchange for a washing machine.' Then, suddenly serious, she added, 'I suspect that most people — at least women — would be willing to renounce their right to vote in exchange for a washing machine. God knows I would.'

Brunetti at first thought she was joking, pushing things over the top as was her wont, but then he realized she was not.

'Would you really?' he asked, incredulous.

'For a vote in this country? Absolutely.'

'And in some other country?' he asked.

This time she ran the fingers of both hands through her hair and lowered her head. She sat as though she were watching the names of the nations of the world scroll by on the surface of her desk. Finally she looked up and said, all playfulness removed from her voice, 'I'm afraid I would.'

Rejoinder or comment had he none, and so he said, 'I've got some things I'd like you to find, Signorina.'

Instantly, she ceased being a statue representing the demise of democracy and was transformed into her usual efficient self. He gave her Giulia Borelli's name and explained her relationship to the murdered man and her job at the slaughterhouse. Though he had little doubt of Vianello's competence, Brunetti did remember that Signorina Elettra was the master, Vianello only the apprentice, and so he added the names of Papetti and Bianchi, explaining who each of them was.

'Is the press going to hound us about this, do you think?' he asked.

'Oh, they've got the uncle, now,' she said. 'So no one writes. No one calls.' Her allusion to the murder case that was currently convulsing the country was clear: a murder within the confines of a close-knit family, with parents and relatives telling different stories about the victim and the accused. Each new day brought additions and subtractions to the list of perpetrators; the press and television were gorged with people willing to be interviewed. It seemed that each day also brought a new photo of some mournful-faced member of the same family holding up a photo of the sweet young victim; then by the next day the photoholder had been transformed by the revelations of yet another relative from mourner to suspect.

The coffee in the bars was flavoured by the story; one could not ride a boat without hearing it discussed. In the early stages, a month ago, when the young woman first disappeared, the policeman in Brunetti wanted to stand on the boat landings and shout, 'It was someone in the family', but he had kept a rigorous, professional silence. Now, when the subject arose, as it did everywhere, he refused to feign surprise at the new discoveries and did his best to change the subject.

Thus, even with Signorina Elettra, he didn't bother to engage and said, instead, 'If anyone from the press does call, direct them to the Vice-Questore, would you?'

'Of course, Commissario.'

He had been curt; of course he had been curt, but he had not wanted to be sucked into yet another discussion of the crime. It troubled him that many people had so readily come to treat murder as a kind of savage joke, to which the only response was grotesque humour. Perhaps this reaction was no more than magic thinking, a manifestation of the hope that laughter would keep it from happening again, or from happening to the person who laughed.

Or perhaps it was an attempt to disguise or deny the deeper revelation made by this murder: the close-knit Italian family was as much a piece of antiquity as were those handmade belt loops and clay dishes. Like them, it had been crafted in a simpler age, made from sturdy materials for people who expected simpler things from life. But now contacts and pleasures were mass-produced and made of less valuable materials, and so the family had followed the path of the church choir and attendance at Mass. Lip service was still paid, but all that remained was a well-remembered ghost.

'I'll be in my office,' Brunetti said, not wanting to stay there and pursue any of the topics they had initiated. When he reached his own office, he moved his chair to the end of his desk to where he had moved the computer he could not stop himself from thinking of as Signorina Elettra's.

He could not bear to learn more about the process he had witnessed that morning, but he was curious to learn about the industry of farming as it existed at present. His curiosity led him through the halls of Brussels and Rome and the impenetrable prose of the various Faceless Deciders of farming policy.

When he tired of that, Brunetti decided to

try his skill by having a look for Papetti, Director of the slaughterhouse at Preganziol, a search which surprised Brunetti with its ease. Alessandro Papetti, it turned out, was not a raw-handed son of the soil with an attachment to husbandry and all things bovine, but the son of a lawyer from Treviso who had taken a degree in *economia aziendale* from the University of Bologna. His first position, understandably enough, had been in his father's office, where he had spent a decade as a tax consultant for his father's business clients. Four years ago, he had been appointed Director of the *macello.*

Soon after his appointment, Papetti had given an interview to *La Tribuna,* the local paper of Treviso, in which he posed for a photo with his wife and three small children. He explained that farmers were the lifeblood of a nation, the men on whose backs the entire nation stood.

Brunetti failed to find any information about Bianchi, and the files of the Treviso edition of the *Gazzettino* gave him only a brief reference from three years ago to the appointment of Signorina Borelli to her position at the *macello.* Signorina Borelli, it was explained, who had earned a degree in marketing and tourism, had left her position at the accounts department of Tekknomed, a small pharmaceutical company in Treviso, to take up her new job.

Treviso and Treviso, Brunetti reflected. But what's in a city?

Idly, he changed sites and brought up the Treviso phone book. In seconds, there it was: Tekknomed. He dialled the number and, after three rings, it was answered by a bright-voiced young woman.

'Good morning, Signorina,' Brunetti said. 'This is the office of Avvocato Papetti. We've been trying to send you an email for the last half-hour, but it keeps coming back as undeliverable. So I thought I'd call and see if you've been having trouble with your server.' Then, injecting concern into his voice, he added, 'Of course, it might be ours, but yours is the only address this is happening with, so I thought I should call and tell you.'

'That's very kind of you, Signore. Hold on a minute and I'll check. Who were you sending it to?'

Prepared for her question, Brunetti said, 'To the people in Accounts.'

'One minute, please. I'll ask them.'

There was a click, a bit of meaningless music, while Brunetti held the line, very happy to be doing so.

She was quickly back and said, 'They

asked if you're sending it to the address you always use: *conta@Tekknomed.it?*

'Absolutely,' Brunetti said, sounding confused. 'Let me try it again and see what happens. If it comes back, I'll call again, all right?'

'Fine. That's very kind of you, Signore. Not many people would bother to take the trouble to call and tell us.'

'It's the least we can do for our clients,' Brunetti said.

She thanked him and was gone.

'Bingo,' Brunetti said as he replaced the phone. But then his habitual caution asserted itself and he changed that to 'Bingo?'

22

'It could be coincidence,' Vianello insisted in response to Brunetti's explanation that Tekknomed — where Signora Borelli had worked — was a client of Papetti's father's legal office.

'She studied marketing and tourism, Lorenzo. And now she's his assistant in a slaughterhouse, for God's sake. Can you tell me how that came about?'

'What are you thinking of accusing her of, Guido? Changing jobs and having an affair?'

'You said it,' Brunetti replied, realizing how weak and petulant his argument was. 'She changed jobs after working for a company her new boss was involved with.'

Vianello gave him a long look before he answered. 'These are times of self-invention, Guido: you're the one who's always telling me that. Young people with degrees, no matter what they're in, are lucky to have a job, any job. She probably got a good offer and agreed to follow him to the new job.' When Brunetti didn't answer, Vianello asked, 'How many of your friends' kids have jobs? Most of the ones I know sit at home in front of their computers all day and have to ask their parents for spending money on the weekend.'

Brunetti raised a hand to stop him. 'I know all that. Everyone knows that. But it's not what I'm talking about. Here's a woman with what was presumably a good job . . .'

'We don't know that.'

'Well, we can find out. And if it was a good job, then she left it to go and do something new.'

'Better salary. Better hours. Closer to home. Hated her old boss. More vacation. Private office. Company car.' Vianello stopped and gave Brunetti a chance to answer, and when he did not, the Inspector asked, 'You want me to give you more reasons why she might have changed jobs?'

'It feels strange,' Brunetti said, sounding, even to himself, like a truculent child grasping at straws.

Vianello tossed his hands in the air. 'All right, all right, so it might sound strange that she'd change jobs like that, but you can't make it be more than that. We don't have enough information to decide what happened. We don't have *any* information. And we won't have it until we find out more about her.'

This small concession was all Brunetti needed. He got to his feet, saying, 'I'll go and ask her to look.'

He had just reached the door, when Vianello, in an entirely natural voice, said, 'She'll probably love that,' and got to his feet to return to his office.

Twenty minutes later, Vianello's reading of that day's *Gazzettino* was interrupted by Brunetti's request that he come up to his office. Upon his assistant's arrival, Brunetti said, 'She did.' He stopped himself from telling Vianello that Signorina Elettra had also found Signorina Borelli's job change suspicious — well, not suspicious, really, but interesting — and told him only that she had said it might take her some time to locate and access her employment records. Her casual use of those verbs reminded Brunetti that some time had passed since either he or Vianello had bothered to question how Signorina Elettra managed to do it: they simply awaited the results of her having done it and were happy to do so. Their reluctance to ask the direct question was perhaps related to the amorphous legality of what she did when conducting her researches. Brunetti turned away from these thoughts with a tiny shake: next thing he knew, he'd be wondering how many angels could dance on the head of a pin.

Vianello said, in the voice Brunetti recognized as the one he used when he wanted to suggest far more than he said, 'You know, we haven't even come close to finding a reason why anyone would want to kill him.' How long, Brunetti wondered, would it be before the Inspector started to talk about the killing as a robbery that got out of hand?

'He came to Venice,' Brunetti said, returning to one of the few certain things they knew. Rizzardi's final report, which they had both read, said only that the dead man, aside from the Madelung's, was in good health for a man of his age. He had eaten dinner some hours before his death and had consumed a small amount of alcohol. Digestion was under way at the time of his death, the pathologist had written, and added that the time the body had spent in the water had obliterated any sign of sexual activity. Given the temperature of that water, the pathologist could do no more than estimate the possible time of death as between midnight and four in the morning.

Though Nava's name and photo had been in the papers that day, along with a request that anyone with information about him should call the police, no one had called.

Vianello took a deep breath. 'The one before him was called Meucci, wasn't he?' he asked.

It took Brunetti a moment to catch up with Vianello's thoughts and realize he was speaking about Nava's predecessor at the slaughterhouse. 'Yes. Gabriele, I think.' He turned to his computer, aware how much his motion imitated Signorina Elettra's swirl when she turned to hers. He stopped himself, just in time, from saying he thought it should be easy to find Meucci, hoping there would be lists of veterinarians, some society which they all joined.

He ended up finding the doctor in the Yellow Pages, under 'Veterinarians'. The *ambulatorio* of Dr Gabriele Meucci was listed at an address in Castello. The number was meaningless until Vianello located it in *Calli, Campi, e Castelli* at the most remote end of Castello, on the Riva di San Giuseppe.

'I suppose people down there must have animals, too,' Vianello said by way of comment on the location. It was as far from the centre of the city as one could get without crossing over to S. Elena, which to both of them might as well have been Patagonia.

'Rather far from Preganziol, I'd say,' Vianello added.

As he switched off the computer, Brunetti noticed that his left hand was trembling. He had no idea of the cause, though by tightening his fingers into a fist a number of times he managed to make it stop. He placed his palm flat on his desk and pushed down on it, then lifted it a few centimetres: it still trembled.

'I think we should go home, Lorenzo,' he said, eyes on his hand and not on Vianello.

'Yes,' Vianello agreed, slapped his hands on his knees and pushed himself to his feet. 'I think it was too much, out there, today.'

Brunetti wanted to say something in return, make some comment — even joking or ironic — about where they had gone, but the words refused to come to him. Events as shocking as those they had seen, he had always heard, left a lasting trace or changed a person in some profound way. Not a bit of it. He had been horrified and disgusted, but he knew he had not been changed, not really. Brunetti had no idea if this was a good thing or not.

'Why don't we meet tomorrow morning, in front of his office?' he suggested to Vianello.

'Nine?'

'Yes. Assuming that he's working.'

'And if he's not?'

'Then we go and have a coffee and a brioche, sit and watch the boats for a while, and then we come to work late.'

'Only if you insist, Commissario,' Vianello said.

As he emerged from the Questura, the accumulated weight of the day descended on Brunetti, and he wished for a moment that he lived in a city where it was possible for a person to call a taxi and not have to pay sixty Euros to do so, no matter how short the ride. Home was, for the first time he could remember, too far to walk, so he went slowly down to the San Zaccaria stop to wait for the Number One.

He held his left hand in a tight fist in his pocket, carefully ignoring its presence there and resisting the urge to take it out and look at it. He had a monthly boat pass, so he did not have to pull out his wallet and extract his travel card.

The boat came and he walked on to it, went inside the cabin and sat. As soon as the vaporetto pulled away from the *embarcadero,* Brunetti's curiosity overcame him, and he took his hand from his pocket. He spread his fingers flat on his thigh, but instead of looking at them, he turned his eyes towards the angel flying above the dome of San Giorgio, still visible in the swiftly fading light.

He felt no tremor against his thigh, but before he looked, he raised his fingers a centimetre above his leg and left them there for a few seconds as he continued to consult with the angel, placed there centuries ago. Finally he looked at his fingers, which were motionless. He relaxed them and let them return to lying on his thigh.

'So many things,' he said under his breath, not quite sure what he meant by that. The young woman beside him, startled, turned and looked at him, then went back to her crossword puzzle. She didn't look Italian, he thought, though he had had only a quick glance. French, perhaps. Not American. And not Italian. She sat on a boat going up the Grand Canal, her eyes on a crossword puzzle, the letters of which were too small to permit him to decipher the language. Brunetti looked back at the angel to see if he had any comment on this, but he did not, and so Brunetti turned to study the façades of the buildings to the right.

When he was a boy, they swam in this canal and in many of the other large ones. He remembered diving into the water at

Fondamenta Nuove, and he remembered that a classmate of his had once swum to the Zattere from the Giudecca because he didn't want to wait for a late-night boat. When Brunetti's father had been a boy, he used to catch *seppie* at the *riva* down at Sacca Fisola, but that was before Marghera, just across the *laguna,* had been completely transformed by petrochemicals. And before the *seppie* were transformed by them, too.

He got off at San Silvestro and walked through the underpass and to the left, bent on getting home, wanting only a glass of wine and something to eat with it. Almonds, perhaps: something salty. And a still white wine: Pinot Grigio. Yes.

No sooner had he let himself into the apartment than he heard Paola call from the kitchen. 'If you'd like a drink, there's something to nibble on in the living room. The wine's open. I'll bring it.'

Brunetti hung up his jacket and followed her suggestion as though it had been a command. When he walked into the living room, he was surprised to see that the lights were on and even more surprised, when he looked out the windows, to see that it was almost completely dark. On the boat, concerned with his fingers, he had not registered the settling in of darkness.

The table in front of the sofa held two wine glasses, a bowl of black olives, one of almonds, some grissini, and a dish with small pieces of what looked like parmigiano. 'Reggiano,' he said aloud. His mother, even in the family's times of blackest financial misery, had refused to use anything but Parmigiano Reggiano. 'Better nothing than something that isn't as good,' she had said, and so he still believed.

Paola came into the room carrying a bottle of wine. He looked up at her and said, 'Better nothing than something that isn't as good.'

Long experience of Brunetti in his sibylline mode caused Paola to smile. 'I presume you're speaking about the wine.'

He held up the two glasses while she poured the wine, then sat beside her on the sofa. Pinot Grigio: he'd married a mind reader. He picked up a few almonds and ate them one by one, loving the contrast set up between the salt, the almonds' bitterness, and the wine.

With no warning, his memory ripped him back to the gravelled space in front of the slaughterhouse, and he caught a whiff of the odour coming from it. He closed his eyes and took another sip of wine; he forced his mind to concentrate on the taste of the wine, the taste of the almonds, and the soft presence of the woman beside him. 'Tell me what you taught today,' he said, kicking off his shoes and leaning back.

She took a long drink, nibbled at a grissino, and ate one of the slivers of cheese. 'I'm not sure I taught anything,' she began, 'but I'd asked them to read *The Spoils of Poynton.*'

'That the one about the lady with all the stuff?' he asked, turning from sibylline to philistine with one well-chosen question.

'Yes, dear,' she said, and poured them both some more wine.

'How did they respond?' he asked, suddenly curious. He had read the book, albeit in translation — he preferred James in translation — and liked it.

'They seemed incapable of understanding that she loved the things she owned because they were beautiful, not because they were valuable. Or valuable for non-financial reasons.' She sipped her wine. 'My students find it difficult to grasp any motivation for human action that is not based on financial profit.'

'There's a lot of that around,' Brunetti said, reaching for an olive. He ate it, spat the pit into his left hand, which he observed was steady as a rock. He set the pit in a small saucer and took another one.

'And they liked the wrong . . . they liked characters different from the ones I like,' she amended.

'There's a very unpleasant woman in it, isn't there?' he asked.

'There are two,' she answered and said that dinner would be ready in ten minutes.

23

A thin rain was falling when Brunetti left his house the next morning. When he boarded the vaporetto at Rialto, he saw that the level of the water was high, even though he had received no message on his *telefonino* alerting him to *acqua alta.* Higher tides at unusual times had become more frequent in the last two years, and though most people — and all fishermen — believed this was the result of the MOSE project's violent intervention at the entrance to the *laguna,* official sources denied this adamantly.

Foa, the Questura's pilot, grew apoplectic on the subject. He had learned the tides along with the alphabet and knew the names of the winds that crossed the Adriatic as well as priests knew those of the saints. For years, sceptical from the beginning, he had watched the metal monster grow, had seen all protest swept away by the flood of lovely European money sent to save the Pearl of the Adriatic. His fishermen friends told him of the new and violent vortices that had appeared in both the sea and the *laguna* and of the consequences of the pharaonic dredging that had taken place in recent years. No one, Foa claimed, had bothered to consult the fishermen. Instead, experts — Brunetti remembered once seeing Foa spit after pronouncing this word — had made the decisions, and other experts no doubt would get the contracts for the construction.

For a decade, Brunetti had been reading yes, and he had been reading no, and most recently he had read of more delays in funding that would delay the project yet another three years. As an Italian, he suspected it would run true to form and turn out to have been yet another building project that served as a feeding trough for the friends of friends; as a Venetian, he despaired that his fellow citizens might have sunk so low as to be capable even of this.

Still musing, he left the boat and began to walk towards the back reaches of Castello. He hesitated now and again, not having been down here for years, so after a time he stopped thinking and let his feet lead the way. The sight of Vianello, wearing a raincoat and leaning against the metal railing of the *riva,* cheered him. Seeing him approach,

Vianello said, with a nod towards the door in front of him, 'The sign says the office opens at nine, but no one's gone inside yet.'

A printed card protected by a plastic shield gave the doctor's name and the office hours.

They stood side by side for a few minutes until Brunetti said, 'Let's see if he's already there.'

Vianello pushed himself away from the railing and followed him to the door. Brunetti rang the bell and after a moment tried the door, which opened easily. They stepped inside, up two steps, and into a small entrance which led in its turn to an open courtyard. A sign on their left carried the doctor's name and an arrow pointing to the other side of the courtyard.

The rain, which outside had been bothersome, here fell on to the newly green grass of the courtyard with gentle kindness. Even the light seemed different; brighter, somehow. Brunetti unbuttoned his raincoat; Vianello did the same.

The courtyard, if it had been part of a monastery, had been part of the smallest monastery in the city. Though covered walkways surrounded the garden, they were no more than five metres long, hardly space enough, Brunetti reflected, to allow a man to make much progress with his rosary. He'd barely have finished the first decade before he'd be back at his starting point, but he'd be surrounded by beauty and tranquillity, at least if he were wise enough to contemplate them.

The acanthus leaves had worn away on the capitals, and the centuries had smoothed the fluting on the shafts of the columns around the garden. Surely this had not happened while the columns were in this protected courtyard; who knows where they had come from or when they had arrived in Venice? Suddenly a goat smiled down at Brunetti: how had *that* column got here?

Ahead of him, Vianello stopped at a green wooden door with the doctor's name on a brass plaque, waited for Brunetti to join him, and opened it. Inside was a room like all those Brunetti had sat in while waiting to see doctors. Opposite them they saw another wooden door, closed now. Rows of orange plastic chairs lined two walls; at the end of one row was a low table with two piles of magazines. Brunetti went over to see if it held the usual copies of *Gente* and *Chi*. Not unless starlets and minor nobles had all been replaced by cats, dogs and, in one instance, a particularly winsome pig wearing a Father Christmas hat.

They sat opposite one another. Brunetti checked his watch. After four minutes, an old woman came in, leading an antique dog so deprived of hair in various places as to resemble the sort of stuffed toy one found in a grandparent's attic. The woman ignored them and lowered herself into the chair farthest from Vianello; the dog collapsed at her feet with an explosive sigh, and both of them immediately lapsed into a trance. Strangely enough, it was only the woman's breathing they could hear.

More time passed, measured by the woman's snores, until Brunetti got to his feet and went to the other door. He knocked on it, waited for Vianello to join him, knocked again, and then opened it.

Across the room, behind a desk, Brunetti saw the top half of what might have been the fattest man he had ever seen. He was slumped back in his leather chair and sound asleep, his head tilted to the left as far as his neck and the chins above it would allow. He was perhaps in his forties, his age disguised by the absence of wrinkles in his face.

Brunetti cleared his throat, but that had no effect on the sleeping man. He stepped closer, and smelled the rancid odour of cigarette smoke mixed with late night, or early morning, drinking. The man's hands were latched across his vast chest, the right thumb and the second and third fingers stained with nicotine up to the first knuckle. The room, strangely enough, did not smell of smoke, only of its after-effect: the same odour came from the man's clothing and, Brunetti suspected, from his hair and skin.

'Dottore,' Brunetti said in a soft voice, not wanting to startle him awake. The man continued snoring softly.

'Dottore,' Brunetti repeated in a louder voice.

He watched the man's eyes for motion: they were set deep in his face, as though they had retreated from the encroaching fat that surrounded them. The nose was strangely thin, but it had been overwhelmed by the encircling cheeks, which pushed up against it and, helped by the engorged lips, came close to blocking his nostrils. The mouth was a perfect cupid's bow, but a very thick, unwieldy bow.

A thin film of sweat covered his face and had so slicked his thin hair to his skull that Brunetti was put in mind of the greasy pomades his father had used on his hair when Brunetti was a boy. 'Dottore,' he said for the third time, this time in a normal voice, his tone perhaps a bit sharp.

The eyes opened; small, dark, curious, and

then suddenly wide with fear. Before Brunetti could say anything else, the man shoved himself away from his desk and got to his feet. He did not leap, nor did he jump, though Brunetti had no doubt that he moved as quickly as his bulk would permit. He pressed himself against the wall behind him and looked across the room at the door, then shifted his gaze back and forth between Brunetti and Vianello, who blocked his path.

'What do you want?' he asked. His voice was curiously high-pitched, either from fear or just from some odd mismatch between his body and his voice.

'We'd like to speak to you, Dottore,' Brunetti said in a neutral voice, choosing to delay an explanation of who they were or the purpose of their visit. He glanced aside at Vianello and saw that the Inspector, in response to the doctor's fear, had managed somehow to transform himself into a thug. His entire body had become more compact and was angled forward, as though waiting only the command to launch itself at the man. His hands, curved just short of fists, dangled beside his thighs as though longing to be given weapons. The habitual geniality of his face had vanished, replaced by a mouth he seemed unable to close and eyes forever in search of his opponent's weakest point.

The doctor's hands, palms outward, rose in front of his chest; he patted at the air, as if to test if it were strong enough to keep these men from him. The doctor smiled: Brunetti recalled a description he had read once of a flower on a corpse, something like that. 'There's got to be some mistake, Signori. I've done everything you told me to. You must know that.'

Suddenly all bedlam was let out on the other side of the door. It started with a thump, a loud roar, and then a high-pitched woman's scream. A chair fell over or was pushed over, another woman screamed an obscenity, then everything was drowned out by a chorus of hysterical barks and growls. There followed a series of yelps, and then all animal noise stopped for a moment and was replaced by an exchange of obscenities in two equally shrill voices.

Brunetti pulled the door open. The old woman stood barricaded behind a fallen chair, her ancient dog trembling in her arms, as she hurled epithets at another woman on the other side of the room. This woman, hatchet-faced and thin as a rail, stood behind two now wildly barking dogs with unusually large, squarish heads. They barked as hysterically as the two women screamed, the only differences being their lower pitch and the trickles of saliva that hung suspended from their lips. For the first time in his career, Brunetti wanted to pull his pistol and fire a shot into the air, but he had forgotten to wear his pistol, and he knew the noise of the shot would deafen every creature in the room.

Instead, he crossed to the two dogs, grabbing one of the magazines as he passed the table. He rolled it into a cylinder, then bent and smacked one of the large dogs across the nose. Given the lightness of Brunetti's blow, the dog's howl was disproportionately loud, and his quick retreat behind the legs of his owner as surprising as it was ignominious. His fellow dog looked up at Brunetti and started to bare his teeth, but a threatening thrust of the rolled magazine sent him to cower beside the other dog.

The thin-faced woman changed target and began to hurl her obscenities at Brunetti, ending in a loud boast that she would call the police and have him arrested. After this, she stopped shouting, sure that she now had the upper hand. Even the two dogs relaxed into this new legal certainty and began to growl, though they remained safely behind the woman's legs.

The still-thuggish Vianello chose this moment to walk into the room, his warrant card shoved in the woman's direction. '*I'm* the police, Signora, and according to the law of 3 March 2009, you have the obligation to carry muzzles with you if you take these dogs into a public place.' He looked around the room, assessing it and her presence in it with the dogs. 'This is a public place.'

The old woman with the dog in her arms said, 'Officer', but Vianello silenced her with a look.

'Well?' he demanded in his roughest voice. 'Do you know what the fine is?'

Brunetti was sure Vianello didn't, so he doubted that the woman did.

One of the large dogs suddenly began to whine; she yanked violently at its leash, silencing it instantly. 'I know. But I thought that in here, inside . . .' She waved vaguely at the walls with the hand that did not hold the leashes. Her voice trailed away. She bent down and patted the head of the first dog, then the other. Their long tails thumped against the wall.

Seeing how automatic her gesture was and the dogs' easy, affectionate response to it must have disarmed Vianello, for he said,

'All right for this time, but be careful in the future.'

'Thank you, officer,' she said. The dogs came out from behind her, wiggling towards Vianello until she pulled them back.

'What about what she said to us?' the old woman demanded.

'Why don't you sit down, ladies, while we finish talking to the doctor?' Brunetti suggested and went back into the doctor's office.

The advantage had been lost: that was obvious to Brunetti as soon as he saw the fat man. He stood by the open window of his office, taking a deep pull from the cigarette he held in his nicotine-stained hand. He looked at the returning men with eyes in which all trace of fear had been replaced by strong dislike. Brunetti suspected it originated not from embarrassment at the fear he had displayed as from what he had discovered them to be.

He continued to draw on the cigarette, saying nothing, until it was a stub that came close to burning his fingers. He shifted it to the very tips of his fingers, took one last long pull, then tossed it out the window. He closed the window but remained standing in front of it.

'What do you want?' he asked in the same

high voice.

'We're here to talk to you about your successor, Dr Andrea Nava,' Brunetti said.

'I can't help you, then, Signori,' Meucci said, sounding uninterested.

'Why is that, Doctor?' Brunetti inquired.

It looked as though Meucci had to fight back a smile as he answered, 'Because I never met him.'

Brunetti, in turn, fought back his surprise at this and asked, 'You didn't have to explain anything to him: who the people at the *macello* were, how things worked, where his office was, supplies, timetables?'

'No. The Director and his staff saw to all of that, I imagine.' Meucci reached into the left pocket of his jacket and pulled out a battered box of Gitanes and a plastic lighter. Flicking it alive, he lit the cigarette, took a deep drag, and turned to open the window behind him. Cool air swept in, spreading the smoke around the room.

'Did you have to leave him written instructions?' Brunetti asked.

'He wasn't my responsibility,' Meucci said. For a moment, Brunetti imagined that the other man could not know Nava was dead and so casually say such a thing. But then he realized that Meucci must know — who in Venice could not, especially someone who had formerly held the man's job?

'I see,' Brunetti answered. 'Could you tell me what your duties were?'

'Why do you want to know that?' Meucci asked, not bothering to hide his irritation.

'So as to understand what it was Dottor Nava did,' Brunetti answered blandly.

'Didn't they tell you that out there?'

'Out where?' Brunetti inquired mildly and glanced aside at Vianello, as if to suggest he remember Meucci's question.

Meucci tried to disguise his surprise by turning to throw his half-finished cigarette out the window. 'At the slaughterhouse,' he forced himself to answer when he turned back to Brunetti.

'When we were there, do you mean?' Brunetti asked pleasantly.

'Weren't you?' was the only thing the doctor could think to ask.

'Surely you know that already, Dottore,' Brunetti said with a small smile and pulled his notebook from his pocket. He opened it and made a note, then looked at the doctor, who already had another lighted cigarette in his hand.

'What can you tell me about Dottor Nava?' Brunetti asked.

'I told you I never met him,' Meucci said, anger held in check, but just barely.

'That's not what I'm asking, Dottore,' Brunetti said, gave another tiny smile, and made another note.

Brunetti's prod seemed to work, for Meucci said, 'After I left the *macello,* I had nothing further to do with it.'

'Or with anyone working there?' Brunetti asked with mild curiosity.

Meucci hesitated only a moment before he said, 'No.'

Brunetti made another note.

This time, Meucci slammed the windows closed after tossing away his cigarette. Turning back to Brunetti he asked, 'Do you have permission to be here, asking me these questions?'

'Permission, Dottore?' Brunetti asked, raising his eyebrows.

'An order from a magistrate.'

Surprise took possession of Brunetti's face. 'Why, no, Dottore, I don't.' Then, with a relaxed smile, he added, 'It never occurred to me to get one. In fact, I thought of the Doctor as a colleague of yours, so I thought you would be able to tell me more about him. But now that you've made it clear that there was never any contact between you, I'll leave you to get to your patients.' Because he had never relaxed enough to sit down, Brunetti could not emphasize his departure by getting to his feet. Instead, he put the cap on his pen and returned notebook and pen to his pocket, thanked the doctor for his time, and left the office.

In the waiting room, the large dogs stood up when the two men came in; the third one slept heavily on. Brunetti took his notebook from his pocket and waved it in the air as they walked in front of the dogs, but they did no more than wag their tails at them. The two women ignored them.

24

'Maybe he's such a bad liar because animals can't tell the difference,' Vianello suggested as they started back towards the Questura. To make it absolutely clear, he added, 'If you can lie to them or not, that is.'

They walked for some time before Brunetti said, 'Chiara's always telling me they have other senses and can read our moods. They even use dogs to detect cancer, I think.'

'Sounds strange to me.'

'The more I live, the more most things sound strange to me,' Brunetti observed.

'What did you think of him?' the Inspector asked with a flick of his head back towards Meucci's office.

'There's no question he was lying, but I'm not sure what he was lying about.'

'He lies a lot,' Vianello said.

This caused Brunetti to stop. 'You didn't tell me you knew him.'

Vianello looked surprised that Brunetti would take him so seriously. 'No,' he said, starting to walk again, 'I meant that I know his type. He lies to himself, I'm sure, about smoking, probably tells himself he doesn't smoke much at all.'

'And the stains on his fingers?'

'Gitanes,' Vianello answered. 'They're famous for being strong, so only a few of them would be enough to cause it.'

'Of course,' Brunetti agreed. 'What else is he lying about?'

'He's probably convinced himself that he doesn't eat much; that he's fat because he has some hormonal disorder, or thyroid condition, or dysfunction of some gland we have in common with the animals, so he'd know about it.'

'They're all possible, aren't they?' Brunetti, who didn't believe it for an instant, inquired.

'Anything's possible,' Vianello answered with heavy emphasis on the second word. 'But it's far more likely that he's fat because he eats too much.'

'And was he lying about Nava?'

'That he didn't know him?'

'Yes.'

At the foot of a bridge, Vianello turned to Brunetti. 'I think so. Yes.' Brunetti remained silent, encouraging the Inspector to continue. 'It's not so much that he was lying about knowing him — though I think he was — as that he was lying about everything about the *macello.* I got the feeling that he wanted to distance himself in every way possible.'

Brunetti nodded. What Vianello said merely put into words his own sense of their meeting with Meucci.

'And you?' Vianello asked.

'It's hard to believe they never met,' Brunetti said. 'They're both veterinarians, so they'd go to the same professional meetings. And if Nava was qualified to take on a job like that, then there must be some common background.' As Vianello started up the bridge, Brunetti added from behind him, 'And Nava must have had questions about the job.'

He fell into step beside the Inspector, saying, 'It's obvious he already knew we'd been to the *macello* and talked to people there. So why did he deny knowing it?'

'How stupid does he think we are?' Vianello burst out.

'Probably very,' Brunetti said, almost without thinking. Being underestimated, he had learned — however unflattering it might be — always conveyed an advantage. If the person doing the underestimating wasn't very bright to begin with — and Brunetti had a sense that Meucci was not — that increased the advantage.

He took his phone from his pocket and dialled Signorina Elettra's number. When she answered, he said, 'I wonder if your friend Giorgio could take an interest in a veterinarian named Gabriele Meucci?'

Giorgio. Giorgio: the man at Telecom, though surely not the man who came to install the phone. Giorgio, who appeared not to have a surname, nor a history, nor any human characteristics other than a slavish need to fulfil Signorina Elettra's every whim and an ability to retrieve or trace any phone call she requested, regardless of country of origin, name of caller, or destination. Did one light a candle to Giorgio; did one send him a case of champagne at Christmas? It hardly mattered to Brunetti, who wanted only to continue to believe in the existence of Giorgio, for to doubt Giorgio's existence created the possibility that the illegal, invasive buccaneering in the telephone records of private citizens and state organizations that had been going on for more than a decade had not been Giorgio's doing but, instead, had had its detectable — and flagrantly criminal — origin in emails originating from a computer traceable to the office of the Vice-Questore of the city of Venice.

'I have to speak to him about something else,' she said blandly. 'I could certainly ask.'

'So kind,' Brunetti said and flipped closed his phone.

He glanced aside at Vianello and saw a thoughtful expression on his face. 'What is it?' Brunetti asked.

'It's like what's in those psychological profiles of serial killers.'

Not willing to admit that Vianello had lost him, Brunetti limited himself to a mere 'In what way?'

'The psycho-people say they start by hurting animals and then go on to killing them, and then it's fires and hurting people, and the next thing you know, they've killed thirty people and buried them in the back garden and never feel regret or remorse for any of it.'

'And your point?' Brunetti asked.

'That's what's happened to us. We started by having her find a phone number for us, when she was supposed to be working for Patta. Then we asked her for another number, and then for some information about the person whose phone it was, and then if they'd made a call to some other number.

And now we've got her looting the records of Telecom and breaking into bank accounts and tax records.' The Inspector stuffed his fists into the pockets of his jacket. 'If I think about what would happen if . . .' He broke off, unwilling to give it voice.

'And?' Brunetti asked, waiting for the comparison with serial killers, who certainly did not show this sort of compunction.

'And we like doing it,' Vianello said. 'That's the frightening part.'

Brunetti waited a full minute for the waves created by Vianello's last remark to abate and for the air around them to grow perfectly still, and then he said, 'I think we should stop and have a coffee before we go back to work.'

As they approached the Questura, they saw Foa kneeling on the wooden prow of the police launch, cleaning the windscreen with a chamois cloth. Vianello called out a friendly greeting and Foa said, addressing Brunetti, 'I've checked the charts, sir.'

Brunetti resisted the urge to say that it was about time that he had; instead he asked, 'And what do they tell you? Us?'

With the ease of a young man who spent most of his time on boats, Foa got to his feet and, bracing his hands on the top of the windscreen, flipped himself over it effortlessly, landing upright on the deck. 'There was a neap tide that night, Commissario,' he said, pulling a sheet of paper from his pocket.

Brunetti recognized a map of the area around the Giustinian Hospital. Holding it towards them, Foa said, 'The tide turned at three twenty-seven that morning, and they found him at six, so if Dottor Rizzardi's right and he was in the water for about six hours, then he wouldn't have gone far from where he went in. Not unless he got slowed down by something.' Then, before either could comment or question, he added, 'That's assuming he drifted back the way he came, which he probably did.'

'And in the slack tide?' Brunetti asked.

'It's longest with the neap tide, sir, so the water would have been still a long time,' Foa said. The pilot tapped at a point on the map. 'This is where they found him.' Then he moved his finger back and forth along Rio del Malpaga. 'My guess is that he went in somewhere on either side of that spot.' Foa shrugged. 'Unless he was snagged for a while on something, as I said: a bridge, a mooring cable, a piling. Unless that happened, then I'd guess he went in not more than a hundred metres from where they found him.'

Over the bent head of the pilot, Vianello and Brunetti exchanged a glance. A hundred metres, Brunetti thought. How many water doors would there be? How many *calli* coming to a dead end at the water? How many unlit angles where a boat could stop and unburden itself of its cargo?

'You have a girlfriend, don't you, Foa?'

'A fiancée, sir,' Foa answered promptly.

Brunetti all but heard Vianello's teeth grinding together as he stopped himself from saying that one did not exclude the other. 'Good. And you have your own boat, don't you?'

'Yes, sir, a *sandolo*.'

'With a motor?'

'Yes, sir,' Foa answered with mounting confusion.

'Good, then what I want the two of you to do is take a camera and go up and down Rio del Malpaga, taking photos of all the water gates.' He pulled the map towards him and pointed to the place Foa had indicated. 'And then go back and walk in front of the houses — both sides of the canal — and find the street numbers of the buildings where the gates are, then give the list to Signorina Elettra.'

'Do you want me to copy the names on

the doorbells while we're there, sir?' Foa asked, and moved a step higher in Brunetti's estimation.

Brunetti thought of how conspicuous this would be. 'No. Only the numbers of the houses you think have water gates, all right?'

'When, sir?' Foa asked.

'As soon as possible,' Brunetti said, then, with a look around them, added, 'Can you do it this afternoon?'

Foa fought to contain his glee at being suddenly promoted to something more closely resembling a policeman. 'I'll call her and tell her to leave work,' he said.

'So can you, Foa. Tell Battisti I said you're on special assignment.'

'Yes, sir,' the pilot said with a smart salute.

Brunetti and Vianello turned away from the smiling officer and entered the Questura. When they reached the bottom of the steps, Vianello stopped like a horse that sees something dangerous lying in its path. He turned to look at Brunetti, unable to hide his emotions. 'I keep thinking about yesterday.' He gave an embarrassed smile and added, 'We've seen much worse. When it was people.' He shook his head at his own confusion. 'I don't understand. But I don't think I want to be here today.'

The simplicity of Vianello's confession

struck Brunetti with sudden force. His impulse was to put his arm around his friend's shoulder, but he contented himself with a pat to his upper arm, saying only, 'Yes.' The word conveyed his own lingering shock after yesterday's visit to the slaughterhouse and today's effort of disguising his deep dislike of Meucci, but chiefly it expressed his longing to return to his nest and have about him the sheer animal comfort of the people he held most dear.

He repeated, 'Yes. Tomorrow we can start from the beginning and talk it all through.' It was hardly sufficient justification for their going home at this hour, but Brunetti didn't care, so strongly had he been infected with Vianello's visceral need to leave. He could tell himself that any lingering smell was merely a phantom of his imagination, but he wasn't fully convinced. He could tell himself that what he had seen in Preganziol was merely the way some things were done, but that changed nothing.

An hour later, a pink-skinned Brunetti stood, a towel wrapped around his waist after his second shower of the day, in front of a mirror in which he did not appear, or if he did, it was as a damp mirage dimly visible behind the condensation. Occasionally a group of water droplets coalesced and raced downwards, opening up a pink slit on the surface. He wiped his hand across the mirror, but the steam instantly covered the place he had swept clean.

Behind him, someone knocked on the door. 'You all right?' he heard Paola ask.

'Yes,' he called back and turned to open the door, allowing a sudden flood of cold, stinging air into the room. *'Oddio!'* he said and grabbed his flannel bathrobe from the back of the door. Not until he was safely wrapped in it did he let the towel fall to the ground. As he reached for it, Paola said from the hall, 'I wanted to see if your skin had started to peel off.'

Then, perhaps seeing the glance he shot her, she came a step forward, saying, 'I was kidding, Guido.' She took the towel from him and draped it over the radiator, saying, 'If you spend half an hour in the shower, I know enough to realize something's wrong.' Slowly, she reached up and pushed his still-wet hair back from his forehead, running her hand over his head and down across his shoulder. 'Here,' she said, opening the linen cupboard and pulling down a smaller towel, 'lean towards me.'

He did; she spread the towel in her hands and placed it over his head. He raised his own hands to cover hers and began to rub it back and forth. Face hidden, he said, 'Would you put the clothes I wore yesterday in a plastic bag for me? And the shirt.'

'Already done,' she said in her most amiable voice.

For a moment, he was tempted to play the scene for all it was worth and tell her to give it to Caritas, but then he remembered how much he liked the jacket, so he uncovered his face and said, 'It should all go to the cleaners.'

Brunetti had told her, yesterday morning, where he and Vianello were going, but she hadn't asked him about it and still did not. Instead, she asked, 'Would you like that sweater you got in Ferrara last year?'

'The orange one?'

'Yes. It's warm; I thought you might like to wear it.'

'After parboiling myself, you mean?' he asked. 'And opening up all my pores?'

'Thus weakening your entire system for the attack of the germs,' she continued, speaking the last phrase with the same silent capital letters with which his mother, for decades, had maintained her belief in the dangers of the body's exposure to excessive temperatures of any sort, especially those caused by hot water.

'At least an assault by those that aren't on perpetual duty outside the open windows of trains so they can launch their attack from *un corrente d'aria*,' he continued, smiling at the memory of his mother's insistence on preaching these two gospels and of the good spirit in which she had always endured his joking and Paola's obvious refusal to believe them.

Stepping back into the hallway, she said, 'When you're dressed, come and tell me about it.'

25

Brunetti was awakened the next morning by a smell; by two of them, in fact. The first was the smell of springtime, a soft sweetness that drifted through the window they had left open for the first time the night before, and the second, quickly dominating and replacing the first, was the smell of coffee, brought to him by Paola. She was dressed to go out, though he could see that her hair was not yet fully dry.

She stood by the bed until he sat up against his pillow, when she handed him the cup and saucer. 'I thought someone should do something nice for you after the days you've had,' she explained.

'Thank you.' Dulled by sleep, that was all he could think of to say. He took a sip, enjoying the mingled bitterness and sweetness. 'You've saved my life.'

'I'm off,' she said, unmoved by his compliment, if that was what it was. 'I have a class at ten, and then the appointments committee meets.'

'Do you have to go?' he asked, wondering what the effect of this would be on his lunch.

'You're so transparent, Guido,' she said and laughed.

He studied the liquid in his cup and saw that she had taken the time to froth the milk she added to his coffee.

'It's a meeting I want to attend, so you're on your own for lunch.'

Stunned, he blurted out, 'You *want* to attend a meeting of your department?'

She glanced at her watch then sat on the edge of the bed. 'Remember I asked you what you had to do if you knew about something illegal that was going to happen?'

'Yes.'

'That's why I have to go.'

He finished the coffee and set the empty cup on the night table. 'Tell me,' he said, suddenly fully awake.

'I have to go so I can vote no about someone who's being considered for a professorship.'

After trying to figure this out, Brunetti said, 'I don't understand how your vote is criminal.'

'It's not my vote that's criminal. It's the

person we're voting about.'

'And so?' he prodded.

'Though not in this country, at any rate. He's been caught in France and Germany, stealing books — and maps — from university libraries. But because he's so well connected politically, they decided not to press charges. But his teaching position in Berlin was cancelled.'

'And he's applied here?'

'He's teaching already, but only as an assistant, and that contract ends this year. He's applied for a permanent position, and today the appointments committee meets to decide whether to appoint him or, indeed, to renew his temporary contract.'

'Teaching literature, I take it?' he asked.

'Yes, something called "The Semiotics of Ethics".'

'Does the syllabus include theft?' Brunetti asked.

'No doubt.'

'And you're going to vote against him?'

'Yes. And I've convinced two other members of the committee to vote with me. That should suffice.'

'You said he's politically well connected,' Brunetti said. 'Aren't you afraid of that?'

She smiled the shark smile he had come to recognize when she was at her most dangerous. 'Not at all. My father is far better connected than his patrons are, so he can't touch me.'

'And the others who are voting with you?' he asked, worried that her crusade would put other people at risk.

'One of them is his father's lover, who loathes him, and there's nothing he can do to her.'

'And the other?'

'Four of his ancestors were doges, he owns two *palazzi* on the Grand Canal, as well as a chain of supermarkets.'

Brunetti recognized immediately the man she meant. 'But you've always said he's an idiot.'

'I said he's a lousy teacher. They are not the same thing.'

'Are you sure he'll vote with you?'

'I told him about the theft of books from a library. I don't think he's recovered yet.'

'Is he still stealing books?' Brunetti inquired.

'For a while, but I had him stopped.'

'How?'

'The library has changed its policy. To enter the stacks, anyone less than a full professor has to have a card. His contract is not permanent, so he has no card and will not be issued one. So if he wants to use a book, he has to ask for it at the main desk, and after he's used it, the librarians keep him there while they check the condition of the book.'

'Condition?'

'In the Munich Library, he sliced out pages.'

'And this man is teaching at the university? Ethics?'

'Not for long, dear,' she said and got to her feet.

Brunetti ambled — there is no better word for it — into the Questura at eleven and went directly to Signorina Elettra's office. 'Ah, Commissario,' she said, 'I've called you twice this morning.'

'Delayed by official business,' he said with a smile.

'I've some information for you, sir,' she said, pushing a few sheets of paper across her desk towards him. Before he could pick them up, however, she added, 'First you might like to look at this,' and hit a few keys on her computer.

Leaving the papers, he came around her desk to look at the screen. He saw a head shot of a woman: dark, sultry, with hair that fell below her shoulders and out of the photo. Her expression was one of mild dissatisfaction, the sort of look which, if seen on the face of a woman as pretty as this one, triggers a masculine impulse to remove it. On a less attractive woman, it would appear as the warning sign it was. Brunetti recognized Giulia Borelli instantly: longer haired, younger, but unconfoundably the same.

He had not heard the sigh that escaped him, but he did hear Signorina Elettra observe, 'She was younger when the photo was taken.'

'What have you found?'

'As you said, sir, she was previously employed by a firm called Tekknomed, where she worked in the accounts department until she left to become the assistant to Dottor Papetti. This is the photo used for her company ID. I'll have a look at him this afternoon.' Brunetti had no doubt about this.

She touched a few keys, and a document appeared on the screen. From what he could make of what he read, it appeared to contain a series of other Tekknomed internal documents, starting with an email from the head of the accounts department, reporting 'certain irregularities' in the accounts kept by Signorina Giulia Borelli. This was followed by an exchange of emails between the head of the department and the president of the company, ending with the president's order that Signorina Borelli be relieved of her duties immediately and that she be denied access to her computer as of the time of receipt of his email. The last was a letter to her from the personnel department, saying that her contract had been cancelled as of the date of the letter.

'They took no legal action,' Signorina Elcttra said, 'so I don't know what she was up to.' She hit a few keys, and a chart filled with numbers came on to the screen. 'As you can see,' she said, tapping at one of the numbers, 'their turnover is seventeen million a year.'

'Lots of opportunity there,' Brunetti observed, then, 'Anything else?'

Nodding towards the papers, she said, 'Her contract of employment with the *macello* guarantees her a car, six weeks of vacation, and a salary of forty thousand Euros, plus a very generous expense account.'

'As a personal assistant?' he asked. 'I tremble at what Papetti must be getting.'

She held up a hand. 'Not until this afternoon, Commissario.'

'Of course,' Brunetti answered and then added, deciding in the instant, 'Vianello and I are going out to see the widow again. Can you have a car at Piazzale Roma in half an hour?'

'Of course, Signore. Should I call her and tell her?'

'Yes, I think we should let her know we're coming this time,' he said and went to get Vianello.

The woman who opened the door to them might have been the elder sister of the woman they had spoken to before. This was evident in the droop of her mouth and the darkness under her eyes as well as in the elderly deliberation with which she moved, like a person under sedation or one recovering from a serious illness. Signora Doni nodded in recognition when she saw the two men. A few beats passed before she extended her hand to them. And then, after that, it took her some time to ask them to come inside. Brunetti noticed how dusty the lenses of her glasses were.

They followed her into the same room. The table in front of the sofa was covered with newspapers neither man had to study to know were opened to the articles about her husband's murder. Littering the open papers were cups. All appeared to have once held coffee; some still did. A kitchen towel lay across the arm of the sofa, with a plate with a desiccated sandwich beside it.

She sat on the sofa this time, absently picking up the abandoned towel, which she spread on her lap and began to fold longitudinally in three. She kept her eyes on the towel while the two men sat on the chairs facing her.

Finally she said, 'Are you here about the funeral?'

'No, Signora,' Brunetti answered.

Eyes still lowered, she seemed to have run out of things to say.

'How is your son, Signora?' Brunetti finally asked.

She looked across at him and made a motion with her mouth that she probably thought was a smile. 'I've sent him to stay with my sister. And his cousins.'

'How did he bear the news?' Brunetti asked, pushing away the idea that someone might some day ask Paola the same question. This was the sister he'd spoken to, who had confirmed Signora Doni's account of their whereabouts on the night of her husband's death.

She gestured with her right hand; the towel waved in the air, calling attention to itself. She lowered it to her lap and started to fold it again, and finally said, 'I don't know. I told him his father had gone to

Jesus. I don't believe it, but it's the only thing I could think of to tell him.' She ran her hand along the two creases in the towel. 'It helped him, I think. But I don't know what he's thinking.' She turned abruptly and replaced the towel on the arm of the sofa.

'Did you come about Teodoro?' she asked, her confusion audible in the emphasis she put on the last word.

'Partly, Signora. He's a nice little boy, and I've thought about him in these days.' This, the Lord be praised, was at least true. 'But we've come, I'm afraid, to ask you more questions about your husband and how he was behaving in the last few months,' he said, having managed to avoid 'the months before he died', which came to the same thing, in the end.

Again, there was a longer lapse than there should have been between question and response. 'What do you mean?'

'You said, when we spoke the other day, Signora, that he seemed troubled, perhaps worried. What I would like to know is whether he gave you any indication of the cause for his . . . his preoccupation?'

This time she managed to resist the towel's allure. Instead, she ran her hand around her watch strap, unclasped it and immediately closed it again. 'Yes, I'd say he was worried, but I told him I didn't want to hear it — this was the last time we talked — I think I told him to go and tell her his troubles, and that's when he said that he thought she was his trouble.'

This was an elaboration of the account she had given last time. Brunetti could not resist the impulse to take a quick glance at Vianello, who sat impassive, listening. Signora Doni looked directly at him. 'Well, she was, wasn't she? I suppose he thought I'd give him the chance to choose between us, either her or me. But I didn't: I just told him to get out.' Then, after a pause, 'The first time and the last time.'

'This last time, Signora, did he say anything about his work?'

She started to answer, but lethargy fell upon her, and she looked down at her watch again. She could have been trying to remember how to tell the time or she could have been thinking about how to answer his question: Brunetti saw no need to hasten her.

'He said it wasn't worth it, taking that job. He said it had ruined everything. I suppose he meant because of meeting her there. I mean, that's what I thought when he said it.'

'Could he have meant something else, Signora?' Vianello broke in to ask.

She must have remembered the good cop because the motion her mouth made this time was closer to a smile. After a long time, she said, 'Perhaps.'

'Do you have any idea what that might have been?' Vianello prodded.

'Once,' she began, looking beyond them at some memory that was not there in the room, at least not with them, 'he said that what they did there was terrible.'

Brunetti had only to remember what they had seen to feel the force and truth of this. 'What was done to the animals?' he asked.

She gave him a tilt-chinned glance and said, 'That's what's so strange. Now, I mean. Now that I think about what happened, I think that maybe he didn't mean what happened to the animals.' She leaned aside again and stroked the towel as though it were some sort of pet. 'The first time he went there, we talked about it. I had to ask him because he loves . . . loved animals so much. And I remember his telling me that it was far less terrible than he feared it would be.' She shook her head. 'I couldn't believe it at first, but he said he'd spent an hour there that morning, to see what went on. And it was less bad than he'd feared.'

An explosive sigh escaped her lips. 'Maybe he was lying to spare me. I don't know.' Her voice had slowed perceptibly.

Brunetti didn't know, either. He had no idea what sort of scene the knackers could have set for the inspecting veterinarian's first day, nor did he know if the inspector would have to return to see the killing or if his only concern was to inspect the resulting meat. He thought of the sense of frenzied action, the shouting and kicking. 'Do you remember anything else he said?' Brunetti asked.

Even with the slowness of her reactions, her hesitation was visible. She touched her watch again, and for a moment he thought she was going to wind it, but then she said, eyes still on her watch, 'Not to me.'

Brunetti was about to ask, when he thought better of it and lifted his chin towards Vianello.

'To your son, Signora?' the Inspector asked.

'Yes. To Teo.'

'Could you tell us what it was?'

'He was telling Teo a bedtime story one night after he brought him home. This was about three weeks ago.' She let that drift away. 'He always did that when they came home.' The last word stopped her. She coughed, then she went on. 'It was always a story or a book about an animal. This one — he must have made it up because we don't have any book like that — was about a dog who wasn't very brave. Things frightened him: cats frightened him, other dogs did, too. In the story he's kidnapped by robbers, who want to train him to help them. They train him to befriend people who are walking on the path through the forest. When the people see this big friendly dog start to walk along with them, they feel safe and keep walking deeper and deeper into the forest. The robbers tell him that, at a certain point, he has to run away, so then they can hurt the people and rob them.

'But even though he's a coward, he's still a dog, and he can never let bad things happen to people. So after all that training, when the robbers finally take him out to help them rob someone, the dog acts like a real dog and turns on the robbers and barks and growls at them — he even bites one of them, though not very hard — until the police come and arrest them. And the man they were going to rob takes the dog back to his old home and tells the family what a good dog he is. They take him back in and they love him, even though he's still not really a very brave dog.'

'Why do you think of the story, Signora?' Vianello asked gently when he understood that she was finished.

'Because, when the story was over, Andrea told Teo that he should always remember the story and never let anyone do bad things to people because that's the worst thing you can ever do.' She stopped and took a deep breath. 'But then I came into the room, and he stopped talking.'

She tried to laugh at herself, but it came out as a cough. 'I mention it because he seemed so serious when he was telling the story. He really wanted Teo to learn that lesson: you never let bad things happen to people, even if the robbers threaten you.'

She gave in to temptation and grabbed the towel. She no longer tried to fold or straighten it but twisted it in her hands as though it were something she wanted to destroy.

However curious he might still have been about the Borelli woman, Brunetti knew it was folly to ask. Instead, he got to his feet and thanked Signora Doni. When she offered to show them to the door, he declined, and they left her to the rags of memory.

26

'What did you make of her?' Brunetti asked as they walked toward the unmarked car parked at the kerb.

'My guess is she's never going to forgive herself, or if she does, it will take a long time.'

'For what?'

'For not having listened to him.'

'Not for having thrown him out?'

Vianello shrugged. 'To a woman like that, it's what he deserved. But not to listen to him when he asked her to: that's what's going to haunt her.'

'I'd say it already does,' Brunetti said.

'Yes. And the rest of what she said?'

Brunetti got into the back seat with Vianello and told the driver to take them back to Piazzale Roma. As the car pulled away from the kerb, he said, 'You mean his saying that taking the job there ruined everything?'

'Yes,' Vianello said, and then added, 'I don't think we should forget about the woman.'

'Perhaps,' Brunetti said, his memory running back over the conversation with Nava's widow.

'Then what else?'

'Lots of things can ruin a job. You hate your boss or the people you work with. Or they hate you. You hate the work,' Brunetti suggested, then added, 'But none of that makes sense, if you think of the story he told his son.'

'Couldn't it just have been a story?'

'Would you tell one of your kids a story like that?' Brunetti asked.

Vianello considered this for a moment and then answered, 'Probably not. I'm not good at stories with morals.'

'Neither are most kids, I'd say,' Brunetti added.

Vianello laughed at this. 'Mine always like the ones where the well-behaved little girl ends up being eaten by the lion and the bad kids get to eat all the chocolate cake.'

'Mine did, too,' Brunetti agreed. Then, back to what was bothering him, he asked, 'So why tell him such a story?'

'Maybe because he knew his wife would be listening?'

'Perhaps,' Brunetti said.

'In which case?' Vianello asked.

'In which case, he was trying to tell her something.'

'Without having to tell her.'

Brunetti sighed. 'How many times have we all done that?'

'And what was he trying to tell her?'

'That he was in a situation where he was being told to do bad things to people, and he thought it was wrong and didn't want to do it.'

'People, not animals?' Vianello asked.

'That's what he said. If he'd wanted to talk about animals, he would have told a story about an animal that had to hurt other animals. Kids have literal minds.'

'You think they care when they're told not to do bad things to people?' Vianello asked, sounding not at all convinced.

'If they trust the person telling them, I think they do,' Brunetti said.

'So how does a veterinarian do bad things to people except by hurting their pets?'

'It was the job at the *macello* that troubled him,' Brunetti insisted.

'You saw the butchers. It wouldn't be easy to cause them pain.'

With that, the two men stopped talking. The ride continued, up on to the overpasses that led from Mestre to the bridge. Then in front of the rows of factories to the right, past the smokestacks that spewed out God knows what for human consumption.

A possibility came to Brunetti, and he said it aloud: 'For human consumption.'

'What?' Vianello asked, his attention summoned back from the giant digital thermometer on the *Gazzettino* building.

'For human consumption,' Brunetti repeated. 'That's what he did at the *macello*. He inspected the animals that were brought in and he inspected the meat that they became. He decided what was acceptable to be sold as food; he declared it fit for human consumption.' His mind on the story Nava had told his son, Brunetti repeated, 'His job was to see that nothing bad happened to people.'

When Vianello said nothing, Brunetti added, 'To keep them from eating bad meat.' Vianello didn't grace this with an answer, and Brunetti asked, 'How much does a cow weigh?'

Vianello still did not answer.

From the front seat, the driver said, 'My brother-in-law's a farmer, Commissario: a good cow weighs up to seven hundred kilos.'

'How much of it can be turned into meat?'

'I'm not sure, Commissario, but I'd guess

about half.'

'Think about it, Lorenzo,' Brunetti said. 'If he refused them or condemned them or did whatever it was a veterinarian is supposed to do, the farmer would lose everything.'

In the face of Vianello's silence, Brunetti asked the driver, 'How much do they get a kilo?'

'I don't know for sure, Commissario. My brother-in-law always calculates that a cow is worth fifteen hundred Euros. Maybe a bit more, but that's the figure he uses.'

Turning to Vianello and responding to his continued lack of enthusiasm, Brunetti said, though he was aware of how disgruntled he sounded, 'It's the first thing we've had that might be a reason to kill him.'

It wasn't until they were on the causeway and the city was in sight that Vianello permitted himself to say, 'Even if Patta doesn't like it as a possibility, I think I prefer assault.'

Brunetti returned his attention to the water on the right side of the car.

As soon as the boat pulled up in front of the Questura, Brunetti and Vianello stepped on to the landing and walked into the building. They entered Signorina Elettra's office together, an arrival that seemed to register on her face as a twin delight.

'You've come for Papetti?' she asked, the question suggesting that, if they had, they'd come to the right place.

'Yes,' Brunetti answered. 'Tell us.'

'Dottor Papetti is married to the daughter of Maurizio De Rivera,' she said, which information Vianello greeted with a low whistle, Brunetti with a whispered 'Ah.'

'I take your noises as indication that you are aware of her father's position and power,' she said.

And who in the North-east was not? Brunetti asked himself. De Rivera was to construction what Thyssen was to steel: the family name sufficed to conjure the product, was almost synonymous with it. The daughter, his only child — unless some other had been slipped into the family while the gossip columnists were heavily sedated — had spent a good deal of her youth under the very public influence of various substances as illegal as they were harmful.

'When was the fire?' Vianello asked.

'Ten, eleven years ago,' Brunetti answered, referring to the fire in her apartment in Rome from which the daughter — he could no longer remember her name — had been saved at the cost of the lives of three firefighters. The public feeding frenzy had lasted months, during which she disappeared from the news, only to reappear a year or so later as a volunteer at some soup kitchen or shelter, apparently having undergone a transformative experience as a result of having been saved at the cost of three lives. But then she had again disappeared from the papers and thus from the public consciousness.

No transformative experience, however, had affected her father, nor his reputation. Speculation continued about his company's repeated winning of contracts for municipal and provincial building projects, especially in the South. And it was in that part of the country that his company's bid was also often the only one to be made.

There were other rumours about him, but those were only rumours.

After giving them time to consider this information, Signorina Elettra went on, 'I've also found an internal memo in which Papetti requests that Borelli be hired, and at that salary.' She seemed barely able to contain her delight at having discovered this.

'If what I think what might be going on is actually going on, then, given what is said about his father-in-law, Signor Papetti is a very brave man,' Vianello said.

'Or a very stupid one,' Brunetti countered.

'Or both,' suggested Signorina Elettra.

'De Rivera's never been convicted of anything,' Vianello said in a neutral voice.

'Neither have many of our politicians and cabinet ministers,' Signorina Elettra added.

Brunetti was tempted to say that none of the three of them had ever been convicted, either, and what did that prove? Instead, he said, 'Shall we merely agree that Papetti's relationship with Signorina Borelli is one he might not want his father-in-law to hear about?' Vianello nodded. Signorina Elettra smiled.

'What else did you find out about him?' Brunetti went on.

'They live very well, he and his wife and their children.'

'What's her name? I've forgotten,' Vianello interrupted.

'Natasha,' Signorina Elettra said evenly.

'Of course,' the Inspector said. 'I knew it was something fake.'

As if the Inspector had not spoken, she went on. 'He has almost two million Euros in various investments, their home is worth at least that, he drives one of their two Mercedes SUVs, and they often go on vacation.'

'It could be De Rivera's money,' Brunetti suggested.

Primly, as if cautioning an over-eager student, Signorina Elettra said, 'The accounts are in his name only. And they are not in this country.'

'I stand corrected,' Brunetti said, then asked, 'Signorina Borelli? Anything else about her?'

'Though she was making less than twenty-five thousand Euros a year at Tekknomed, she somehow managed to buy, during the years she worked there, two apartments in Venice and one in Mestre. She lives in the one in Mestre and rents the ones in Venice to tourists.'

'And Tekknomed chose not to bring charges against her when she left,' said a reflective Brunetti. 'She must have known a great deal about their accounts.' Then, to Signorina Elettra, 'Her bank accounts?'

'I'm continuing my researches, Signore,' she said primly.

'Is there any evidence that her relationship with Papetti is sexual?'

She allowed herself a cool glance. 'It's impossible to find those things in the records, sir.'

'Yes, of course,' Brunetti answered. 'Continue your researches, then.' To Vianello, he said, 'I want to talk to Papetti.'

'You have the endurance to go back to the

mainland?' Vianello asked with a smile.

'I'd like to talk to him before more time passes.'

'If you go, you should go alone,' Vianello said. 'It's less threatening.' He took a step towards Signorina Elettra and asked, 'Do you think we could have a look at the records of the *macello* at Preganziol while the Commissario is away?'

Her response was an exercise in modesty. 'I could try.'

Leaving them to it, Brunetti went downstairs and out to the boat.

27

Brunetti marvelled again at how it was possible for people to live like this: driving around in cars, getting stuck behind long columns of other cars, eternal victims of the vagaries of traffic. And the air, and the noise, and the overwhelming ugliness of what he passed. No wonder drivers were prone to violence: how could they not be?

Signorina Elettra had called and made an appointment with Dottor Papetti, explaining that Commissario Brunetti was on the mainland that day and could easily stop by to talk to him about Dottor Nava: luckily, Dottor Papetti had no appointments that afternoon and would be in his office. She explained that Commissario Brunetti knew the way to the slaughterhouse.

Though the driver took Brunetti the same way, he recognized little of what they passed, road-memory or road-skill not being a talent he had acquired. He thought he'd seen one of the villas, but from a distance many of them looked the same. He did, however, recognize the lane that led to the slaughterhouse and then the gates behind which it stood. And, though it seemed less strong now, Brunetti also recognized the smell that swept at him from the back of the building.

This time it was Dottor Papetti who met him at the door. He was a tall man with receding hair that exaggerated the narrowness of his face and head. His eyes were round and dark and belonged on a fatter face. The lips were thin and drawn back in a formulaic smile. The shoulders of his suit were padded in a way that was out of fashion but that still managed to disguise his thinness. Brunetti glanced down and saw that his shoes were handmade; the narrowness of his feet probably made this necessary.

After surprising Brunetti with the strength of his handshake, Papetti suggested they go to his office. Papetti walked along beside him with the free-jointed motion of a heron in water; his head, on an inordinately long neck, shoved forward with every step. Neither man spoke; intermittent noises came from the back of the building.

Opening the door to his office, Papetti stepped back and said, 'Commissario, please have a seat and tell me how I can help you. I'm sorry I couldn't be here during your visit.'

Brunetti passed in front of him, saying, 'I'm very glad you could find time to see me now, Dottor Papetti.' Once both were seated, Brunetti added, in a voice from which he could not banish his gratitude, 'I'm sure a man with your position has many responsibilities.' Papetti smiled modestly in response to this: his smile made Brunetti remember a line he had read, he thought, in Kafka, about a man who had seen people laugh, 'and thought he knew how to do it'.

'Luckily,' Papetti began, 'well, luckily for you, two people cancelled meetings this afternoon, so I found myself with an opening in my schedule.' He tried another smile. 'It doesn't often happen.'

His words at first created only a wild surmise, and then memory brought it to him: it was Patta's voice the man was using. But was it Patta at his most cordial or his most devious?

'As my secretary must have told you, I'd like to speak to you about Dottor Nava,' Brunetti said, as one overburdened bureaucrat to another.

Papetti nodded, and Brunetti continued,

'Since he worked for you, I thought you might be able to tell me something about him.' Then, in a display of openness and candour, Brunetti said, 'I've spoken to his widow, but there was very little she could tell me. I don't know if you're aware of this, but they've been legally separated for some months.' He waited to see what Papetti would say to this.

After a hesitation so brief as barely to have existed, he said, 'No, I'm afraid I didn't know that,' rubbing the fingers of his left hand across the back of the right. 'I knew him only because of his work at the *macello,* so I was not familiar with his private life.'

'You knew that he was married, though, didn't you, Dottore?' Brunetti asked in his mildest voice.

'Oh,' Papetti said with an attempt at an airy wave of the hand, 'I suppose I must have known, or at least assumed; most men his age are, after all. Or perhaps he mentioned his children. I'm sorry, but I don't remember.' Then, after the briefest pause, with what was meant to be a look of concern, 'I'd like you to extend my condolences to his widow, Commissario.'

'Of course, of course,' Brunetti said with a nod that acknowledged Papetti's feelings.

Brunetti let some time pass and then

asked, 'Could you tell me exactly what Dottor Nava's duties at the *macello* were?'

Papetti's answer came so fast it seemed he had been prepared for this question. 'His job was really that of an inspector. He had to see that the animals that come to us were fit for slaughter, and then he had to inspect samples of the meat that came from them.'

'Of course, of course,' Brunetti said, then with the eagerness of a novice, he went on, 'Your position must afford you some knowledge of the way all slaughterhouses work, Dottore. In general, that is. The animals arrive, are unloaded . . .' Brunetti paused with another friendly smile and said, 'We didn't get much of an idea.' Trying not to look embarrassed, he said, 'My Inspector, he . . .' He stopped and shrugged and then went on, 'So please understand that I'm speaking out of ignorance here, Dottore. I'm merely trying to imagine how it might be; I'm sure you know far better than I.' Trying his best to look uncertain, Brunetti asked, 'Now, where was I? Oh, yes, the animals are unloaded or led in or however it is they're brought there. And then, presumably, Dottor Nava would examine them to see that they are healthy, and then they would be taken into the slaughterhouse and killed.' Dull people are repetitive, Brunetti knew, hoping that Papetti also believed this.

Papetti seemed to relax at this chance to remain far away from the particular. 'That's more or less what happens. Yes.'

'Are there problems that you might encounter, or that Dottor Nava might have?'

Papetti pursed his lips in a gesture of thought and then said, 'Well, as far as the slaughterhouse is concerned, if there should be a difference between our records of the number of animals brought in and what the farmers claim: that might be one. Or if there are delays in processing that force the farmers to keep their animals here longer than planned, with the resulting costs: that's another.' He uncrossed and recrossed his legs and said, 'As for Dottor Nava, his concern would be any violation of EU regulations.'

'Could you give me an example, Signore?' Brunetti asked.

'If the animals suffer unnecessarily or if the proper standards of cleanliness aren't maintained.'

'Ah, of course. Now it makes sense to me. Thank you, Dottore.' Brunetti was pleased at how he must look, finally understanding all of this.

As if in response to Brunetti's willingness to understand, Papetti said, 'We like to think of ourselves as working with the farmers to help them receive a just price for the animals they've raised and brought to us.'

Brunetti, enjoining himself to avoid the danger of overreaching, stopped himself from saying that he could not have put it more accurately. Instead, he muttered, 'Indeed,' and then said, 'But if I might take us back to Dottor Nava, did you ever hear anyone at the *macello* say a word against him?'

'Not that I can recall,' Papetti answered instantly.

'And you were pleased with his work?'

'Absolutely,' Papetti said with another swipe at the back of his hand. 'But you have to understand that my function is primarily administrative. My direct contact with the people who work here is somewhat limited.'

'Would any of the workers have informed you if there had been anything irregular in Dottor Nava's activities?' Brunetti asked.

After some consideration, Papetti said, 'I don't know, Commissario.' Then, with a modest smile, he added, 'I doubt that's the kind of information that would be passed on to me.' Could mere gossip percolate to so high a point?

Keeping his voice as casual as it had been since he began speaking to Papetti, Brunetti asked, 'Do you think they'd tell you about Nava's affair with your assistant, Signorina Borclli?'

'How do you . . . ?' Papetti said, then did something Brunetti had never seen an adult do: he clapped both hands across his mouth. Roundness is an absolute. So Papetti's eyes could not grow rounder, but they could grow larger. They did, and his face grew whiter as the blood drained from it.

He tried. Brunetti had to give him credit for that. Papetti laced his voice with indignation and demanded, 'How do you dare say that?' but it was a feeble attempt: both men knew it was too late in the game to try to change either his reaction or his words.

'So they did tell you, Dottore?' Brunetti said, finally permitting himself the smile of the wolf. 'Or was it perhaps Signorina Borelli herself who told you?'

At first, from the noise Papetti was making, Brunetti thought the man was choking, but then he realized it was the sound of a man fighting off tears. Papetti sat with one hand over his eyes, the other draped across his bald forehead and skull in what seemed to be an attempt to hide. The noise persisted, gradually subsiding into deep heaves as Papetti caught his breath, then heavy breathing as he sat, his head and face still protected from Brunetti.

After some moments, Papetti took his hands away. The round eyes were encircled by red patches, and two more had appeared in the middle of his cheeks.

He looked at Brunetti and said, voice shaking, 'You have to leave.'

Brunetti sat immobile.

'You have to leave,' Papetti repeated.

Slowly, Brunetti got to his feet, aware of who this man's father-in-law was and aware from his own family of the lengths to which a wife's father might go in defence of his daughter and his grandchildren. He took out his wallet and removed one of his cards. Taking a pen from Papetti's desk, he wrote his *telefonino* number on the front of the card, then placed it on the desk between them.

'This is my number, Dottore. If you decide you want to tell me more about this, you can call me whenever you wish.'

Outside, Brunetti found the driver leaning against the door of the car, eyes narrowed as he faced into the sun. He was eating an ice cream cone and looking very pleased with it. They drove back to Venice.

28

Feeling that to have been out to the mainland twice in one day — regardless of how inconclusive the meetings had been and regardless of the fact that thousands of people did the same two trips every day — was more than a full day's work for him, Brunetti decided he did not have to return to the Questura. Instead, when the driver let him out at Piazzale Roma, he offered himself the chance to go for a walk and the chance to get home by any route he chose, so long as it got him home on time for dinner.

The softness of the late afternoon encouraged him to walk in the vague direction of San Polo, turning or stopping where whim indicated. He had known this part of the city decades ago, when he took the train daily to Padova to attend his university classes and chose to walk back and forth to the station because it saved him — how much had it been then? — the fifty lire of boat fare. It had been enough for a sweet drink or a coffee; he recalled with the affection age brings to the weaknesses of youth how he had chosen coffee only when with his classmates, giving in to his normal preference for sweet drinks when alone and there was no one to judge his choice unsophisticated.

For a moment, he considered stopping for one of those drinks, if he could only remember their names. But he was a man and had laid aside the things of childhood, and so he stopped for a coffee, smiling at himself as he poured in the second envelope of sugar.

He emerged into Campo Santa Margherita, by day the same, normal *campo* it had been for centuries, with fruit and fish stands, a *gelateria,* a pharmacy, shops of all sorts, and the odd, elongated shape that made it such a good place for children to run after dogs or other children. Because he had given himself free time, Brunetti turned his mind away from the chaos that now plagued the *campo* at night and that had driven people he knew to sell their family homes, if only to escape the noise.

Had Gobbetti still been there, he would have stopped to buy a chocolate mousse to take home, but they had sold the business, and the *pasticceria* that had replaced them had not replaced the mousse. How replace the sublime?

The boats were moored on the other side of Ponte dei Pugni, one for fruit and one for vegetables, and he tried to remember if he had ever known them *not* to be there. If not, and they were permanently there, were they — at least in the philosophical sense — still boats? Musing on this, he got halfway across Campo San Barnaba before he decided he would like to go home and enjoy the rest of the evening's softness from his balcony. He passed in front of the *calle* that led to his parents-in-law's *palazzo* without giving a thought to stopping to see them. The idea was in his mind to go home, and go home he would.

To Brunetti's great relief, everyone was there when he arrived, and to his greater relief, after they said hello and kissed him, they left him to whatever he chose while they went about the business of their lives. He poured himself a glass of white wine and took a chair out on to the balcony, where he sat for an hour, watching the light dim and disappear, sipping at his wine, and being grateful that the people he loved all had lives and things to busy themselves with that had nothing at all to do with the dreadful lies and deceptions with which his days were filled.

The next morning dawned sweetly for Brunetti, though that sensation diminished the nearer he got to the Questura and what he decided would have to be another conversation with Patta. He realized he had no choice but to tell his superior what he had learned and where those facts had led his suspicions. Like the composer of an opera, he had notes and arias, a range of singers, the sketch of a plot, but there was as yet no coherent libretto.

'She's Maurizio De Rivera's daughter, and you think her husband knows something about a murder and isn't telling you?' Patta erupted after Brunetti recounted his conversation with Papetti. Had Brunetti told him that the liquefaction of the blood of San Gennaro was a hoax, Patta could have been no more indignant.

'You know who he is, don't you, Brunetti?' his superior demanded.

Ignoring this, Brunetti said, 'He might want to know what sort of man his daughter is married to.'

'The truth's the last thing a man wants to know about the man his daughter's married to.' Then, after a pause so long that Brunetti sensed Patta was taking careful aim, Patta let fire. 'You should know that.'

Brunetti failed to contain his response, but he did manage to limit it to a glance, quickly turned away. It must, however, have sufficed to show Patta that he had finally gone too far, for he added immediately, in a transparent attempt to back-pedal, 'You've got a daughter, after all. You'll want to believe she's married to a good man, won't you?'

Brunetti's heart was still pounding at the insult, so it took him some time to find an answer. Finally he said, 'De Rivera might have different standards from other fathers, Vice-Questore. If his daughter or her husband were involved in this killing in any way, he might not be bothered by things like obstruction of justice, lying to a public official in the pursuit of his duties, perhaps even direct support in the commission of the crime.' Then, after a pause, he added, 'After all, he's been tried for the first two.'

'And acquitted,' Patta snapped back.

Brunetti ignored the remark and went on, 'Nava was stabbed in the back and somehow taken to a place where he could be pushed into a canal. That suggests the participation of two people.' Brunetti was calmer now and in greater control of his voice.

'And why does this have to involve Papetti?' Patta asked loftily.

Brunetti stopped himself from blurting out that it simply *felt* right, well aware of how far he was likely to get with that. 'It doesn't necessarily, Dottore. But he knows something, or he knows things, that he's not telling. He knew about the affair between Nava and Borelli: his surprise that I knew about it was evidence of that. And if he recommended her for the job as his assistant, then she's got some hold on him,' Brunetti said, dismissing out of hand the possibility of the generosity that is one of the first signs of love.

Patta drew his lips together in a tight, outthrust circle, a habit Brunetti had come, over the years, to see as a visual suggestion that he was going to consider things reasonably. The Vice-Questore raised his right hand and studied his fingernails. Brunetti had no idea whether he actually saw them or if this was merely another physical manifestation of thought.

At last Patta lowered his hand and relaxed. 'What do you want to do?'

'I want to bring the Borelli woman in here and ask her a few questions.'

'Such as?'

'I won't know that until I have some more

information.'

'What information?' Patta asked.

'About some apartments she owns. About Papetti and Nava and how she got her job as Papetti's assistant. And how her salary was decided. About the slaughterhouse and how well she knows Dottor Meucci,' he added, a scenario taking shape.

'Who's he?' Patta demanded, giving evidence that he had not read the reports on the case.

'Nava's predecessor.'

'What's she got, this Borelli woman — a thing for veterinarians?'

Brunetti was tempted to smile at hearing Patta so unthinkingly ask this very interesting question.

'I've no idea, sir. I'm merely curious in a general way.'

'In a general way?' Patta repeated slowly. 'Meaning?'

'Meaning, sir, that I don't have a clear idea yet of how all of these people are connected or of what continues to hold them together. But something does, because no one is telling me anything.' Speaking more to himself than to Patta, Brunetti said, 'All I need is the way in.'

Patta set his palms firmly on his desk. 'All right, bring her in and see what she has to say. But, remember, I want to know anything you learn about Papetti before you act on it.'

'Of course, Vice-Questore,' Brunetti said and repaired to the outer office, where he saw the face of Signorina Elettra rising behind the screen of her computer.

'I've accessed the files of the ULSS office in Treviso, sir, since they keep the same records the slaughterhouse does,' she said. 'It was easier than trying to get into those of the *macello*.' Thoughtfully, she added, 'Besides, in the unlikely event that any traces of my presence were left, it's always better to leave them in a government agency than in a private business.'

Not wanting to offend Signorina Elettra, who was perhaps waiting for him to query her use of 'accessed' or 'always', perhaps even 'unlikely event', Brunetti limited himself to a mild 'Tell me.'

'I've gone back four years, sir, and to make it easier to read, I've put it into a graph.' She nodded to the screen.

She moved the mouse, clicked, clicked again, and a line graph appeared, above which was written 'Preganziol'. The months of the year were listed at the top; the side held numbers that ascended from 0 to 100.

The line began, in January four years

before, at three and zigzagged its way to four the following month, then wiggled back to three the next. This pattern continued for the next two years. In the third year it followed the same erratic path upwards to five before sinking back to three, where it remained until November, when it catapulted up to eight and, rising steadily, finished the year at twelve. The line jumped off from January and hit thirteen, stayed there for a month, and then in March moved up to fourteen. The chart ended that month.

'So whatever this number reflects,' Brunetti said, 'it moved upward suddenly at about the time Nava began working at the *macello* and continued to do so . . .' He leaned forward and tapped at the end of the line, '. . . until the month before his death.'

Signorina Elettra scrolled the page down, allowing Brunetti to read the caption: *Percentage of animals rejected by the competent authority as unfit for slaughter.*

'Unfit for slaughter.' Which probably meant the same thing as 'Unfit for human consumption.' So there it was. The cowardly dog had defied the robbers, but this cowardly dog had not managed to turn on the robbers and save anyone, and the family where he had been living had not been able to take him back in and love him again, even though he still wasn't very brave.

'So he was doing his job,' Brunetti said, then added, to Signorina Elettra's confusion, 'just like the dog.' But he quickly added something she did understand, so clear was it made by the graph: 'And his predecessor was not.'

'Unless we're back in Exodus and plagues were unleashed upon the land and pestilence upon the herds the day he started working there,' she added.

'Unlikely,' Brunetti observed, then asked, 'Anything else about Signorina Borelli?'

'Aside from the list of her properties, I now have some information about her investments and her bank accounts.'

'Plural?'

'Here in the city, one in Mestre where her salary is deposited, and one in the postal banking system.' She smiled and said, with badly disguised contempt, 'People seem to believe that no one would think to look there.'

'And what else?' he asked, so familiar with her manner that he knew there were still treats to be revealed.

'Meucci. Not only has he made three phone calls to Signorina Borelli's *telefonino* in the last two days, but it turns out that he is not a veterinarian at all.'

'What?'

'He spent four years at Padova, took and passed most of the exams, but seems not to have taken the last four, and there's no record that he took his degree from the university or that he passed — or ever applied to take — the state exams.'

Brunetti was about to ask how it was possible for the provincial department of health to give him a job as a veterinarian at a slaughterhouse or by what means he had set up a private practice, but he stopped himself in time. Few weeks passed without the revelation of some fake doctor or dentist; why should the species of the patient make fraud any less likely?

He decided on the instant. 'Call his office and find out if he's there: ask if you can bring your cat in or something like that — just find out if he's there. If he is, send Foa and Pucetti over to ask him if he'd like to come in to talk to me.'

'I'd be delighted, sir,' she said, then, 'Have a look at the papers about Signorina Borelli, why don't you?'

Brunetti took the folder, intending to go to his office to read through the papers, but instead he went to the officers' room to give more precise instructions to Foa and Pucetti, telling Pucetti to be careful to address Meucci as 'Signore' and not 'Dottore'. After that, still carrying the file, he went down to the bar at Ponte dei Greci and had a coffee and two *tramezzini.*

Back in the office, he called Paola and asked what they were going to have for dinner. To please her, he asked how she was feeling about having orchestrated the non-renewal of her colleague's contract.

'Like Lucrezia Borgia,' she said and laughed.

Brunetti spent some time looking for a tape recorder, which he found in the back of his bottom drawer. He checked that it worked and placed it very conspicuously on his desk. He opened the file then and began to read but had got as far only as the prices paid for Signorina Borelli's apartment in Mestre and the first one in Venice when he heard a sound at his door.

Looking up, he saw Pucetti and, beside him, Meucci. If he were a tyre, then some of the air had been let out of him; this was most evident in his face, where the eyes seemed to have grown larger. His cheeks had sagged and hung loose above the soft little mouth. Less flesh pressed against the retaining wall of his collar.

His body seemed smaller, as well, but that might have been because of the dark woollen jacket that had replaced his voluminous lab coat.

Pucetti waited at the door while Meucci entered. The door closed; the only sound was the officer's retreating footsteps.

'Come in, Signor Meucci,' Brunetti said coolly. He leaned across the desk and clicked on the tape recorder.

The man came slowly forward, as timidly as a young wildebeest forced to step into tall grass. As he approached Brunetti's desk, his eyes moved around the room in search of the danger he knew was there. Slowly he lowered himself into a chair. Brunetti thought the noise was a sigh, but then he realized it was the sound of Meucci's flesh-crammed clothing as it rubbed against the sides and back of the chair.

Brunetti observed the man's hands, which remained fixed to the arms of the chair. The stained fingers were wrapped under the arms and so the hands looked like normal hands, however swollen with fat.

'How did you obtain your job at the *macello,* Signor Meucci?' Brunetti asked. No greeting, no politeness, only the simple question.

Brunetti watched Meucci consider various

possibilities, and then the fat man said, 'The opening was announced, and I applied for it.'

'Were you asked to submit supporting documents with your application, Signore?' Brunetti asked, giving special emphasis to the last word.

'Yes,' Meucci answered. The fact that he did not answer with an indignant 'of course' told Brunetti that he would have no trouble with this interview. Meucci was a defeated man who wanted only to limit the damage he was going to endure.

'And the absence of evidence that you were a doctor of veterinary medicine did not serve as an obstacle to your application for that position?' Brunetti asked with the mildest interest.

Meucci's right hand moved to the pocket of his jacket, then slipped inside to take what comfort it could from the feel of his packet of cigarettes. He shook his head.

'You have to speak, Signore. Your answers must be audible so that the stenographer can record them.'

'No,' Meucci said.

'How was that possible, Signore?'

As he looked at Meucci, Brunetti was filled with the strange sensation that the man was melting. He sat lower in his chair, though he had made no motion that suggested he was shifting in his seat. His mouth seemed to have grown smaller before it pronounced that last monosyllable. His jacket hung loosely from his shoulders.

'How was that possible, Signore?'

Brunetti heard the crunching sound as Meucci's hand closed on the packet of cigarettes. 'No one showed me any papers. I didn't sign anything that said you could ask me these questions.' Something resembling anger could be heard in Meucci's voice.

Brunetti gave an understanding smile. 'Of course, Signor Meucci. I understand that. You are here voluntarily, come in to aid the police in their investigations.' Brunetti slid the tape recorder back towards him. 'You're free to go whenever you please.' He clicked off the tape.

Eyes locked on the tape recorder, Meucci asked, the anger evaporated, 'What happens if I do?' It was a simple request for an answer, not a demand. Lost men had no demands to make.

'Then you leave us with no choice but to inform the police in Mestre and the ULSS and, for good measure, the Guardia di Finanza, just in case you haven't been bothering to pay taxes on what is probably — given your lack of a licence to function as a veterinarian — an illegal practice.'

Brunetti pushed his chair back and crossed his legs. Not being in a particularly theatrical vein that day, he failed to lean back and latch his fingers behind his head while staring at the ceiling. 'Let me see what my various colleagues might make of this. Impersonation of a public official, to begin with.' Then, seeing Meucci open his mouth to protest, 'You serve as a public official at the *macello,* Signore, whether you know it or not.' He saw Meucci register the truth of this.

'Let's see what else we have here, shall we? Illegal exercise of a profession. Fraud. Taking money under false pretences.' Brunetti allowed a menacing smile to cross his face. 'And if you've ever written a prescription for any of your patients, then there would be the illegal procurement of drugs; and if you've ever given an inoculation to an animal and been paid for it, there is also the illegal sale of and administration of drugs.'

'But they're animals,' Meucci protested.

'Indeed they are, Signor Meucci. Thus your lawyer will have an intriguing argument to present at your trial.'

'Trial?' Meucci asked.

'Well, it's likely to come to that, wouldn't

you say? You'll be arrested, of course, and your practice closed, and I imagine your clients — to make no mention of the management of the *macello* — will all sue you to return the money you took from them illegally.'

'But they *knew,*' Meucci bleated.

'Your clients?' Brunetti asked with feigned astonishment. 'But then why would they bring their animals to you?'

'No, no, not them. The people at the *macello.* They knew. Of course they knew. That was all part of it.'

Brunetti leaned forward and held up his hand. 'Shall I turn on the tape recorder before we continue this conversation, Signor Meucci?'

Meucci pulled the cigarettes out of his pocket and clasped his hands around the packet. He nodded.

Willing to accept a gesture as a response, Brunetti switched on the machine.

'You've just told me that the people at the *macello* in Preganziol hired you even though they knew you were not a veterinarian. That is, they employed you as a veterinarian while knowing that you had no licence. Is this correct, Signor Meucci?'

'Yes.'

'They knew you had no licence?'

'Yes,' Meucci said, then he snapped, 'I just told you that. How many times do I have to tell you?'

'As many as you like, Signor Meucci,' Brunetti said amiably. 'Hearing it repeated might serve to remind you that such an interesting fact needs some explanation.'

When Meucci did not speak, Brunetti asked, 'You said that the opening for the job was announced. Could you tell me how you learned of that announcement?'

Here it came, Brunetti knew: the moment when the person being questioned began to weigh the relative risk of little lies. Forget something here, leave out a name, change a date or a number, pass over a meeting as having been insignificant.

'Signor Meucci,' Brunetti said, 'I'd like to remind you how very important it is that you tell us everything you remember: all of the names and where and when you met the people, and what was said in your conversations. To the best of your ability.'

'And if I can't remember?' Meucci asked, but Brunetti heard fear in the question, not sarcasm.

'Then I'll give you time until you do remember, Signor Meucci.'

Meucci nodded again, and again Brunetti let the gesture serve in place of assent.

'How did you learn about the job at the *macello?*'

There was no hesitation in Meucci's voice as he said, 'The man who had it before I did called me one night — we were friends at university — and said he was going to quit, and he asked me if I would be interested in taking the job.'

'Did this friend know that you had not finished your studies?' Brunetti asked.

He saw Meucci prepare to lie and held up his right forefinger in a gesture his elementary religion teacher used to make.

'Probably,' Meucci finally said, and Brunetti gave him some credit for not wanting to shop a friend.

'And how did this occur, that you replaced him?'

'He spoke to someone there, and then I went out to the *macello* one day for an interview. It was explained what I had to do.'

'Was any mention made of your missing qualifications?'

'No.'

'Did you have to submit a curriculum vitae?'

After the briefest of hesitations, Meucci said, 'Yes.'

'Did you say in it that you had a degree in

veterinarian medicine?'

Voice softer, Meucci repeated, 'Yes.'

'Did you have to submit proof — photocopies of your degree?'

'I was told that wasn't necessary.'

'I see,' Brunetti said, then asked, 'Who told you this?'

Meucci, apparently unaware of what he was doing, took a cigarette out of the pack and put it in his mouth. He took out a lighter and lit the cigarette. Years ago, Brunetti had seen an old man step down from a train that had stopped at a station and light up, take three incredibly deep drags on a cigarette, then, at the sound of the conductor's whistle, pinch it out and put it back in the packet. Dragon breath issuing from his mouth, the old man had pulled himself back into the train just as it started to move. He sat and watched Meucci smoke the entire cigarette with the same blind avidity. When there was only the smallest stub left and the front of his jacket was covered with spilled ash, Meucci looked across at Brunetti.

Brunetti opened his middle drawer, took out a box of Fisherman's Friend, and poured them out. He shoved the box across to Meucci and watched as he stubbed out the cigarette.

'Who was it that told you the degree wasn't necessary?'

'Signorina Borelli,' Meucci said and lit another cigarette.

29

'She's Papetti's assistant, isn't she?' Brunetti asked, as if unfamiliar with her.

'Yes,' Meucci said.

'Who brought up the subject of your degree?'

'I did,' Meucci said, removing his cigarette from his mouth. 'I suppose I was nervous that she would find out, though Rub . . .' he stopped before pronouncing his predecessor's full name, as if too stunned by what was happening to realize his name would be public information. 'My colleague assured me it wouldn't matter. But I couldn't believe it. So I asked her if she had checked my file and if it was satisfactory.' He gave Brunetti a look that asked for his comprehension. 'I suppose I needed to know, really, that they knew I didn't have the licence, and that it didn't matter and wouldn't come back to haunt me.' Meucci looked away from Brunetti and out the window.

'And did it?' Brunetti asked with what sounded like real concern.

Meucci shrugged, crushed out his cigarette and reached for another, only to be stopped by Brunetti's glance.

'What do you mean?' Meucci asked, stalling.

'Did anyone at the *macello* ever try to make use of that information?'

Again Brunetti watched the fat man consider lying, saw him weigh the alternatives: which was the greater danger? Which would cost him less, the truth or a lie?

Like a drunkard who pours a bottle of whisky down the kitchen sink as proof of reformation, Meucci placed the crumpled packet of cigarettes on Brunetti's desk and lined it up carefully beside the tape recorder. 'It happened during my first week,' he said. 'A farmer from Treviso brought in some cows: I don't remember now how many: maybe six. Two of them were more dead than alive. One looked like it was dying of cancer: it had an open sore on its back. I didn't even bother to do an exam: anyone could see it was sick: skin and bones and saliva dripping from its mouth. The other one had viral diarrhoea.'

Meucci looked at the cigarettes, and went on. 'I told the knacker, Bianchi, that the farmer would have to take those two cows back and destroy them.' He looked at Brunetti and raised one of his hands towards him. 'After all, it was my job. To inspect them.' He stopped and made a heaving motion that could have been a shrug or an attempt to extricate himself from the constriction of the chair.

'What happened?' Brunetti asked.

'Bianchi told me to wait there with the cows and went to get Signorina Borelli. When she came and asked me what was going on, I told her to look at the cows and tell me if she thought they were healthy enough to be slaughtered.' His voice was filled with the sarcasm he could not use with Brunetti.

'And what did she say?'

'She barely looked at them.' Meucci, Brunetti could see, was back there, at the *macello,* having this conversation again. 'And she said,' he began, moving forward to bring his mouth closer to the tape recorder, 'she said, "They're as healthy as your application, Signor Meucci." ' He closed his eyes at the memory. 'She'd always called me Dottor Meucci before that. So I knew she knew.'

'And?' Brunetti asked after some time.

'And I knew that it had,' Meucci answered.

'Had what?'

'Come back to haunt me.'

'What did you do about the cows?' Brunetti asked.

'What do you think I did?' Meucci demanded indignantly. 'I certified them.'

'I see,' Brunetti said, forbidding himself to allow the words 'safe for human consumption' to pass his lips. He remembered then that Nava's wife had said her husband ate fruit and vegetables. 'And after that?' he asked calmly.

'After that I did what I was told to do. What else did you expect me to do?'

Ignoring that, Brunetti asked, 'Who told you what that was?'

'Bianchi was the one who told me that the average rate of rejection was about three per cent, so that's where I stayed: some months a little more, some a little less.' He paused to hoist himself up in his chair. 'At least I tried to condemn the worst of them. But so many of them were sick. I don't know what they feed them, or what medicines they pump into them, but some were disgusting.'

Ignoring the temptation to comment that this had not prevented Meucci from approving their entry into the food chain, Brunetti said, 'Bianchi told you, but someone must have told him.' When Meucci said nothing, Brunetti prodded him. 'Don't you think?'

'Of course,' Meucci answered, snatching back the cigarettes and lighting one. 'It was Borelli who gave him the orders: that's obvious. And that's what I did. Three per cent. Sometimes a little bit more, sometimes a little bit less. But always right around there.' It sounded, this time, like a kind of incantation.

'Did you ever speculate about who might be giving Signorina Borelli the orders?' Brunetti asked.

Meucci shook his head quickly, then said, 'No. That wasn't my business.'

Brunetti let a suitable amount of time pass and then asked, 'For how long did you do this?'

'Two years,' Meucci snapped, and Brunetti wondered how many kilos that represented in cancerous and diseased meat.

'Until what?'

'Until I went into the hospital and they had to hire someone else,' Meucci said.

He cared nothing about the cause, but aware of how useful a display of concern would seem, Brunetti asked, 'Why were you in the hospital, Signor Meucci?'

'Diabetes. I collapsed at home, and when I woke up I was in Intensive Care; it took them a week to find out what was wrong with me, and then two weeks to get me stabilized, and then a week at home.'

'I see,' Brunetti said, unable to say that he was sorry.

'At the end of the first week, they hired Nava.' He looked at Brunetti and said, 'You didn't believe me, did you? When I said I never met him? Well, I didn't. I don't know how they found him or who recommended him.' Meucci took visible pleasure in being able to say this.

'But you were lying when you said you didn't know I had been out to the *macello,* which means you were lying when you said you didn't keep in touch with anyone there.' He waited for Meucci to respond, and when he didn't, Brunetti snapped the whip. 'Doesn't it?'

'She called me,' Meucci said.

Brunetti thought it unnecessary to ask him whom he meant.

'She said she wanted me to go and work in Verona,' Meucci said with lowered eyes. 'But I told her about the diabetes and told her my doctor said I couldn't work until they had me stabilized.'

'Is that true?' Brunetti asked.

'No, but it got me out of having to go to Verona,' he said, sounding pleased with himself.

'To do the same thing?' Brunetti asked. 'In Verona?'

'Yes,' Meucci said. He opened his mouth to proclaim his virtue in having refused, but when he saw Brunetti's expression, he said nothing.

'Is she still in touch with you?' Brunetti asked, keeping to himself his knowledge that Meucci had called her.

Meucci nodded, and Brunetti pointed to the tape recorder. 'Yes.'

'What for?'

'She called me last week and said that Nava was gone and said I had to come back until they could find someone suitable.'

'What do you think she meant by "suitable"?' Brunetti asked calmly.

'What do *you* think she meant?' Meucci asked, finally using sarcasm with Brunetti.

'I'm afraid I'm the person who does the asking, Signor Meucci,' Brunetti said coldly.

Meucci sulked for a moment but then he answered. 'She wanted someone who would maintain the three per cent.'

'When did she tell you this?'

Meucci thought about this, then said, 'She called me on the first — I remember the date because it was my mother's birthday.'

'What did you say?'

'I didn't have much choice, did I?' Meucci asked with the petulance of a sixteen-year-old. And with the same moral clarity.

'If she wanted you to go to Verona,' Brunetti said, trying to clarify this, 'does it mean she's involved with other *macelli*?'

'Of course,' Meucci said, giving Brunetti a look that suggested *he* was the sixteen-year-old. 'There are five or six of them. Two near here and four more, I think, out around Verona: anyway, in the province. They belong to Papetti's father-in-law.' Then, unable to resist the temptation to goad Brunetti by showing that he knew something the other man did not, he asked, 'How else do you think Papetti would get a job like that?'

Ignoring Meucci's provocation, Brunetti asked, 'Have you ever been to any of the others?'

'No, but I know Bianchi's worked at two of them.'

'How do you know that?'

Surprised, Meucci said, 'We got on well, working together the way we did. He told me about it, said he preferred Preganziol because he knew the crew better.'

'I see,' Brunetti said neutrally, then asked, 'Do you know if she and Papetti are involved with them all?'

'They visit them occasionally.'

'Together?' Brunetti asked.

Meucci laughed out loud. 'You can put that idea out of your head, Commissario.' He laughed so long it started him coughing. Panicked, he tried to get up but remained trapped in the chair, which he managed to lift from the floor in his attempt to stand. Brunetti rose to go around his desk to try to do something, but Meucci forced himself to sit back. The coughing spluttered out. He reached over and took a cigarette, lit it, and pulled life-saving smoke deep into his lungs.

Brunetti asked, 'Why shouldn't I think about it, Signor Meucci?'

Meucci's eyes narrowed, and Brunetti saw the pleasure he could not disguise at having information that might be useful to Brunetti. Or to both of them. Meucci might be a coward, but he was not a fool.

Nor, it seemed, did he want to waste time. 'What do I get in exchange?' Meucci asked, stabbing out his cigarette.

Brunetti had known that something like this was bound to come, so he said, 'I leave you alone at your private practice, and you don't work in a slaughterhouse again.'

He watched Meucci calculate the offer,

and he watched him accept it. 'There's nothing between the two of them,' he said.

'How do you know?'

'She told Bianchi.'

'I beg your pardon?' Brunetti said.

'Yes, Bianchi. They're friends. Bianchi's gay. They just like one another, and they gossip together like teenagers: who they've had, who they'd like to have, what they did. She told him all about Nava and how easy he was. It was like a game to her, I think. Anyway, that's the way it sounded when Bianchi told me about it.'

Brunetti made sure he looked very interested in what the other man was saying. 'What else did Bianchi tell you?'

'That she tried with Papetti, but he almost wet his pants, he was so frightened.'

'Of her?' Brunetti asked, though he knew the answer.

'No, of course not. Of his father-in-law. He ever screw around on his wife, the old man would probably see he never did any screwing again.' Then, reflective and expansive, Meucci added, 'After all, the old guy's turned a blind eye to the way Papetti's been screwing the company for years, so it's obvious that it's only his daughter he cares about. She's in love with Papetti, so De Rivera lets him do whatever he wants. I guess it's worth it to him.'

Brunetti made no comment and, instead, asked, 'Why'd she bother with Nava?'

'The usual thing. She wanted him to approve the animals so they could get their cut from the farmers. The way it worked with my friend.'

'And with you,' Brunetti reminded him.

Meucci did not respond.

'But not with Nava?' Brunetti asked.

The thought of that restored Meucci's good humour and he said, 'No, not with Nava. Bianchi told me she was like a hyena. She fucked him, even told Bianchi how he was: not so great. And then he wouldn't do what she asked him to do. So she threatened to tell his wife. But it didn't work: he told her to go ahead, he still wouldn't — he said he couldn't, can you imagine that? — do it.'

'When did she threaten to tell his wife?'

Meucci closed his eyes to think. Opening them, he said, 'I don't remember exactly: at least a couple of months ago.' Seeing Brunetti trying to work out the timing, he said, 'She told Bianchi it took her almost two months to get him to fuck her, so it would have been after that that she asked him to approve the animals.'

Brunetti, deciding to change tack, said, 'The animals that are brought in — the sick ones, that is — why did Signorina Borelli want you to declare these animals healthy?'

Meucci stared at him. 'I just told you,' he said. 'Don't you get it?'

'I'd prefer that you explain it to me again, Signor Meucci,' said an imperturbable Brunetti, conscious of the future use that might be made of this recording.

With a small snort of disbelief or contempt, Meucci said, 'They pay her, of course. She and Papetti get a part of what they're paid for the animals once they're declared healthy. And since she works there, she knows exactly how much they get.' Before Brunetti could ask, he said, 'I have no idea, but from things I've heard, I'd guess their cut is about twenty-five per cent. Think about it. If the animal's condemned, the owners lose everything they would have got for it, and they have to pay to have it destroyed and then disposed of.' With an expression he probably supposed demonstrated virtue, Meucci said, 'I think it's a fair price, when you consider everything.'

After a reflective pause, Brunetti said, 'Certainly,' then, 'I hadn't thought of it that way.'

'Well, maybe you should,' Meucci said with the tone of the person who always had to have the last word.

Brunetti picked up his phone and dialled Pucetti's *telefonino* number.

When the young man answered, Brunetti said, 'Come up here, would you? I'd like you to take this witness downstairs to wait while a stenographer makes a copy of his statement. When it's ready, have him read it and sign it, would you? You and Foa can witness it.'

'Foa's gone, sir. His shift ended an hour ago, and he's gone home. But he gave me the list,' Pucetti said.

'What list?' Brunetti had to ask, still lost in the world of animals.

'The addresses of the houses along the canal, sir. That's what he told me.'

'Yes, good,' Brunetti said, remembering. 'Bring it up when you come, will you?'

'Of course, Commissario,' Pucetti said and hung up.

30

When Pucetti was gone, taking Meucci with him, Brunetti forced himself to resist the urge to open Foa's list immediately. Better to start with a careful reading of the file Signorina Elettra had compiled on Signorina Borelli. Four years at Tekknomed, which firm she left suddenly and under a cloud, only to move effortlessly into a much more highly paid position as the assistant to the son of Tekknomed's lawyer. Though he scorned the same prejudice in Patta and would confess his own only to Paola and then only when bamboo shoots were shoved under his fingernails, Brunetti considered a slaughterhouse an unseemly place for a woman to work, especially one as attractive as she. That being the case, one had then to consider what inducement might have taken her there.

Brunetti turned a page and studied the information on the properties she owned.

Neither her salary at Tekknomed nor that at the slaughterhouse would have allowed her to buy even one of them, let alone all three. The apartment in the centre of Mestre was one hundred metres. The two apartments in Venice were slightly smaller but, if rented to tourists and well managed, would earn her a few thousand Euros a month. So long as this rental income was not reported to the tax authorities, the total sum would equal her salary at the *macello,* no mean achievement for a woman in her early thirties. Added to this would be sums she was earning — though the use of that verb left Brunetti uncomfortable — from the various farmers who brought unhealthy animals to the slaughterhouse.

His mind fled to the scandal in Germany some years before of the dioxin-laden eggs that resulted from the deliberate contamination of livestock food. And then he remembered a dinner party soon thereafter at which the hostess, one of those upper-class women who grew more ingenuous with each passing year, had asked how people could possibly do such a thing. It had been with considerable restraint that Brunetti had stopped himself from shouting down the table at her: 'Greed, you fool. Greed.'

Brunetti had always assumed that most

people were strongly motivated by greed. Lust or jealousy might lead to impulsive actions or violence, but to explain most crimes, especially those that took place over time, greed was a better bet.

He set the file aside and picked up the list Pucetti had given him of the owners of the houses on either side of the Rio del Malpaga that corresponded with the water doors he had seen. The search for their names, Brunetti assumed, would have taken hours of patient research among the chaotic records in the Ufficio Catasto.

He ran his eye down the first page, not at all sure what he was looking for or, indeed, that he was looking for anything. Near the middle of the second page, his eye fell upon the name 'Borelli'. The hairs on the back of his neck rose as a chill slithered across his flesh. He set the papers down very gently and spent some time aligning them with the front edge of his desk. When that was done to his satisfaction, he stared at the opposite wall and shifted pieces of information around, fitting them into different scenarios, leaving pieces out or shifting them to new places.

He reached for the phone and dialled the number on the front of the folder on his desk. She answered on the third ring.

'Borelli.' Direct, no nonsense, just like a man.

'Signorina Borelli,' he said, 'this is Commissario Brunetti.'

'Ah, Commissario, I hope you saw everything,' she said in a voice entirely without nuance or suggestion of hidden meaning.

'Yes, we stayed,' Brunetti said. 'But I doubt we saw everything that goes on there.'

That gave her pause, but after a moment she said, 'I'm not sure I understand you entirely, Commissario.'

'I meant that we still don't have a full understanding of everything that goes on at the slaughterhouse, Signorina.'

'Oh,' was all she said.

'I'd like you to come in to the Questura and talk about it.'

'I'm very busy.'

'I'm sure you can make time to come in and have a talk,' Brunetti said, voice level.

'But I'm not sure that I can, Signore,' she insisted.

'It might be easier,' Brunetti suggested.

'Than?'

'Than my asking a magistrate for an arrest warrant and having you brought here under duress.'

'Duress, Commissario?' she asked with

what she tried to make sound like a flirtatious laugh.

'Duress.' No flirting. No laugh.

After pausing long enough to allow Brunetti to add something if he chose, she finally said, 'Your tone makes me wonder if I should bring a lawyer with me.'

'As you please,' Brunetti answered.

'Oh my, as serious as all that?' she said, but she didn't have the gift of irony, and the question fell flat.

Brunetti knew what she would say and what she would do. Greed. Mindless, atavistic greed. Think what a lawyer would cost. If she could talk her way out of it, there would be no need of a lawyer, would there? So why pay one to come along? Surely she was smarter than some timeserving policeman, wasn't she?

'When would you like me to come in?' she said with sudden docility.

'As soon as you can, Signorina,' Brunetti replied.

'I could come in after lunch,' she conceded. 'About four?'

'Very good.' Brunetti was careful not to thank her. 'I'll expect you then.'

He went immediately down to Patta's office and told him about Signorina Borelli's apartment on the canal where the dead man was found. Recalling the missing shoe and the scrapes on the back of Nava's heel, Brunetti said, 'The scientific boys might want to go over the place.'

'Of course, of course,' Patta said, quite as though he was just about to suggest it.

Leaving it to his superior to get the magistrate's order, Brunetti excused himself and returned to his own office.

When the man at the front door called Brunetti at ten minutes after four to tell him he had a visitor, Brunetti said that Vianello would go down to meet her, having arranged it this way to ensure the Inspector's presence during their conversation.

Brunetti looked up when he saw them at the door: the large man and the small woman. He wondered about that, had wondered about that ever since the idea had first come to him. He had taken another look at Rizzardi's report and seen that there were holes in Nava's shirt and traces of cotton fibres in the wounds. So it had not been a lovers' quarrel, or at least not one that had taken place in bed. The trajectory of the wounds — Brunetti doubted that was the correct word — had been upward, so the person standing behind him had been shorter than he.

Habit brought Brunetti to his feet. He said

good afternoon and waved them to the chairs in front of him; Vianello waited and when she was seated took the other chair and pulled out his notebook. She looked at the tape recorder, then at Brunetti.

Brunetti switched the machine on and said, 'Thank you for coming in, Signorina Borelli.'

'You didn't leave me much choice, did you, Commissario?' she asked, her tone halfway between anger and light-heartedness.

Brunetti ignored the tone, just as he ignored the idea that this woman could have any lightness of heart, and said, 'I explained the choices open to you, Signorina.'

'And do you think I've made the right one?' she asked, almost as if she could not break herself of the habit of flirtatiousness.

'We'll see,' Brunetti responded.

Vianello crossed his legs and riffled through the pages of his notebook.

'Could you tell me where you were on Sunday evening?'

'I was at my home.'

'Which is where, Signorina?'

'Mestre, Via Mantovani 17.'

'Was anyone with you?'

'No.'

'Could you tell me what you did that

evening?'

She looked at him, then off towards the window, while memory returned to her. 'I went to the cinema, an early showing.'

'What film, Signorina?'

'Città aperta,' she said. 'It was part of a Rossellini retrospective.'

'Did anyone go with you?' Brunetti asked.

'Yes. Maria Costantini. She lives in the building next to mine.'

'And after that?'

'I went home.'

'With Signora Costantini?'

'No. Maria was going to have dinner with her sister, so I went home alone. I had some dinner, then I watched television, and I went to bed early. I have to be at work early: at six.'

'Did anyone call you that evening?'

She considered that, then said, 'No, not that I recall.'

'Could you give me an idea of your duties at the *macello* in Preganziol?' Brunetti asked, as if he'd heard enough about her activities on Sunday evening.

'I'm Dottor Papetti's assistant.'

'And your duties, Signorina?'

Vianello filled the room with the sound of a turning page.

'I plan the timetable for the workers, both

the knackers and the cleaning crew; I keep track of the numbers of animals brought in to the *macello,* of the total quantity of meat that is produced each day; I keep the farmers current with the directives that come down from Brussels.'

'What sort of directives?' Brunetti interrupted to ask.

'Methods of slaughtering, how the animals are to be brought in to the *macello,* where and how they are to be kept if they have to wait a day, or more, before slaughter.' She looked at him and tilted her head to one side as if asking him if she should continue.

'The matter of price, Signorina, of what a kilo of a particular cut of meat is worth: who determines that?'

'The market,' she answered immediately. 'The market and the season and the quantity of meat available at any given time.'

'And the quality?'

'I beg your pardon,' she said.

'The quality of the meat, Signorina,' Brunetti said. 'Whether an animal is healthy and can be slaughtered. Who determines that?'

'The veterinarian,' she said, 'not me.'

'And how does he judge the health of an animal?' Brunetti asked as Vianello turned another page.

'That's what he went to university for, presumably,' she said, and Brunetti realized he had goaded her or come close to doing so, surprised at himself for choosing this word.

'So that he can identify animals that are too sick to be slaughtered?'

'I should certainly hope so,' she said, but she said it too forcefully, making it sound false, not only to Brunetti but, he suspected, to herself.

'What happens if he judges that an animal is not suitable to be slaughtered?'

'Do you mean not healthy enough?' she asked.

'Yes.'

'Then the animal is given back to the farmer who brought it, and he is responsible for disposing of it.'

'Could you tell me how that is done?'

'The animal has to be slaughtered and destroyed.'

'Destroyed?'

'Burned.'

'How much does this cost?'

'I have no . . .' she started to say, then realized how hollow that would sound and changed her sentence. '. . . way to give you a fixed sum for that. It would depend on the weight of the animal.'

'But, presumably, it would be a significant sum?' he asked.

'I would think so,' she agreed. Then, reluctantly, 'As much as four hundred Euros.'

'So it's in the best interests of the farmers to bring only healthy animals to the *macello*?' Brunetti asked, making it a question, though it really was not.

'Yes. Of course.'

'Dottor Andrea Nava was employed as the veterinarian at the *macello*,' Brunetti began.

'Is that a question?' she interrupted.

'No, it is a statement,' Brunetti said. 'My question is what your relationship with him was.'

The question seemed not to surprise her in the least, but she paused a bit before she answered. 'He was employed by the *macello*, as I was, so I suppose you would say we were colleagues.'

Brunetti folded his hands neatly on the desk in front of him, a gesture he had seen his professors use when a student failed to supply an adequate answer. He remembered, as well, the technique of the long silence, one that almost invariably proved successful with the most insecure students. He looked at Signorina Borelli, at the view from his window, and then back to her.

'And that was the extent of it?' he asked.

If he had only imagined her response to the thought of hiring a lawyer, this time he could watch her think the problem through. She wanted to stall him so as to have more time to work out how much she could admit, though surely she must have known this question was bound to be asked.

Finally she shrugged and gave a raffish smile. 'Well, not really. We had sex a few times, but it was nothing serious.'

'Where?' Brunetti asked.

'Where what?' she asked, genuinely confused.

'Where did you have sex?'

'A couple of times at his place, the one above his office, and in the changing room at the *macello*.' Then, as an afterthought, 'Once in my office.' She tilted her chin to one side and gave his question the thought she believed it deserved. 'I think that's all.'

'How long did this affair go on?' Brunetti asked.

She looked up at him, either surprised or pretending to be. 'Oh, it wasn't an affair, Commissario. It was sex.'

'I see,' Brunetti said, accepting the reprimand. 'How long did it go on?'

'From a few months after he started work until about three months ago.'

'What caused it to end?' Brunetti asked.

She dismissed the question, perhaps even the answer, as uninteresting. 'It stopped being fun,' she said. 'I thought it would be convenient for us both, but the first thing I knew, he was talking about us as a couple, with a future.' She shook her head at this. 'You'd think he'd forgotten he had a wife and child.'

'You hadn't forgotten it, Signorina?' he asked.

'Of course not,' she said hotly. 'That's why married men are so convenient: you know either one of you can end it when you want, and no one's hurt.'

'But he didn't see it that way?'

'Apparently not.'

'What did he want?'

'I have no idea. As soon as he started talking about a future, I told him it was over. *Finito. Basta.*' She moved around in her chair, rather like an angry chicken fluffing out its feathers. 'I didn't need that.'

'You mean his attentions?' Brunetti asked.

'The whole thing: call them attentions if you want. I didn't want to listen to his guilt and his remorse and how he was betraying his wife. And I wanted to be able to go out to dinner or for a drink without having the man I was with looking over his shoulder every second, as if he were a criminal.' She sounded genuinely angry; Brunetti had no doubt that she was, and had been, though perhaps not for those reasons.

'Or as if you were,' Brunetti said.

That stopped her. She hesitated, and just as it became too late for her to ask what he meant, she finally forced herself to say it. 'What do you mean?'

As if she had not spoken, Brunetti went on, 'You said that one of his duties was to inspect the animals brought into the *macello* to see if they were healthy enough to be slaughtered.'

Taken aback by his change of pace, she agreed, 'Yes.'

'From the time Dottor Nava took the position as veterinarian at the *macello,* there was a sudden increase in the number of animals declared unfit to be slaughtered.' He paused, and when she did not acknowledge the truth of this, he broke into the silence of her hesitation by saying, 'Before he began to inspect the animals, the average rate of rejection — if I might call it that — was about three per cent, yet as soon as Dottor Nava began, that rate tripled, then quadrupled, and then went even higher.'

Brunetti studied her response: none was evident. 'Can you explain that, Signorina?'

She brought her lips together, as if in consideration of his question, and then said, 'I think you'll have to ask Bianchi about that.'

'You didn't know about the increase?' he asked with false surprise.

'Of course I knew about it,' she said, unable to disguise her satisfaction in being able to correct him. 'But I had, and have, no idea of the cause.'

'Did you speculate about what it might be?' Brunetti asked, expecting that she would try to answer this: it would make sense for someone in her position to be involved in the discussion.

After some time, she said, 'I don't like to say it.' And then didn't.

'Say what?' Brunetti asked.

With great evidence of reluctance, she said, voice hesitant, 'One of the suggestions that was made — I don't remember who made it — was that maybe the farmers were trying to unload sick animals on the new veterinarian. That they thought they'd test the new man and see how severe he was.' She gave an awkward smile, as though embarrassed to have to give voice to this example of human duplicity.

'The test went on a long time,' Brunetti said drily. At her look, he added, 'The numbers kept rising, didn't they?' Then, before she could answer, he added, 'Right up until his death.'

She raised her brows to acknowledge either ignorance or incomprehension. But she said nothing.

Vianello turned another page. Signorina Borelli and Brunetti looked at one another, each waiting for the other to speak. For a moment, neither did.

But then Brunetti asked, wanting to have it in her own words, 'Could you tell me something about your relationship with Dottor Papetti?'

This question surprised her. ' "Relationship"?' she asked.

'He hired you as his assistant after you were let go from your previous job, presumably without any good recommendation.' That Brunetti had this information seemed to surprise her even more. 'Thus my question: "Relationship".'

She laughed. It was an honest, musical laugh. When she stopped, she said, voice tight with the anger she was growing tired of suppressing, 'You men really can think of only one thing, can't you? He was my boss; we worked together; and that's all.'

'So there was no sexual link between you, as there was with Dottor Nava?'

'You've seen him, haven't you, Commissario? You think any woman would find him attractive?' Then, as if to expand the impossibility, 'Desirable?' She laughed again, and Brunetti finally understood the biblical passage, 'They laughed him to scorn.' Then, with acid audible in her voice, she added, 'Besides, he knows if he ever looked at another woman, his little Natasha's daddy would have his legs broken the same day.' She began another sentence, perhaps having to do with other things that his father-in-law would do, but contented herself with a mere 'Or worse.'

'So you were never lovers?'

'If you find these questions get you excited, Commissario, I have to put an end to your pleasure. No, Alessandro Papetti and I were never lovers. He tried to kiss me once, but I'd rather fuck one of the knackers.' She gave him a saccharine smile. 'Does that answer your question?'

'Thank you for coming in, Signorina,' he said. 'If we have more questions, we'll ask to speak to you again.'

'You mean I can go?' she asked and immediately saw this was the wrong thing to say.

Impulsive, Brunetti thought. Very pretty and probably charming when she wanted to be or when it served her purposes. He looked at her attractive face and thought of what she had said about Nava and was chilled to realize that the appearance of cold-heartedness was not an attempt to distance herself from Nava but simply the way she was.

Both men got to their feet, and then she did. Vianello opened the door for her. She turned away from Brunetti silently and walked from the office. Vianello followed her, and Brunetti went to stand by the window.

A few minutes later he saw the top of her head appear on the pavement below him, and then the rest of her as she walked to the left and disappeared.

Still watching the place where she had been, he heard Vianello come back. 'Well?' the Inspector said.

'I think it's time we had another conversation with Dottor Papetti,' Brunetti said. 'But let's do it here. He's sure to be more uncomfortable.'

31

The next morning, Papetti, unlike his personal assistant, arrived in the company of his lawyer. Brunetti knew Avvocato Torinese, a solid, reliable criminal lawyer with a clean reputation. Brunetti had been expecting one of the many sharks which lurked in the waters of criminal justice in the city and in the wider world and was pleased to see Torinese, who, though clever and capable of legal surprises, played more or less by the book; one did not have to fear bribed witnesses or false medical claims.

The two men sat facing Brunetti, Vianello sitting on a wooden chair he carried over from beside the closet. Once again, there were both the tape recorder and Vianello's notebook; and then Torinese took a tape recorder from his briefcase and placed it not far from Brunetti's.

Brunetti studied the two men for a moment: even seated, Papetti towered over his lawyer, who was by no means a short man. Torinese snapped his briefcase closed and set it to the left of his chair. Brunetti and Torinese both leaned forward at the same moment and switched on their tape recorders.

'Dottor Torinese,' Brunetti began formally, 'I'd like to thank you and your client, Dottor Papetti, Alessandro Papetti, for coming to see me so quickly. There are certain matters I would like to clarify, and I think your client can be of service to me in this.'

'And those matters are?' Torinese asked. He was about Brunetti's age, though he looked older, with his horn-rimmed glasses and hair slicked back from a widow's peak. No tailor in Venice had the talent to have made his suit, nor had any of the shoemakers made those shoes. The thought of expensive shoes brought Brunetti's mind back to the matter at hand.

'First, there is the murder of Dottor Andrea Nava, who worked at the slaughterhouse of which Dottor Papetti is the director,' he supplied. 'I've already spoken to Dottor Papetti about this, but since then I have come into possession of new information, and that makes it necessary for me to ask the Dottore more questions.' Brunetti knew that the demon of formality had taken over his speech, but in his awareness that everything they said would eventually be printed out, signed, dated, and entered into the public record, he could not behave otherwise.

He saw Torinese preparing to speak and so went on, 'Avvocato, I would like, if you would permit it, not to have to filter everything through you.' Before the lawyer could object, Brunetti said, 'I believe this would make things easier, both for me and for your client. You have the right, of course, to interrupt whenever you see fit to do so, but it would be better for your client — and I can ask only that you invest me with your confidence in this — if we could speak directly.'

As Torinese and Papetti exchanged a glance, Brunetti's mind wandered to a phrase — he wondered why his thoughts kept retreating to the Bible — 'You have been weighed in the balance.' He waited, wondering whether the two men would find him wanting.

Apparently they did not, for Papetti, after a brief nod from his lawyer, said, 'I'll speak to you, Commissario. Though I must say it's like speaking to a different man from the one who came to my office.'

'I'm the same man, Dottore: I assure you

of that. I'm merely better prepared than I was the last time we spoke.' Presumably, if Papetti now believed he was not an incompetent, he would be better prepared, as well.

'Prepared by what?' Papetti asked.

'As I told Avvocato Torinese, by new information.'

'And prepared *for* what?' Papetti asked.

Brunetti turned his attention to Torinese and said, 'I will set the example for this conversation by telling you both the truth.' And then to Papetti, 'To find out the extent of your involvement in the death of Dottor Nava.'

Neither man showed surprise. Torinese, after decades of experience with sudden accusations of all sorts, was probably immune to surprise. Papetti, however, looked distressed but failed to disguise it.

Brunetti went on, speaking to Papetti, suspecting he had not had time to explain everything to Torinese. 'We are by now aware of what was going on at the *macello*.' Brunetti paused, to give Papetti the opportunity to ask for an explanation of that, but he did not.

'And, given that we are now talking about murder, the legal consequences to anyone who attempts to obscure the truth of anything surrounding the murder are much more severe, something I'm sure needs no explaining to you.' When he saw that they understood, he added, 'I'm sure the men who work at the *macello* will understand this as well.' Brunetti paused to let this register. 'Thus I assume,' he continued, 'that the men who work there, especially Bianchi, will be willing to tell us what they know, either about the murder or the lesser crimes.' Brunetti was careful not to name these lesser crimes, curious to see how Papetti would react.

Torinese, for all his training and experience, could not stop himself from glancing at his client. Papetti, however, ignored him, his attention on Brunetti, as if willing him to reveal more.

Brunetti slid the papers on his desk closer and studied them for a moment, then said, 'I'd like to begin by asking you, Dottor Papetti, to tell me where you were on the night of the seventh.' Then, just in case Papetti might have trouble recalling the date, he clarified by saying, 'That's the night between Sunday and Monday.'

Papetti glanced aside at Torinese, who said, 'My client was at home, with his wife and children.' The fact that Torinese was able to answer this question meant that Papetti had both expected it and understood its importance.

'I expect you can prove this,' Brunetti observed mildly.

Both men nodded, and Brunetti did not bother to ask for details.

'That, as you must know,' he said, speaking directly to Papetti, 'is the night Dottor Nava was killed.' He let this register before saying, 'We can, of course, confirm your statement by an examination of the records of your *telefonino*.'

'I didn't call anyone,' Papetti said, and then, aware that his response had come too quickly, added, 'At least I don't remember calling anyone.'

'As soon as we have the authorization from a magistrate, we can help you remember, Dottor Papetti. As well as whether you received any calls,' Brunetti said with his blandest smile. 'The records will also tell us where the phone was during that night, if it was moved away from your home for any reason.' He watched Papetti as the realization smashed upon him: the computer chip in his phone left a geographic signal that could be traced and would be traced.

'I might have had to go out,' Papetti said; the look Torinese gave him was a confirmation to Brunetti of the lawyer's ignorance. And a moment later, the hardening of his look was confirmation of his anger at this fact.

'To Venice, by any chance?' Brunetti inquired in a voice so light and friendly it held out the promise that he would follow an affirmative response with a series of suggestions for quaint points of artistic interest in the city.

Papetti seemed to disappear for a moment. He stared at the two tape recorders so intently that Brunetti all but heard the gears in his mind working as he tried to adjust to the new reality created by his *telefonino*'s betrayal.

Papetti began to cry but seemed unaware of it. The tears ran down his face and chin and under the collar of his freshly ironed white shirt as he continued to watch the red lights on the tape recorders.

Finally Torinese said, 'Alessandro, stop it.'

Papetti looked at him, a man old enough to be his father, a man who was perhaps a professional colleague of his father, and nodded. He wiped his face with the inside of his sleeve and said, 'She called me. On my *telefonino.*'

At this point, Torinese astonished Brunetti by saying, 'The phone records will all have the exact times, Alessandro.' The sadness in his voice made it clear to Brunetti that he must be a colleague, perhaps a friend, of Papetti's father, perhaps of the man himself.

Papetti returned his attention to the tape recorder. As if speaking for the first time, he said, 'I had dinner with a friend in Venice. It was for business. We were at Il Testiere and they know him, so they'll remember us, that we were both there. After dinner, my friend went home and I went for a walk.'

He looked across at Brunetti. 'I know that sounds strange, but I like being in the city by myself, with no people, and I wanted to be alone.' Before Brunetti could ask, he added, 'I called my wife and told her how beautiful it was. That will be on your records, too.'

Brunetti nodded, and Papetti went on. 'She called me about midnight.' Brunetti did not ask Papetti to confirm that he was speaking about Signorina Borelli: the records would do that.

'She told me to meet her at the new dock on the Zattere, down by San Basilio. I asked her what she wanted, but she wouldn't tell me.'

'Did you go?' Brunetti asked.

'Of course I went,' Papetti said savagely. 'I always have to do what she says.'

Torinese cleared his throat, but neither Brunetti nor Vianello said a word.

'When I met her there, she took me back to a house. I'm not sure where it is.' Having said that, Papetti looked around and explained, 'I'm not Venetian, so I get lost.'

Brunetti permitted himself a nod.

'When we went in, there was a kind of entrance hall, with windows at the back and a few stairs. Going down, not up. She took me over, and I saw a man's feet sticking out of the water, on the steps. His feet and legs. But his head was in the water.' Papetti looked at the floor.

'Nava?' Brunetti asked.

'I didn't know when I first saw him,' Papetti said, raising his eyes to Brunetti's. He shook his head and added, 'But I knew. I mean I didn't see, but I knew. Who else could it be?'

'Why did you think it had to be Nava?' Brunetti asked. Torinese sat quietly, his face wiped of all expression, as though he were on a train, eavesdropping on a conversation in the seat in front of him.

Papetti repeated dully, 'Who else could it be?'

'Why did she call you?'

Papetti held up his hands and looked at them, one after the other. 'She wanted to put him in the canal, but she couldn't open the water door. It was . . . the metal bar that held it closed . . . was rusted shut.'

Brunetti decided to let Papetti decide when to speak again. At least a minute passed, during which Torinese examined the backs of his own hands, which were placed on his thighs.

'She had tried to hit it open with the heel of his shoe. But it wouldn't open. So she called me.'

'And what did you do?' Brunetti asked after a long wait.

'I pulled it open. I had to step into the water to get close enough to the door to open it.'

'And then?' Brunetti asked.

'Then we pushed him out into the water; then I closed the door and bolted it.'

'And Signorina Borelli?' Brunetti asked. One of the tape recorders made a whirring noise and the red blinked off. Torinese leaned forward and pushed a button: the red light went on again.

'She told me to go home, said she was going home.'

'Did she tell you what happened?'

'No. Nothing. She asked me to open the door and then to help her push him down the steps.'

'And you did.'

'I didn't have any choice, did I?' Papetti

asked and looked down again, silent.

Papetti licked his lips, sucked them into his mouth, then licked them again. 'We've known one another a long time.'

Calmly, Brunetti asked, 'And that gave her that much power over you?'

Papetti opened his mouth, but no sound emerged. He gave a small cough and said, 'I once . . . I once did something indiscreet.' And then he stopped.

'With Signorina Borelli?' Brunetti asked.

'Yes.'

'Did you have an affair with her?'

Papetti's eyes widened in shock. 'Good God, no.'

'What happened?'

Papetti closed his eyes and said, 'I tried to kiss her.'

Brunetti shot a glance at Vianello, who raised his eyebrows.

'That's all?' Brunetti asked.

Papetti looked at him. 'Yes. But it was enough.'

'Enough for what?'

'For her to get the idea.' When Brunetti failed to understand, Papetti said, 'About telling my father-in-law.' Then after a moment, he added, 'Or she planned it and that's why she asked for a ride home. She said her car was in for servicing.' Papetti ran both hands across his scalp. 'Or it really was. I don't know.' Then, fiercely, 'I'm a fool.'

Brunetti said nothing.

Voice unsteady, Papetti said, 'He'd kill me.' Then he asked, 'What else could I do?'

It seemed to Brunetti that he had passed his entire life hearing people ask that same question. Only once, about fifteen years ago, had a man who had strangled three prostitutes said, 'I liked it when they screamed.' Though it had chilled Brunetti's blood to hear it then, and still did to remember it, the man had at least spoken the truth.

'After you put the body in the water, what did you do, Signor Papetti?' he asked, deciding there was no way to prove or disprove Papetti's story. What was not in question was the woman's power over him.

'I went back to Piazzale Roma and got my car and went home.'

'Have you seen Signorina Borelli since then?'

'Yes. At the *macello.*'

'Has either of you spoken about this?'

Puzzled, Papetti asked, 'No, why should we?'

'I see,' Brunetti answered. Turning to Torinese, Brunetti said, 'If you have anything to say to your client, Avvocato, my colleague and I can leave you here for a while.'

Torinese shook his head, then said, 'No, I have nothing to say.'

'Then I would like to ask Dottor Papetti,' Brunetti went on, 'to tell me something more about the way things work at the *macello*.' Torinese, he noticed, was understandably surprised by his question. His client had just confessed to helping to dispose of the body of a murder victim, and the police wanted to know about his job. To prevent Papetti from wasting time and energy by looking surprised too, Brunetti said, 'Certain suspicions have arisen about the safety of the meat being produced there.'

'Suspicion is not the same thing as information,' Torinese interjected, making one of those distinctions that earn lawyers hundreds of Euros an hour.

'Thank you for that point of law, Avvocato,' Brunetti answered.

The lawyer looked across at Brunetti as if in search of clarification. 'Forgive me for being vulgar, Commissario, but am I correct in assuming that we are involved in a bargaining session here?' Knowing his gesture would not appear on the tape, Brunetti gave a small nod. 'In which case I would like to know what sort of an offer you might be making my client in return for whatever information he might have to give you.'

Brunetti had to compliment the man on the eloquence of his vagueness: 'assuming', 'would like', 'might', and 'might' again. For a moment, he considered decapitating Torinese and using his smoked head as a bookend, so perfect did he find his attention to the niceties of language. Casting away that thought, he said, 'The only offer I can make is the continued goodwill of your client's father-in-law.'

That stopped them. Papetti's mouth dropped open, and Brunetti thought he was going to begin to cry again. Instead, he looked at Torinese, as if waiting for him to speak, then back at Brunetti. 'I don't know what . . .' he started to say.

Torinese gave his client a quick look and tried to take over. 'If you could clarify your statement, Commissario, I'm sure both my client and I would be very pleased.'

Brunetti waited for the colour to return to Papetti's face; when it did, he said, careful to speak to Torinese, 'I'm sure your client understands my meaning. The last thing, the very last thing, I would like to see happen is for Dottor Papetti's father-in-law to misunderstand the nature of his relationship with any of the employees at the *macello.*' Papetti stared at him, face blank, mouth open just the least little bit.

Brunetti gave him the merest glance and returned his attention to the lawyer. 'That Dottor Papetti's father-in-law would confuse professional intimacy with intimacy of another kind: I dread the possibility that something like that might happen.' He smiled to show his opinion of the rashness of men and of how terribly prone to it some of them were. 'Such a misunderstanding might upset Signor De Rivera, to make no mention of his daughter, Dottor Papetti's wife, and I would never want to feel in any way responsible for the possible consequences of that error.' He turned to Papetti and gave him a smile that was an exercise in compassionate fellow feeling. 'I couldn't live with myself were that to happen.'

Papetti's right hand lifted and moved towards his head, but he caught it in time and returned it to his thigh. Ignoring the glance Torinese shot him, he said, 'She started an affair with Dottor Nava after he began to work at the slaughterhouse.'

'She started it?' Brunetti asked, placing special emphasis on the personal pronoun.

'Yes.'

'Why?'

'To get a hold on Nava. She knew he was

married, and it was obvious that he was a decent man.' Papetti shook his head at his lawyer to stop him from speaking. 'We had to pay the ones who came before him; not all that much, but still we paid them. She wanted to save money, so she began the affair, and then, when she was sure that Nava was deeply involved with her,' he began, leaving the three other men in the room to imagine what this might entail, 'she told him she was going to tell his wife that they were lovers unless he changed his behaviour at the *macello*.'

'Changed it how?' Brunetti asked to nudge him along.

'Stopped condemning so many animals as unhealthy.'

'Why would she want to do that?' Brunetti asked, aware that Torinese's head was moving back and forth as if he were watching a tennis match.

'Because she was . . .' Papetti began but was cut short by a savage glance from Brunetti. 'Because she and I,' he amended, 'were paid by the farmers to see that most of the animals brought in for slaughter would be accepted.'

No one spoke, all of them waiting to see how much more he would reveal. 'There was a certain amount of money involved.'

Before anyone could ask, he said, 'A lot of money.'

'What was your share?' Brunetti asked, using a soft voice and asking in the plural.

'Twenty-five per cent,' Papetti said.

'Of?'

'Of the price the farmers got if the sick animals weren't condemned and could be slaughtered.'

Though Torinese tried to disguise it, Brunetti could see that he was startled, perhaps even something stronger than that.

'These animals, Dottor Papetti, the ones that Dottor Nava condemned: what sort of diseases did they have?'

Evasively, Papetti said, 'The usual ones.'

Torinese, in a voice that had suddenly grown dry, asked, 'What ones?'

'TB, digestion problems, cancer, viruses, worms. Most of the diseases animals can have. Some of them looked like they'd been eating contaminated fodder.'

'And what happened to them?' Torinese asked almost as if he could not stop himself.

'They were slaughtered,' Papetti said.

'And then?' Again, it was his lawyer who asked the question.

'They were used.'

'As?'

'Meat.'

Torinese gave his client a long look and then turned his attention away from him.

'And this was a profitable business for you and Signorina Borelli?' Brunetti asked.

Papetti nodded.

'You have to speak your answer, Dottore,' Brunetti informed him. 'Or else it won't appear on the transcript.'

'Yes.'

'Did Dottor Nava agree to stop condemning the animals?'

It took some time, but finally Papetti said, 'No.'

'Did you and Signorina Borelli discuss the financial consequences of his refusal?'

'Yes.'

'And what did you decide to do?'

Papetti thought about this before he answered. 'I wanted to fire him. But Giulia — Signorina Borelli, that is — wanted to try to threaten him first. I told you: she'd already begun an affair with him as a kind of insurance policy if he didn't agree to do it, so she threatened to tell his wife.'

'What happened?' Brunetti asked.

Papetti rolled his eyes back in his head, as if imitating the actions of a lunatic. 'He told his wife. Or at least that's what he told Giulia: that he went home and told her about the affair.'

'And what did the wife do?' Brunetti asked, sounding completely ignorant about the matter.

'She told him to get out,' Papetti said in the voice one uses for recounting signs and portents, wonders and miracles.

'And?'

'He left. And the wife went ahead and asked for a legal separation.' Unable to stifle his astonishment, he said, 'For an affair.'

'And, surely, you both must have been concerned that Nava would tell someone what was going on,' Brunetti said calmly, stating the most natural thing in the world.

Papetti pursed his lips and then rubbed at them, seeking the proper way to say it. 'I didn't think I was at much risk,' he finally conceded.

'Because of your father-in-law's connections?' Brunetti asked. Torinese was back, watching the match again.

Papetti raised his hands and let them fall to his thighs again. 'I'd rather not say. But I didn't have to worry, not really.'

'About an investigation?'

Papetti nodded.

'Protected by someone concerned with public health?' Brunetti asked.

Papetti's grimace was strained. 'I'd really rather not say.'

'Did Signorina Borelli share your sense of ease about an investigation?'

Papetti thought for a long time, and Brunetti saw the moment when he realized the profit to be had. 'No,' he said.

Before Brunetti could formulate another question, Papetti went on, 'She was angry — I think I could say very angry — about the loss.'

'Loss?' Torinese asked from the sidelines.

'Of money,' Papetti said in a quick, impatient voice. 'That's all she cares about, really. Making money. So as long as Nava was there, she was losing a lot of money every month.'

'How much?' Brunetti asked.

'Close to two thousand Euros. It depended on how many animals were brought in.'

'And she objected?' Brunetti asked.

Papetti actually sat up higher in his chair before he asked, 'Most people would, don't you think?'

'Of course,' Brunetti acquiesced in face of the reprimand, then asked, 'How was it left between you?'

'She said she'd try to talk to him one more time. Maybe persuade him to quit. Or to ask him if he'd let Bianchi do some of the inspecting.'

'He knew what was going on, this

Bianchi?' Brunetti asked, quite as though it were in doubt.

'Of course,' Papetti shot back.

'And it was left like this? That she would ask him?'

'Yes.'

'And was any of this on your mind when she called you at midnight and said she had to see you?'

Papetti shrugged. 'I suppose it was. But I never thought she'd do something like that.'

'Like what, Signor Papetti?' Brunetti demanded.

All Papetti could do was shrug.

32

Well, thought Brunetti, here we are. Two of us and two of them, and everything is clear, at least clear to anyone who wants to understand. He looked across at Torinese: the lawyer had returned to the contemplation of his hands, sufficient sign that he now had a more comprehensive idea of his client's involvement in the story of Dottor Andrea Nava. Brunetti leaned forward and switched off both tape recorders: neither Papetti nor Torinese objected.

The silence expanded, each moment making it more difficult to break. Brunetti decided to see where it led. Vianello, he noticed, kept his head down, eyes on his notes. Torinese continued the study of his hands, while Papetti looked at his lawyer and then, it appeared, at the feet of Brunetti's desk.

After an eternity, Papetti said, clearing his throat before he spoke, 'Commissario, you mentioned your concern for my father-in-law.' Did his voice grow less steady as he pronounced that title?

Brunetti met his eyes but said nothing, waiting.

'Could you be clearer about what you mean? Specifically, that is.'

'I mean that your father-in-law, when the information about Signorina Borelli reaches the press, might come to the hasty conclusion that there was something other than a common economic interest between the two of you.' He gave a smile, the sort men use when it's just men talking together, and about women. 'She's a very attractive young woman, and she certainly sounds available.' That word, which would usually, in a conversation among men, sound like a promise, now fell upon Papetti's ears like the threat it was.

Papetti cleared his throat again. 'But I never . . .' He smiled, as if he remembered that he was in a room with other guys and there was a way they had to talk to one another. 'I mean, it's not that I didn't want to. You know that. As you said, she's an attractive woman. But she's not my type.' No sooner had Papetti spoken, and in that manner, than Brunetti saw the shadow of his father-in-law fall across his face. Quickly,

Papetti added, 'Besides, it's obvious that she's more trouble than she's worth.'

Well, Brunetti thought, Nava certainly discovered that, didn't he? But he said, 'My concern, Dottore, is not so much our understanding in this room,' and he waved his hand at the other two men, neither of whom looked up, 'as that your father-in-law should not draw the wrong conclusion.'

'That can't happen,' Papetti declared, but it came out as a plea rather than a statement.

'I certainly share your concern, Dottore,' Brunetti said in an expression of male fellow feeling. 'But the press, as we all know, prints what it wants and insinuates what it will.' Then he gave in to the temptation to provoke Papetti. 'Your father-in-law would probably be able to prevent these reports from appearing,' Brunetti began and paused before adding, 'though it might be better to keep even the hint of suspicion from occurring to him.' The expression on Papetti's face made Brunetti ashamed of what he was doing. What's next, you put him in a cage and poke him with a stick?

Papetti shook his head and kept on shaking it as he considered the possible consequences of his father-in-law's misunderstanding. Finally, like a man who confesses to stop the pain, he asked, 'What do I have to do?'

If this was the taste of victory, Brunetti did not like it, but still he said, 'In the presence of your lawyer, you confirm and sign the transcript of what you've just told me about the way you and Signorina Borolli paid the veterinarians at the slaughterhouse to approve as healthy animals that were not. And about how she began an affair with Dottor Andrea Nava in hopes of being able to persuade him to do the same.' He gave Papetti a chance to acknowledge understanding or compliance, but the man remained motionless, his face blank.

'You've also explained Signorina Borelli's decision to threaten him by revealing the affair to his wife, and Dottor Nava's response to that.' He waited for Papetti's nod, and at that he said, 'I also want you to sign the transcript of what you told me about her call to you and the help you gave her in disposing of the body of Dottor Nava.'

Brunetti stopped and looked at Papetti's lawyer, who might as well not have been in the room for all the attention he seemed to be paying to what was going on around him. 'You will sign this account, and your lawyer will sign it as a witness.' That, to Brunetti, seemed clear enough.

'And if she claims we were having an affair?' Papetti asked in a tight voice.

'I've a statement that confirms what you've said about what was going on at the slaughterhouse, and Signorina Borelli's lack of sexual interest in you,' Brunetti said and saw the shock on both men's faces.

'Thus the newspapers could report that the police have excluded that possibility,' Brunetti offered. 'For we do.'

As if someone had walked over his grave, Torinese raised his head and asked, 'Could report or will report?'

'Will report,' Brunetti guaranteed.

'What else?' Torinese asked.

'Do I want or do I give?' Brunetti asked.

'Want.'

All Brunetti wanted was enough to convict Borelli of having killed Dottor Nava. The rest — the diseased meat, the corrupted veterinarians, the farmers and their contaminated earnings — he would gladly hand over to the Carabinieri, who had the NAS for such things: they could handle it better than he. And the boys in Finance could be given a chance to pick the bones of their illegal earnings.

'I want her,' he said.

Torinese turned to his client and asked, 'Well?'

Papetti nodded. 'I'll tell them anything they want.'

Brunetti would not allow the ambiguity of this and said instantly, 'If you lie, in your own favour, or against her, I'll toss you to your father-in-law so fast you won't have time to raise your hands to protect yourself.'

Vianello's head snapped up at Brunetti's tone, the other two at his words.

Torinese got to his feet. 'Is that all?' he asked. Brunetti nodded. He looked at Brunetti and, after some time, the lawyer nodded in return, a gesture Brunetti could not interpret.

'If you'll go downstairs with Inspector Vianello,' Brunetti said, 'he'll bring you the printed statement as soon as it's ready. When you sign it, you can both go.'

There was much shuffling of feet, then chairs scraped against the floor. But no one spoke and no one shook hands. Torinese put his tape recorder in his briefcase. The three men left the office; Brunetti walked over and closed the door, then went to his desk and called Signorina Elettra and told her he wanted Patta to have a magistrate issue an order for the arrest of Signorina Giulia Borelli.

In the afternoon, Bocchese called to say that

the crime squad had spent most of the morning at the apartment on the Rio del Malpaga. There was no sign of anything suspicious in the apartment itself, which Bocchese said looked like the sort of place that would be rented to tourists by the week, but in the ground floor entranceway, which had a wooden door opening on the canal, they had found traces of blood and, on one of the steps leading down to the water, twin furrows in the algae covering it. Yes, the technician answered, the marks might have been left by the feet of a body being dragged down the steps. The furrows were being tested for traces of what might be leather; he had already retrieved Dottor Nava's shoe from the evidence room and, if they did find traces of leather that had survived the rise and fall of repeated tides, he would check to see if the marks on the shoe and on the steps matched.

They were dredging the canal just in front of the door, and a diver was on the way to have a look farther out in the water. Anything else?

Brunetti thanked him and hung up.

Not for an instant did it occur to Brunetti that she would attempt to flee: she might want to run from the legal risk, but a woman like her would never leave her property behind. She owned three apartments, had bank accounts, probably had more money stashed somewhere else: a woman ruled by greed would not take the chance of losing all of that or losing control over it. Where could she go? There was no indication that she spoke another language nor that she had some other passport, so she could not slip away to another country to establish a new life. She would stay and she would try to get away with it, even if it meant having to pay the huge costs of a defence lawyer. Brunetti did not doubt that she would attempt to embroil Papetti in the murder. But Papetti's father-in-law, believing that the crime was only murder and not the far more heinous crime of betraying his daughter, would surely not baulk at hiring the best defence lawyers for his daughter's husband.

Half an hour later, as Brunetti still stood at the window, his phone rang.

It was Bocchese. 'We found a *telefonino* on the bottom step, Commissario. It must have fallen out of his pocket when he went into the water. Anyone could see it in the daylight, lying there.'

But not at night, Brunetti thought. 'Is it his?' he asked.

'Probably.'

'Is it still working?'

'Of course not. The water would stop it instantly,' Bocchese said.

'Can you retrieve the information from it to tell when that happened?'

'No,' Bocchese said, dashing Brunetti's hopes of constructing an accurate chronology of the events of the night of Nava's murder.

'But . . .' Bocchese said in a voice that sounded, to Brunetti, almost flirtatious.

'But what?'

'You really don't understand these things, do you?' Bocchese asked.

'What things?' Brunetti asked, wondering what procedural possibility he had overlooked.

'Everything.' Bocchese made no attempt to disguise his exasperation. 'Computers, *telefonini*. Everything.'

Brunetti refused to answer.

In a voice suddenly grown more accommodating, Bocchese said, 'Then let me tell you. If his phone was connected to his network — and phones are — even yours — then his connection to it would have been broken within the first three minutes after the phone went into the water.' Before Brunetti could suffer the embarrassment of having been so close, Bocchese went on,

'But the network will have the records of all the calls he made, or received, up until that time.' He let Brunetti think about that for a moment and then asked, 'Will that be enough?'

Brunetti closed his eyes, flooded with gratitude though with no idea where to direct it. 'Yes,' he answered. 'Thanks.'

33

The day after Giulia Borelli was arrested for the murder of Dottor Andrea Nava, whose *telefonino* had stopped working ten minutes before Signorina Borelli telephoned to Alessandro Papetti, who was on the other side of Venice when he answered, Vianello and Brunetti drove out to Mestre to attend the funeral of Dottor Nava. Because there was heavy traffic, Brunetti and Vianello reached the church only a few minutes before the funeral was to begin. The driver slowed to a stop half a block away and the two men got out, then walked quickly to the church and up the stairs, hurrying under the gaze of the saints and angels looking down on them. Entering, it took them some time to adjust to the dimmer light; at the front of the church, six dark-suited men were just setting the coffin in place on the wooden trestles before the altar.

Propped up on either side of the coffin

were two enormous wreaths of red and white flowers, each crossed by a purple sash bearing the name of the donor and the proper sentiment. Carpeting the steps of the altar were countless bouquets of spring flowers of all conceivable colours. Few appeared to be the careful confections produced by florists; instead they were simple bouquets of the sort of unruly flowers that grew at the side of the road. Many of them had a home-made quality to them: bows not neatly tied, simple field grasses used as background to the bright flowers.

The church was crowded, and the two men had to take places in the third aisle from the back. The people there moved quickly to the right to make room for them, and an old woman beside Brunetti smiled and nodded to them as they slipped in beside her.

The priest emerged from a door on the left, two white-robed altar girls and one boy behind him. He walked to the pulpit, pushed back the long white sleeves of his surplice, and tapped the microphone a few times. The *thwank thwank thwank* sounded through the church. He was a youngish man, with a full beard and some streaks of grey in his hair. He cast his eyes across the assembled mourners, raised both hands in a gesture either of welcome or blessing, and began.

'Dear brothers and sisters in Christ, dear friends and companions: we are here today to say goodbye to our brother Andrea, who to many of us was far more than a friend. He was healer and helper, someone who comforted us when we were worried about our friends and who dedicated himself with love and devotion to taking care of them, and of us, for he knew that we are all children of the same God, who delights to see the love we bring to one another. He cured us all, he healed us all, and he helped us all, and in those instances when his powers could not heal our friends, it was Andrea who advised us when it was time to help our friends make their last journey, and who always stayed with us so that neither we, nor they, would be alone when they started on their way along that road. Just as he helped us bear the unhappiness of their parting from us, let us hope that our friends will help us bear the unhappiness of his parting from us.'

Brunetti looked away from the priest and began to study the profiles and the backs of the heads of the people in front of him. As he did so and as he allowed his mind to drift away from the voice of the priest, he was struck by how noisy this crowd was. Usually a church, no matter how large and no matter how many people, was silent in the presence and presentation of death. But this group was restless and made a great deal of noise moving about nervously in their pews. In the enclosed place, the restless scratching and scraping of the old was too easily heard.

And somewhere in the church, one of the mourners must have been fighting back tears: the muffled, grunting noises were unmistakable. Brunetti shifted his gaze to the people on the left side of the church and saw, near the front, someone who appeared to have bunched a sweater over his shoulder. But when he took a more careful look, Brunetti saw that it was a grey parrot, and then he noticed, four aisles behind, a bright green one, somewhat smaller. As if Brunetti's attention had caught its attention, the grey one opened its beak and said, *'Ciao, Laura,'* and then, in quick repetition, *'Ciao, ciao, ciao.'*

The green one, hearing that voice, called back, *'Dammi schei,'* almost as if it believed the Venetians there, understanding him, would obey and give him money. Astonishing as Brunetti found the presence and voices of the birds, even more so was the fact that no one among that large number of people seemed to find it at all strange nor turned to look at either of the parrots.

He heard a noise from below him, and looked down to see the black paw of a large dog move across the floor and grow still just a few centimetres from his own left foot. Across the aisle, a beagle jumped up on the pew, put his front paws on the top of the one in front, and leaned out into the aisle to stare ahead of him.

He tuned back into the voice of the priest, who was now saying, '. . . examples of the love and wit of God, to give us these beautiful companions and enrich our lives with their love. We are enriched, as well, by the love we give to them, for to be able to love them is to be given a great gift, just as the love they have for us is a gift that comes ultimately from God, source of all love. And so, before we begin the ceremony that will help our brother Andrea begin his passage home to God, let us all exchange the sign of peace, not only with one another, but with the patients he cared for, who have come here today to join us as we pray for the soul of our brother Andrea. They too want to say their final farewells to the friend who for so long and with such kindness took such loving care of them.'

The priest left the pulpit and came down

past the altar, the acolytes close behind him. He bent to kiss a woman in the first row and caressed the head of the cat she held on her shoulder. Next he crouched down to run his hand along the ear of an enormous black Great Dane, who climbed to his feet at the touch of the priest's hand, the dog's head now higher than his. The sound of his tail slapping the side of the pew resonated through the church. The priest stood up and moved to the other side of the aisle, where he embraced Nava's widow, then bent and kissed Teo's upraised face. As if summoned by the boy's evident need, the Great Dane walked across the aisle and leaned against Teo, who wrapped one arm around the dog's shoulder and rested his head on his black neck.

The priest embraced a few more people and ruffled a few more ears and then returned to the altar to begin the Mass. It was a dignified affair, with only the voice of the priest and the response of the congregation to be heard: no music and no singing. The green parrot sat on the shoulder of his owner as the man approached the altar to take communion, and the priest seemed not to mind in the least. Brunetti joined in the recitation of the Lord's Prayer and was happy to shake the hand of the old woman and of Vianello, on his other side.

There was no singing until the Mass was finished and the priest had circled the coffin, swinging the censer and sprinkling holy water from the aspergillum. Having returned to the altar, he raised his head and looked at the choir loft, then lifted one hand. At that sign, the organ softly began to play a tune Brunetti neither recognized nor found in any way lugubrious. The organist had not played more than a few notes when, from the front of the church, an agonized sound broke out, a howl of such pain and grief as almost to be unbearable. It rose higher than the notes of the organ, as if to remind the organist just why they were all there: not to listen to pretty music but to express the agony of bereavement.

From the same place came the sound of a man's voice saying, quite sharply, 'Artù, stop that,' and then Brunetti, tall enough to see over the people's heads, saw a handsome man in a dark suit bend down and rise up, his arms clasped around an even more handsome golden brown dachshund, who had had the courage and the love to express the grief felt by so many of those assembled there at the loss of their good and gentle friend.

The organist stopped playing, as if accepting that the dog had given clearer voice to the sentiments of the congregation. The priest, as though the interruption had been to his liking, came down from the altar again and walked around to the front of the coffin. The six dark-suited men returned from their places at the back of the church and lifted the coffin to their shoulders. Following the priest in solemn silence, they carried their dearly beloved brother Andrea from his last visit to the patients who had loved him. Behind him they came: old ladies carrying their cats in cages, the young man from the veterinarian clinic with the one-eared rabbit in his arms, the Great Dane, Teo walking beside him with his arm over his shoulder, the dog Brunetti now recognized as Artù.

Outside, people clustered on the steps, animals held by arm or leash, as the men carried the coffin down the steps and slid it into the back of a waiting hearse. Signora Doni and Teo paused at the door of the car idling behind it while a tall man came and attached a leash to the collar of the Great Dane.

Teo kissed the dog's head and got into the car. His mother followed him inside. Other people stepped into cars that Brunetti, in his hurry to get into the church, had not noticed parked there. The beagle emerged from the church and, at the bottom of the steps, came to stand directly in front of Artù: they confronted one another, tails erect and bodies tensed. But then, as if conscious of the situation in which they found themselves, neither barked; they contented themselves with giving one other a thorough sniffing and then sat down side by side in quiet amiability.

The back doors of the hearse closed: not a slam, but certainly not a quiet sound. The engine started, followed by the firing into life of the engines of the cars behind it. Slowly it pulled away from the kerb, followed by the cars of Dr Nava's family and patients. Brunetti saw that the cars were almost all light-coloured: grey and white and red. Not a single one was black. Though Brunetti found that fact somehow comforting, it was the sight of the green parrot disappearing down the street on the shoulder of his owner, the man arm in arm with a woman, that lifted his heart and wiped it clean of any funereal gloom.

ABOUT THE AUTHOR

Donna Leon is the author of twenty-one novels featuring Commissario Guido Brunetti. She has lived in Venice for thirty years.

The employees of Thorndike Press hope you have enjoyed this Large Print book. All our Thorndike, Wheeler, and Kennebec Large Print titles are designed for easy reading, and all our books are made to last. Other Thorndike Press Large Print books are available at your library, through selected bookstores, or directly from us.

For information about titles, please call:
(800) 223-1244

or visit our Web site at:
http://gale.cengage.com/thorndike

To share your comments, please write:
Publisher
Thorndike Press
10 Water St., Suite 310
Waterville, ME 04901